EVERLASTING

Class

EVERLASTING

A KISSED BY AN ANGEL *novel*

TULLAMORE

0 9 MAY 2023

ELIZABETH CHANDLER

SIMON AND SCHUSTER

A **pulse** book

First published in Great Britain in 2012 by Simon & Schuster UK Ltd
A CBS COMPANY

Published in the USA in 2012 by Simon Pulse,
an imprint of Simon & Schuster Children's Division, New York.

alloy**entertainment**

Produced by Alloy Entertainment
151 West 26th Street, New York, NY 10001

Simon & Schuster UK Ltd
1st Floor
222 Gray's Inn Road
London
WC1X 8HB

www.simonandschuster.co.uk
www.simonandschuster.com.au

Simon & Schuster Australia, Sydney
Simon & Schuster India, New Delhi

Simon Pulse, and colophon are registered trademarks of
Simon and Schuster UK Ltd
A CIP catalogue copy for this book is available
from the British Library.

ISBN: 978-1-47111-564-6

1 3 5 7 9 10 8 6 4 2

Printed and bound by CPI Group (UK) Ltd, Croydon CR0 4YY

For Françoise Bui—
Here's to lunches in Macmillan's cafeteria,
the many books that have passed through our hands
since then, and a treasured friendship.

Prologue

GREGORY WAS CERTAIN NOW: IVY KNEW ABOUT HIM. She had finally realized he was inside Beth's mind. His pleasure doubled. After all, what satisfaction was there in hurting Ivy if she didn't know *he* was doing it?

Vengeance is mine.

Each day he was growing stronger and more skillful. From the moment he began prowling Beth's mind, she had fought him, but he was wearing her down. Beth would soon obey him, body and soul. Let Ivy call to Tristan for help—Angel Tristan was gone. And the ever-loyal Will had turned against her.

To get Ivy alone—that excited Gregory just as it had when he was walking the earth in his own body. Beth must have felt his excitement: Her body trembled.

While he gained control over Beth's mind, it would be amusing to use some of his old tactics. To create dread—to slowly torture Ivy's mind and soul—would be nearly as much fun as killing her. And he would kill her. He would win this time.

Vengeance is mine, he thought, and felt deep satisfaction as Beth's lips moved silently with his words: *Soon. Soon.*

One

"INCREDIBLE!" CHASE EXCLAIMED, HIS GRAY EYES assessing Ivy with mock admiration.

Ivy, Will, and Beth squeezed together on their picnic blanket to make room. Chase had arrived at the last minute, claiming a place on the bayside beach among the Fourth of July revelers. Somehow, he always seemed to find them.

"Last year your boyfriend was murdered," Chase went on, his eyes bright with amusement. "This year you hook up with a cold-blooded killer. That's quite a dating résumé for a nice girl like you!"

Ivy wanted to tell him off; instead, she shook her head as if she could hardly believe how badly she had been deceived. "It's horrifying! I was totally fooled by Luke. I never thought he was capable of violence."

"It was obvious to me," Chase replied.

Will, who had been aimlessly drawing in the sand, threw aside the stick he'd been using. He lifted his head, his brown eyes narrowing with dislike. Ivy knew why.

Chase had been curious about the stranger who had washed up on Lighthouse Beach and skeptical about Luke's amnesia. But it was Will who had repeatedly warned her that a guy found badly beaten and unconscious, who claimed he had no idea how it happened, probably had a dark past. Ivy had attributed Will's warnings to his habit of being protective of her. When she had ended her romantic relationship with Will, she'd chalked up his actions to jealousy. But in the end, Will's decision to report Ivy's new love to the police had appeared to be the right one. Luke McKenna was on the run, wanted for strangling his ex-girlfriend.

"It's over now," Will said. "Let's drop the subject."

"I was just thinking—" Chase persisted.

"It's over!" Will snapped.

Ivy knew that, given what Will and the others didn't know, Will's anger with her was justified. The fact that he was able to keep it down to a simmer and continue to work with her at the Seabright Inn was evidence of his strong character. Last summer, when Tristan had died, Will had risked his life to save Ivy from Tristan's murderer, Gregory. As far as her friends knew, Ivy had recently broken up with Luke because she had been deceived once more by a "cold-blooded killer."

"It's not over," Beth said.

Everyone turned to her.

"He will have revenge."

The skin on Ivy's arm prickled. Was Beth talking about Luke—or Gregory?

"Luke got his revenge when he strangled that girl," Chase replied. "He's on the lam. If he has half a brain, he's far away by now."

Luke McKenna *was* far away, Ivy thought. He had drowned the night Tristan crawled to shore in Luke's body. But where was Tristan?

Ivy prayed he was somewhere safe, a place where the police would never find him and charge him with Luke's crime. But safety meant he was far away from here, far away from her. She ached as much as she had the first time she had lost him.

Withdrawing from the conversation, Ivy gazed out at the dark water of Cape Cod Bay. Now and then a small flare discharged, brightening the outlines of a barge laden with fireworks. People impatiently checked the time on their cell phones and watches. Finally, a bright missile shot up from the barge, and every face turned toward the sky.

"Oh!" the spectators exclaimed in one breath. Color exploded against the night sky, bright red bars ending in a circle of stars. Ivy watched the fireworks' falling sparks: pure bits of light suddenly going dark and drifting into nothingness.

Why was Tristan inside Luke's body? she wondered. Lacey claimed that Tristan had fallen the night he used his angelic powers to give life to Ivy. Was he a dark angel now? Ivy's heart rebelled at the thought. Tristan had acted in pure love. Her stepbrother, Gregory, had acted with jealousy, greed, and deadly anger. Last summer, trying to murder her, he had killed Tristan instead. For a time, Gregory had pretended to grieve with and comfort Ivy. He'd acted the part of loving older brother with her younger brother, Philip, just to get to her. If Gregory had had his way, he would have killed them both. It was Gregory who had died and become a demon, not Tristan.

A cascade of colors brought her back to the present. Purple splashed over brilliant green, gold spilled over purple. *The sky is raining fire*, she thought. She turned to look at Beth and caught her breath: Her best friend gazed back at her, fire and darkness in her eyes. A series of booms drew Beth's attention. A finale of garish explosions bathed Beth's upturned face in a sinister radiance.

It was over; smoke hung heavily over the still bay. A moment of silence was followed by applause and a blast of boat horns. People around them stood up, talking excitedly about which firework was their favorite.

"I've seen better," Chase said as they crossed the beach toward Wharf Lane. "In Jackson Hole— "

"Life must be a continual disappointment to you," Will observed, "since you've always seen and experienced something better."

Chase shrugged. "Why pretend? I dislike false modesty. Don't you, Elizabeth?" he added, draping his arm across Beth's shoulders.

Beth slid out from under his arm, and he laughed. The more Beth tried to get away from Chase, the harder he pursued her. Initially, her reunion with a boy she had known since middle-school summers on the Cape had left Beth in awe. Somehow gawky Chase Hardy had morphed into a tall, broad-shouldered guy with sea-mist eyes and dark curly hair. He could have dropped out of any one of the romances Beth liked to write. But since the night of the séance, Beth had changed, withdrawing from him, from Ivy, from most everyone but Will.

Watching Chase and Beth together, Will frowned. Ivy wondered if it was his dislike for Chase or his surprise at Beth's behavior that prompted his reaction. The old Beth, the most sensitive person Ivy knew, would have let a cobra rest on her shoulders if she feared she might otherwise hurt its feelings.

For the last week Ivy had kept her discovery about Beth's secret, hoping she was wrong—knowing she wasn't—looking for the right moment to talk with Will about their friend. In retrospect, it seemed so clear: Beth, a natural medium, would be the easiest mind for Gregory to slip into. Still, everything about Beth, her voice and softly rounded face and feathery sweep of light-colored hair, was gentle. It was only when Ivy dared to look into Beth's darkening eyes that she could believe Gregory was present in her friend.

Chase fell into step with Will as they started up Wharf Lane, discussing movies. Ivy walked beside Beth, who kept her face averted, as if she were interested only in the dark hedges and stone walls that lined the narrow road. The lane ended at Route 6A, where a large Victorian house occupied one corner and an old church perched on the other. Will had parked in the pebble lot behind the church.

"Hold up," Will said, pausing at the edge of the lot. "I want to take a look at this place." An artist, he was always on the hunt for interesting landscapes and buildings.

They followed him as he circled the church. It was small, with just three sets of elongated double windows on each side, steep rooflines, and triangular dormers. A square bell tower anchored the corner of the wooden building, its high porch covered by a trussed roof forming the entrance to the church. The wood that sheathed the bell tower was laid in narrow bands, the first story running horizontally, the second vertically, with the boards below the bell cut in wavy lines as if an expert baker had iced the blocky tower with a delicate knife.

The church's doors were locked—Will tried them. Chase stood at the bottom of the steps, looking bored. Beth backed away from the building, her arms folded and shoulders hunched as if she were cold.

"This isn't a church anymore," Ivy said, reading a lawn placard. "They're raising money to restore the building and use it for community events." She walked back to where Beth stood and gazed upward into the tower's shadows, seeing a faint outline against the night sky. "It looks as if it still has its bell."

"'Ask not for whom the bell tolls,'" Chase quoted in a fake British voice. "'It tolls for thee.'"

Beth glanced over her shoulder apprehensively, then her eyes rose to the bell. "It will toll when it's time," she said softly.

"John Donne, seventeenth-century poet and homilist," Chase continued. "He's talking about how we don't see our own connection to other humans, how each person whose life has been lost is our loss and—"

"I see it," Beth said. Then she added so quietly only Ivy could hear, "Soon. The bell will toll soon."

The skin on the back of Ivy's neck felt cold. Sometimes, when Beth "saw" things, she *foresaw* them. Was she speaking as herself or for Gregory? Was she seeing his plan? Was someone going to die soon?

Ivy laid a hand on her friend's arm. "Beth—"

Beth shook it off and walked away, taking the long route, circling the church counterclockwise back to the car.

"Angels protect her," Ivy prayed. "Angels protect us all."

Two

TRISTAN WAS RUNNING. FROM WHAT, TO WHERE—HE didn't know. A heart that wasn't his pounded in his chest. His legs moved with the swiftness of someone who had been used to running, dodging, and hiding.

But Tristan couldn't get away—couldn't put distance between himself and the voices—murmuring, menacing, inhuman voices. He stopped for a moment, trying to decipher words, but all he could hear were emotions: misery and rage.

He started running again, crashing through bushes,

snapping branches underfoot, sending a cascade of stones rolling over the edge of a ravine. But the noise he made did nothing to muffle the voices. No matter what he did they were there, just above his threshold of hearing.

Out of breath, Tristan stopped a second time and found himself on the top of a ridge, looking down a steep hillside of rocks and trees. Suddenly, he remembered: The night he and Will had raced to the train bridge to save Ivy, the voices had rung in their ears. Demons, he'd thought.

Though his weary legs were heavy and unsteady beneath him, Tristan continued to run. He saw Ivy on the bridge as he had seen her that misty night last autumn, high above the rocks and river. He raced toward her, calling her name. He tripped, and the voices shrieked with delight as he tumbled headlong, falling, falling—

Tristan jerked awake. It was a dream, *just a dream*, he said to himself. Still he cowered against the large roots of a fallen tree. Looking around him in the moonlit night, he saw that he was lying halfway down a hillside of rocks and trees. He knew where he was now: Nickerson State Park, Cape Cod, where he had hidden when he'd first escaped the hospital.

Several weeks earlier, when he was found barely alive at the ocean's edge and brought to the hospital, not knowing his own name, the doctors had thought he had amnesia. But the life he couldn't recall had been Luke McKenna's, not his, and slowly he had remembered the details of his own life as Tristan. He had remembered Ivy.

He knew he'd died once when he was with Ivy. Returning as an angel, his mission had been to warn her about Gregory. With the help of Beth and Will, and an angel named Lacey, Tristan had succeeded. Then he'd moved on to the Light.

So why had he returned? Tristan remembered saving Ivy a second time, when his angelic powers healed her the night of the accident on Morris Island. Ivy had told him that Gregory was back with the powers of a demon, and Tristan believed he had been sent to help Ivy again. But if that was true, why, after healing her, had he been stripped of all angelic powers—and worse, placed in the body of an accused murderer? How could he help her while on the run from the police?

It felt like a cosmic test, one that was rigged against him. And the voices were taunting him, dooming him to failure. Were the voices the dark thoughts of Gregory?

The only thing Tristan knew for sure was that he loved Ivy and could not bear to leave her again.

Three

"HOSE ME DOWN, IVY," KELSEY SAID. "I'M FRYING."

"Maybe if you didn't use baby oil, you wouldn't," Dhanya suggested, gracefully stretching her legs and pointing her toes, then flipping the page of a thick novel. She sat in an Adirondack chair she had dragged around the side of the inn to a stretch of grass next to the Seabright's Unloading Zone, where Ivy was washing her car. Kelsey, whose beach towel lay next to Dhanya's chair, stood up and surveyed her arms and legs, then twisted around to look at her shoulder. Her black bikini displayed her shapely body

14

to perfection—muscles as well as round breasts and hips.

If Kelsey had been sunning when Michelangelo was sculpting, he'd have immortalized her, Ivy thought. Then she raised the hose and splashed water over Kelsey.

"Not the hair!" Kelsey cried.

Ivy laughed, and touched her own cloud of dark gold hair, which got even frizzier than Kelsey's auburn mane. "Give it up, Kelsey. It's hopeless with a whole ocean nearby."

The Seabright Inn, owned by Kelsey and Beth's aunt, sat on a bluff above and behind the dunes in Orleans. Aunt Cindy's level yard ended with bushes and scrub trees, which protected the sands of the bluff and prevented a view of the ocean, but everywhere the sea's presence was felt in its damp and salty breath. The Atlantic's deep blue could be seen from the inn's porch, where the girls and Will served breakfast every morning, and from the second floor rooms, which they cleaned and straightened for the guests.

They worked five days each week, six during busy weeks, taking turns on getting weekdays off. Their workday began at six thirty a.m. in the inn's kitchen. Today they had finished at two, but with the Fourth of July crowds on the Cape, they had been working hard and decided to hang out at the inn. Will had returned to sketch in his room in Aunt Cindy's converted barn. Beth had stayed behind in the girls' cottage, which was nestled among the trees on the side of the inn facing the road.

Beth's increasingly frequent desire to be alone made Ivy uneasy. She read it as a sign that Gregory's power over Beth was growing. Last year, when Tristan had first slipped into Beth's mind, she had fought him. But eventually, realizing the presence was Tristan and therefore angelic, she had allowed him to work through her. Beth must have sensed that this new presence was evil; she, herself, had said that Gregory was here. Had he grown too powerful for her to resist? Ivy had tried to stay close, but Beth had rebuffed every attempt Ivy made to talk to her.

In the past week Dhanya and Kelsey had stayed close to Ivy, trying to be supportive after the police came for Luke. Ivy suspected she had risen several notches in Kelsey's eyes, now that she believed Ivy had been seduced by a "gorgeous fugitive from the law."

Sparkling with hose water, Kelsey returned to her beach towel, adjusting it slightly, perfecting the angle at which the sunlight touched her skin.

"You're getting burned," Dhanya warned.

"Dhanya, chill! I don't want to hear it, not from someone born with a tan. You can't possibly understand what it is like to have skin like Snow White."

"Well, she got her prince, didn't she?" Dhanya asked.

Kelsey lay back on her towel, then grinned. "Yeah, I guess so. Ivy, we need to find you a prince."

Ivy, surprised, shot water at the car door she had just finished drying.

"You've put in a whole week of mourning," Kelsey continued. "Don't you think that's enough?"

Ivy almost laughed.

"Come with us tonight. Some of Bryan's teammates have come out to the Cape and will be at Max's party. College guys, hockey players!"

"Can't wait," muttered Dhanya. "I wonder if they have front teeth."

"You are such a snob, Dhanya!"

Ivy smiled. "Don't want to shock you, but I also prefer guys with front teeth."

Kelsey snorted. "You need to let go, Ivy. No regrets, over and done—move on! And you, Dhanya, need to close your novels and get real." Talking with her eyes closed, Kelsey looked like some mythological prophetess spouting advice. "As for missing teeth, you're way off. College hockey is a sport of skill and discipline, requiring smarts as well as toughness. I'm sure that Bryan's friends are just like Bryan."

"So how can you resist?" a deep voice asked.

Dhanya turned around and instantly blushed. Kelsey sat up.

Bryan's laugh was loud and friendly. "But maybe Max is more your type," he suggested to Dhanya.

"I don't think so," said Max, having followed Bryan around the side of the inn.

Max and Bryan, who had become friends at college, were polar opposites. Bryan, with dark hair and green eyes, was medium height, powerfully built, and good-looking; brimming with confidence, his game face was a roguish smile. Max had a leaner build and countered his monochrome looks—light brown hair, light brown eyes, and year-round matching tan—with expensive and tropically colored clothes. Recently, however, after learning that Dhanya found him "tacky," he'd started sporting more traditional preppy attire.

"How'd you find us?" Kelsey asked.

"Beth," Bryan replied, "though she didn't exactly volunteer the information. We could hear her in the kitchen. When she didn't respond to our calling, we invited ourselves in."

"She gets like that when she's writing," Kelsey said. "Totally spacey."

Max and Bryan exchanged glances, then shrugged. Ivy guessed that they saw a strangeness in Beth that Will stubbornly denied and Kelsey conveniently ignored.

"Is everyone coming to Max's tonight?" Bryan asked.

Kelsey started smoothing on more oil, although her body was already glistening with it. "Wouldn't miss it!"

"Dhanya?"

"Yes."

Bryan turned to Ivy and she shook her head. "Sorry."

His green eyes glinted with mischief. "Does that mean we can call you if Kelsey gets stinking drunk again?"

That was how it had all started. Three nights after Gregory re-entered the living world through a séance meant to be just a game, Kelsey and Dhanya had gotten drunk at one of Max's wild parties. On the way to pick up their roommates, Ivy and Beth had been struck by a hit-and-run driver. The paramedics and doctors couldn't explain how Ivy had survived, but she knew the source of the miracle: Tristan's kiss.

Ivy dried the door of her rental car, then straightened up and turned toward Bryan. He talked a big game about drinking, but she had come to realize he drank a lot more caffeine than alcohol. "No, it means you'll have to help keep that from happening."

He smiled. "You mean babysit her?"

"If that's what it takes," Ivy replied. "Aunt Cindy has reached the end of her rope with us."

Bryan nodded. "My uncle would have booted you all out by now. Partying, totaling your car, then dating a killer who claims he has amnesia."

"He *did* have amnesia," Ivy replied.

"You're sure?"

"Positive." Ivy slopped suds on the trunk of the white VW. She winced every time she thought of Aunt Cindy's description of her: a "good girl" who showed "absolutely no judgment" when it came to people. Ivy wanted to argue that it was perceptiveness and positive instincts rather than lack of judgment that had made her trust a stranger before she knew his story. But Tristan's safety required her to remain silent; it was impossible to defend herself.

"Have you heard from Luke?" Max inquired.

"No."

"Do you *want* to hear from him?" Bryan asked, picking up an extra sponge, washing a patch she had missed.

Ivy met Bryan's eyes. She thought she saw a flicker of sympathy, then he threw his wet sponge at Kelsey, who had been watching them with a jealous pout.

"Why would I want to hear from a murderer?" Ivy asked, dropping her sponge in the bucket, picking up the hose.

"Because to you," Bryan replied, "he wasn't a murderer."

"I was totally taken in. I acted like a fool."

Bryan studied her until she looked away. "We all make mistakes, Ivy. Don't beat yourself up about it."

"That's exactly what I've been telling her," Kelsey interjected. "So how many hot hockey players am I going to meet tonight?"

Bryan turned to Kelsey. "You already know one," he replied, smiling. "But if I'm not too busy with some of the girls coming from Boston, how about I introduce you to my teammates?"

"I'm counting on it. I have a few questions to ask them about you."

They teased on. Max attempted without success to get Dhanya to talk about the novel she was reading; if he had looked a little harder at its cover, he might have realized it was a steamy romance. Ivy finished up the car as soon as she could and drove it back to the inn's lot.

It was tempting to continue on to Nickerson State Park, where she thought Tristan might be hiding, but she couldn't chance it. Four times in the last seven days, the police officers who had tried to arrest Tristan had phoned Ivy. Twice, the woman officer, in plainclothes and an unmarked car, had stopped by the inn, saying she was just "touching base." Ivy couldn't go anywhere without feeling as if someone was watching her. A week ago the police had guessed correctly that "Luke" would return to her; it made sense that they would keep an eye on her for a while longer.

When you love someone and want to be with him, Ivy thought, patience was a lot harder than courage. Taking a risk was easy compared to waiting and not knowing. If she were risking only *her* safety, she'd be searching for him now. *Tristan, be safe,* she prayed as she walked toward the cottage.

It was quiet when she entered the small, shingled building. "Beth? Are you home?"

Receiving no reply, Ivy headed to the kitchen, directly behind the living room, and fixed a glass of iced tea, which she carried toward the steps. The old cottage had a central hearth with steep steps built against the chimney, rising from the kitchen to the second floor. As Ivy started up the stairway, Beth rushed down, moving so quickly that Ivy had to flatten herself against the wall to avoid being bowled over.

"Beth!"

The cold drink sloshed over Ivy's hand and onto Beth's shoulder as she passed, but Beth kept going, hurrying across the kitchen and out the back door. Ivy stared after her. If she hadn't glimpsed Beth's face, she would have guessed it was fear driving away her friend. But Ivy had seen the intense anger, and it was Ivy who felt afraid—worried that Gregory was slowly driving Beth insane.

After wiping up the tea, Ivy continued to the cottage's second floor, one large bedroom with a small bathroom across from the central chimney. A bed occupied each corner, Dhanya's and Kelsey's beds under the sloping roof to the right, Ivy's and Beth's to the left. Ivy sniffed for burnt candles, then glanced toward Dhanya's bed, under which the Ouija board was kept, but there was no indication that Beth had consulted it again.

Retrieving a clean T-shirt, Ivy was surprised to find the contents of her bureau drawer in disarray. Shrugging off the suspicion that someone else had been sorting through her things, she changed clothes and carried her music bag to her bed. She kicked off her flip-flops, then slipped on the shoes she wore for piano.

Needles of pain pierced the sole of Ivy's foot. Her right knee gave way. Dropping down on her bed, she yanked off her shoe. For a moment she just stared at the underside of her foot, the skin glistening with dark blood and splinters of glass. It shocked her, seeing this again. Last summer, before killing her cat Ella, Gregory had cut the tender pads on her paws. As a warning to Ivy, he had spread broken glass on her bathmat. It was like a recurring nightmare: Worse than the physical pain was the horror of feeling trapped in a sequence she knew would get much worse.

Grimacing, Ivy freed a shard of glass with her fingers, then hopped to the bathroom, where she used tweezers to remove tinier pieces. Her foot burned from the lacerations and her breath quickened, but she was almost too stunned to cry. She bathed her foot with cool water. When she patted it dry, she winced, the glass still in her skin, then went back to work with the tweezers.

After applying antibiotic and bandages, Ivy limped back to her bed and sank down on it. Her heart was filled with dread—as Gregory had known it would be. She imagined he had taken great pleasure in planning this.

"Tristan!" Ivy called out, but he no longer had the power to hear her.

Ivy tried to block the image of Beth breaking the glass and placing it in the front of the shoe, where it wouldn't be discovered until Ivy slipped it on. She shook it lightly, then picked out a glittering thorn.

She couldn't wait till Will got over his anger with her. She would show him now. She had to get Will to listen and to help her fight back, before Gregory went too far, before it was too late for both Beth and her.

Four

TRISTAN'S CLOTHES HAD DRIED FROM THE PREVIOUS night's dip in Ruth Pond. Now the heat of late afternoon made him wish he could swim again, but he remained in a thickly wooded area, as far as possible from the hiking trails. Although hungry, he'd restrained himself when he stole food from campsites—a roll here, a piece of meat there— never taking enough for campers to notice and report, never enough for the police to see a suspicious trend in the park.

He couldn't see Ivy; the police would be watching, waiting for him to show up. He knew he should leave Cape Cod, but he couldn't bear to put distance between them. Maybe it was better to see her one last time and let the police find him. But then there was Gregory: If captured by the police, Tristan would be leaving Ivy alone with Gregory. He had to stay here and stay hidden.

In the last week, Tristan had begun to remember more of his life and the time immediately after it. He'd recalled the help of an angel named Lacey. Was she still around? When he'd met her, she had put off finding her mission for two years, allowing herself to be continually sidetracked by adventures and pranks. It would be three years now, and yet, having known her, he wouldn't be surprised if she was still in this world.

"Lacey," he called out softly, tentatively. "Are you there? Can you hear me? Lacey, I need your help."

Leaves rustled. An insect hummed close to his ear. The dark green canopy of oak and pine nearly blocked out the sky. Tristan felt earthbound and isolated.

"Well, look at you," a familiar voice greeted him. "Goldilocks with a beard!"

"Lacey!" Tristan grinned and tried to locate her voice. A tree branch about six feet above his head bore purple leaves. Tristan took a step back to gaze at the branch. The violet haze spun and dropped to the ground.

"I wish I could touch you. I wish I could hug you," Tristan said. "I've lost my angel powers. All I see is a purple mist."

To his amazement, a girl with long hair—tinged purple—wearing leggings and a tank top materialized, becoming as solid as the tree trunks around him. Tristan reached out, his hand touching and folding around a smaller hand with long purple nails. He pulled Lacey close and felt a warm body. "It's great to see you."

She suddenly pulled away from him.

"I missed you, Lacey."

She took another step back. "I guess I would have missed you, too, if I hadn't been so busy."

"Yeah? Posting strange photos on the electronic billboard in Times Square? Terrorizing girls playing in a cemetery? Remember the Baines's big party, when you gave Ella a voice, ordering a bowl of milk from the bartender?"

She smiled. "Those were good times."

"So I guess you haven't gotten around to finding your mission," he observed.

"Don't be too quick to judge," Lacey told him. "Maybe I didn't move on to the Light like you, but at least I didn't regress to a body—*someone else's body*."

Tristan nodded.

"How's life as a murderer and fugitive?"

"Not much fun," he replied. "How'd you know about that?"

"Newspaper, Internet. I'm never far from somebody's iPad. Took you long enough to contact me, Tristan."

He felt a little defensive. "I didn't know who I was."

"If you hadn't just said how much you missed me, I'd have thought you wanted a favor."

"Actually," Tristan began—

"Uh-oh."

"Lacey, I really need your help."

She grimaced. "What do you think this is, a sequel? During my Hollywood years, I never let myself get trapped in a role."

Remembering Lacey's acting career differently than she did, Tristan raised an eyebrow but decided not to correct her. "Ivy believes that Gregory is back."

"Which means—let me guess—Ivy's in danger."

He ignored the sarcastic tone. "It's hard for me to help her." He turned to look behind him, hearing hikers laughing and talking in the distance. "If the police catch me—"

"The police are the *least* of your problems!"

"Keep your voice down," he warned.

Lacey leaped and caught hold of the branch above his head, as easily as if she had the bones and sinews of a cat.

"Lacey, if anyone saw that—"

"Keep your voice down," she said, and hung there for a moment, watching. "They're gone." She dropped softly onto the carpet of pine needles. Reaching toward him, she twisted a lock of his hair around her finger. "Tristan, did it ever occur to you that someone beat up that sexy body

28

you're hauling around, left it to die, and will be real unhappy to find it still moving? If I were you, I'd cut off these pretty gold waves and try some brunette Just for Men. The beard helps. They make dye for beards, too."

Tristan smiled at her, looking into her dark eyes, marveling at how solid she was. Again, she backed away.

"I'm planning to disguise myself," he said, "but I need to stay here and stay completely hidden for as long as it takes the police to decide I've left the Cape."

She snapped her fingers and pointed at him. "Now *there's* an idea. Get off the Cape. Get as far away as you can. I'll reschedule appointments with my clients to give you a hand with that."

"I can't leave Ivy."

"Sure you can."

"Not when she's in danger."

Lacey shook her head in disgust. "Well, then, you have what might be called an eternal problem."

"Meaning?"

"Who do you think is producing this film? I doubt Number One Director is amused by the changes you made in the script."

"I don't understand."

"You broke the rules, Tristan. When Ivy was in that car accident, you played God. Dead chicks are supposed to stay dead. You gave Ivy the kiss of life."

"But I wasn't trying to save her. I wasn't trying to restore her life. I just wanted to hold her again."

"Pitiful."

"I wanted to—to touch her face one more time. All I wanted was one last kiss—"

"Absolutely pitiful."

But Lacey's voice quavered as she attempted to dish out scorn, and when she turned away from Tristan, he caught her by the arm. "You don't really believe that, do you? You understand, Lacey, I know you do. Because you loved someone too—I remember now. Just before I left, you said—"

She pulled her arm away from him. "The difference between you and me is that I've come to my senses since then."

He studied her, the way she kept her face averted. "Angels shouldn't lie," he said.

She swung around. "That's good, coming from someone whose angelic powers are gone. Don't you get it, Tristan? You're fallen! You're not materializing like I am—you're lugging around a ninety-eight point six. You're a *fallen* angel."

Tristan inhaled sharply. So he hadn't come back with a mission to save Ivy from Gregory? Despite the fact he had lost his powers, he'd assumed that deep down he was the same Tristan who had walked into the Light, not someone sent back in punishment. He leaned against the trunk of a tree, slowly lowering himself to a crouch, thinking.

"I'm telling you, this is your last chance," Lacey said.

He looked up. "Last chance to do what?"

Meeting his eyes, her certainty faded. "I—I'm not sure. But you died once. I think this time you're playing for eternity."

With his fingers Tristan stirred the leaves and needles on the ground next to him. In the height of summer, when everything was green and alive, twisted leaves and brown needles still lay on the forest floor, death and life mixed together by the continual cycle of the seasons. Did humans and angels travel in a circle or a straight line into eternity? He didn't know, and he didn't understand his own nature, half dead, half alive. The only thing he knew was that he loved Ivy.

"Lacey, would you carry a message to Ivy?"

"Did you hear anything I just said?"

"Yes."

"You're wearing me out, Tristan. In more ways than one," she added, lifting her hands. Her skin was translucent. "I can stay materialized a little bit longer each time, but . . ."

He watched her fade. "Lacey, you okay?"

The purple shimmer circled a tree and peeked out at him, as if playing hide-and-seek.

He smiled. "Would you do something for me so Ivy knows I'm still here?"

"Something like what?" she grumbled.

"Leave a shiny penny on her pillow, or drop one in her

hand—anywhere she'll notice it and know it's for her. The day I found the bright penny in the pond, I remembered the first time I kissed her—the afternoon she dove for a penny in the school pool. All the memories started coming back then. Give her a shiny penny. She'll know what it means."

Lacey's purple mist moved in a slender twist up through the trees. "It's a good thing I'm tired out, Tristan," she said, her voice growing fainter with the distance, "or I'd smack you upside the head."

Five

"MAX!" IVY EXCLAIMED. "I DIDN'T HEAR YOU COME IN."

After finding the broken glass in her shoe and deciding she would talk to Will, Ivy had stayed upstairs, composing herself, figuring out exactly what she should say. When she descended to the kitchen, she was surprised to see Max standing in front of an open cupboard.

"I was filling Dhanya's water bottle and getting myself something to drink," he explained, holding up a drinking glass. "Is everything okay?"

"Yeah. Sure." *Chill*, she told herself. She hadn't heard

him because she had been preoccupied—or because he hadn't wanted to bother her and was trying to be quiet—not because he was sneaking around. "There's raspberry iced tea in the fridge and some lemonade packets in the cupboard next to that one."

"Can I fix you something?" he asked.

The first time Max had come over for a barbecue, he had hung around Dhanya, expecting her to wait on him. Ivy wondered if Dhanya had noticed his new manners. "No, but thanks."

He glanced curiously at the shoe she carried. Before he could ask why she was carrying just one, Ivy hurried toward the back door.

"Ivy," he called.

She turned around.

"My house is big. Come to the party with Kelsey and Dhanya—if you get tired of it, you can hang out in the library or something. There are lots of rooms where you can go and lock the door. I've left my own parties at times," he added with a smile and shrug.

"Thanks. Probably not tonight, but I'll keep that in mind."

Exiting through the back door, Ivy walked through the trees surrounding the rear of the cottage, not emerging into the open until she reached the renovated barn. Two of the barn's guest suites faced the garden and the inn, and the third faced the small wooded area that buffered the inn from Cockle Shell Road. Will's room, a lean-to that had been added to the barn, had the least scenic view, a shed used for storage.

As she approached the lean-to, Ivy heard two voices. She hesitated, then crept forward till she stood directly beneath Will's window. Beth was talking.

"Don't you see how much Ivy has changed?"

"Everybody changes," Will replied. "Maybe Suzanne was the only one who could admit it to herself, when she went off to Italy. The three of us were hoping things would stay the same till we got to college, but we were growing apart faster than we realized."

"No. It's more than that. There's something wrong with Ivy. When she met Luke, she turned against you, Will. And now she's turning against me."

"How do you mean?"

"She—she blames me for Gregory's return."

Ivy bit her lip, wanting to argue.

"She says I was the one who invited him in on the night of the séance."

I never said that! Ivy protested silently. *All of us were to blame.* She rested her shoulder against the rough-planked wall. Why was Beth saying this?

Ivy heard a chair scrape back, then the springs on the bed creak. Other than Will's desk chair, the bed was the only place to sit in his art-crammed room.

35

"Beth, when I was trying to warn Ivy about Luke, I told her about Suzanne's e-mail and how Suzanne was feeling haunted by Gregory and having dreams the way you were. I thought Ivy needed to be scared into thinking sense. I wanted her to see that she was blindly trusting another guy who didn't deserve it, the same way she had trusted Gregory. But this idea that Gregory has *actually* come back. . . . It's a little far-fetched."

"Last year you believed that Tristan came back."

"I *heard* Tristan. I saw his glow. There were signs."

"I have a sign," Beth replied.

"You do?"

"Open your hand," she told him.

There was a long pause. Ivy leaned forward, straining to hear.

"Glass." Will spoke the word softly. "Broken glass."

"She put it in my shoe."

Ivy drew back, caught off guard, the shoe in her own hand spilling a piece of glass on the grass next to the barn.

"Ivy? I can't believe it," Will said.

"Gregory made her do it. I'm scared, Will. I keep thinking about last year, when Gregory left glass for Ivy to step on. He's come back. Why else would she do this to me?"

"Ivy?!"

"She hasn't been herself since she met Luke," Beth insisted. "It was like he cast some kind of spell on her."

Ivy heard Will walking back and forth in the room. "Where were your shoes when you found this?" he asked.

"In the bathroom."

"So maybe someone broke a drinking glass and cleaned it up but didn't realize that fragments had fallen into your shoe."

Beth didn't respond right away. "You're loyal, Will," she said at last, "and I admire that. After all Ivy has done to you, you're still loyal to her."

Ivy heard paper crumpling and knew Will was destroying something he had drawn.

"I'm just trying to make sense of things," he said.

"Or trying to convince yourself that Ivy is the person you've never stopped loving."

Ivy swallowed hard, feeling afresh the pain she had inflicted on Will and herself. Would there ever be an opportunity to do right by Will? How could she ask him to listen and believe her one more time?

"I love her, too," Beth went on, "but I can see she's pulled away from both of us. I can't trust her anymore."

Ivy leaned against the barn wall, her mind reeling. Had Gregory put the glass shards in *both* of their shoes, trying to drive a wedge between them as he had once driven a wedge between her and Suzanne? As an angel, Tristan had learned to materialize his fingers. Could demons develop the same powers?

Or was Gregory influencing Beth's mind, getting her to speak for him, beating Ivy to the punch when it came to telling Will about the glass? Now that Beth had suggested that Ivy, under Gregory's influence, was playing games with her, it would be nearly impossible for Ivy to persuade Will that, in fact, Gregory was inside *Beth*.

No matter how Gregory did it, Ivy thought, as she walked back to the cottage, he'd won this round. He'd succeeded in turning her best friends against her.

Six

THE SCAR, SLICING ACROSS TRISTAN'S THROAT JUST beneath his jaw, was mostly covered by his beard now. His bruises were gone. Last night, he had spent hours hacking at his thick, wavy hair with a fishing knife stolen from a campsite. The ragged remains could barely be seen under a baseball cap he'd found on a path around Flax Pond. He wore a faded Red Sox T-shirt taken from a camp clothesline and looked like a lot of other guys on Cape Cod; still, as Tristan got in line at the hospital cafeteria, he felt as if the word WANTED was blazoned across his chest.

Yesterday, after Lacey had gone, Tristan had done a lot of thinking about the person who had beaten up the "ninety-eight point six" he was carrying around. Luke McKenna had a history, and until Tristan knew the details of that deadly night—as well as what had occurred before—he was a sitting duck.

As far as Tristan knew, the person Luke had fought hadn't reported it to the police. Why? Perhaps Luke's opponent was also wanted by the law. Or maybe his opponent had died, and Luke had two murders on his head. Perhaps they had been on a boat, and Luke had thrown the victim over, tied to a weight so he would never be found.

What were Luke and this unknown opponent fighting over—money, power? Perhaps someone who loved Corinne, Luke's ex, was taking revenge for her murder. There were too many possibilities and too few facts. Tristan couldn't ask the police for the details of the night he was brought, unconscious, to the hospital. There was only one person he could risk approaching: Andy, the nurse who had taken care of him.

The smell of clam chowder and French fries made Tristan's mouth water, but, careful with his money, he bought only a cup of coffee. Picking up a newspaper someone had left behind, he sat with his back to a bright spread of windows, aware that it would be hard for someone looking into the light to see his face. Sometimes it bothered him how many tricks he had learned while trying to stay under the radar.

He wondered how long he could camp out at the cafeteria without being noticed. Andy might not be working today, but Tristan couldn't risk going to his floor to find out. So he waited, pretending to read, pretending to sip his coffee, looking over the edge of his cup, checking out the people who came into the cafeteria. He envied them, workers who were tired and hungry, but luckier than they would ever realize, able to eat with friends and go where they wanted without looking over their shoulders.

At last, forty-five minutes later, Andy walked in with two women, all of them in nurses' scrubs. Tristan was surprised by the lump in his throat when he saw the sandy-haired, squarely built nurse. Despite the comically short robe Andy had lent him, Tristan hadn't realized how stocky he was. When Tristan came to the hospital he had been as helpless and scared as a baby, scared to the point of nastiness, and had trusted no one except Andy. He owed the nurse big time.

Andy glanced around the room, looking for a free table. He paused for a moment when he caught Tristan looking at him. Tristan quickly lifted up his newspaper, feeling like a detective in a corny movie.

Would Andy talk to him? Would he call the police? Even if Andy hadn't read one of the newspapers that were everywhere in a hospital, someone must have said to him, "Hey, remember that patient you took care of? The one who skipped out on you? He's wanted for murder."

It took just fifteen minutes for the nurses to finish their lunch, but it seemed like an eternity to Tristan. When the three of them carried their trays to the drop-off station, Tristan stood up and followed, quietly calling Andy's name.

The nurse turned and gazed at Tristan with the same quick, assessing look he had worn when Tristan was his patient.

"Sorry," said Tristan, "but I had to ditch the robe."

Andy's eyes widened, then he turned to his companions, who had started toward the hall. "I'll see you upstairs," he called to them. When they had moved on, he turned back. "Guy?" he asked, using the name Tristan had been given when he didn't know his identity.

Tristan nodded.

"Jesus! What are you doing here? Tempting fate?"

"I have to talk to you. Can you sit—just for a minute— please?" Tristan gestured to the table where he had left his coffee. Andy followed him.

For a moment they sat quietly, Andy taking the seat against the window, Tristan facing away from the crowd in the cafeteria.

"You look well," Andy said in a low voice.

"I owe you my life."

"Don't exaggerate."

"I'm not. I—"

"You do owe me the robe I gave you so you wouldn't moon the other patients in your hospital gown."

Tristan laughed a little, and Andy smiled, his tan face lighting up, his expression younger than the weathered lines around his eyes. Then he glanced around. "You've got a lot of explaining to do, but you'd better cut to the chase. Hospitals are full of nosy people. Why are you here?"

"I need information. When I came in, what was my medical condition?"

"I didn't see you until you were brought up to my floor."

"But you must have read the reports from the ER."

Andy nodded. "You'd swallowed a lot of saltwater. Because you were so confused when you regained consciousness, we thought there was brain trauma, but the scans showed nothing. Have you gotten back your memory?"

Tristan shook his head. "No. I can't recall anything from the life of a guy named Luke."

Andy studied him curiously, perhaps because of the way Tristan had phrased it. But Tristan didn't see how he could add that the guy named Luke wasn't him—not without the nurse recommending he reconsider seeing the hospital psychiatrist.

"You don't remember . . . anything?" Andy asked slowly.

"You mean like committing murder? No."

43

"Your blood alcohol level was elevated," the nurse said. "Everyone has a different threshold for inebriation, depending on their physical makeup and their history of drinking, but I remember being surprised your number wasn't much higher. You were unconscious for a long time. You had lost blood, but not an excessive amount—the knife wound wasn't as deep as it appeared. You could have been knocked out by a blow to the head, but as I said, there were no signs of a serious blow. Despite the seawater you swallowed, there were no signs of oxygen deprivation from being underwater for an extended period of time. You were a true medical puzzle.

"And speaking of medical puzzles," Andy added, "how's Ivy?"

"You knew?" Tristan asked, surprised. He hunched over. "They put her in the paper, didn't they?"

"No. They didn't. Under eighteen, they protect your identity. But Ivy came to see me the same afternoon you left here. And besides, the day I sent her friends and her to the solarium, hoping to cheer you up, I saw your face when you shot out of there." Andy smiled. "She'd gotten under your skin. *And* I saw you go back after her friends left."

"You don't miss much," Tristan said.

"No, just my patients checking out by way of the stairwell," Andy replied dryly. "Guy—Luke—there's one more thing. We did toxicology tests and no drugs showed up.

44

But there are drugs, not the kind people use by choice, that don't leave an identifiable chemical trace in the body. The one I'm familiar with is used for medical purposes—it temporarily paralyzes the patient. Some patients react to it afterward with muscle twitches, especially when awakening. It's one of those things you observe as a nurse, and I observed it with you."

"Did you tell that to the police?"

"When you were here, the police were interested only in what the first responders and doctors had to say, not a lowly nurse." Andy met Tristan's eyes. "Do you understand what I'm telling you?"

Tristan nodded slowly as he realized what this information meant. "That I might have been given a drug that would keep me from running or swimming to safety, a drug that would prevent me from fighting back." A chill swept over him. "That this thing that landed me in the hospital, it wasn't just an argument that got out of hand or a fight between two drunk guys. It was premeditated murder."

"And the person who tried it the first time," Andy said, "might try it again. Be careful."

Tristan heard the soft beep of Andy's pager.

The nurse ignored it. "Do you have a safe place to go?"

"Yes," Tristan lied.

"You're sure?"

"Yes."

The beeper sounded a second time, and Andy glanced at it. "Sorry. I've got to get upstairs."

"Are you going to tell the police you've seen me?"

"What do you think?"

Tristan stood up, picked up his coffee, and swirled it around in the paper cup. "I don't understand why you wouldn't report being contacted by a murderer."

Andy nodded. "And I don't understand why, on one morning, I was given two patients with strange medical histories, a guy who still can't remember anything about the killer he is supposed to be, and a girl who should have been dead on arrival but left the hospital with barely a scratch. I truly don't understand it. But twenty-three years of nursing have taught me to respect miracles and simply do what I'm trained to do—heal."

"Thank you."

"However," Andy added as they parted, "I might report the stolen robe."

Seven

"GO AHEAD! REALLY, I MEAN IT. I CAN FINISH THE BEDS,"
Ivy told Dhanya and Kelsey at two o'clock that afternoon,
shooing them down the inn's second floor hall. After serving
breakfast, she, Kelsey, and Dhanya had vacuumed rooms,
wiped out sinks, and changed towels, while Will took care
of the suites in the barn. Now Will was outside with Beth,
finishing up the yard work. Ivy wondered if Aunt Cindy had
noticed Beth's strangeness and purposely assigned her niece
a job that kept her away from the guests.

"I'm not in a hurry. I can handle what's left," Ivy said.

"But I thought you were going with us to Chatham," Dhanya protested.

"Another day," Ivy replied. "Promise."

Kelsey dumped a load of folded sheets in Ivy's arms. "C'mon, Dhanya, we're wasting time. Gather ye daisies while ye may."

"It's *rosebuds*, Kelsey. Gather ye rosebuds," Dhanya told her friend. With one last glance at Ivy, she followed Kelsey down the back steps.

It had been nine days since Tristan had escaped arrest. Ivy felt as if it was getting harder rather than easier: the not knowing, the creeping fears that something had happened to him and she would never know. She preferred work to lying in the sun—she preferred any activity to sitting still and thinking.

Ivy had just begun to separate the clean sheets for today's check-ins when Aunt Cindy called to her from the stairway landing.

"Ivy, would you come downstairs? Ms. Donovan's here."

Aunt Cindy never called Rosemary Donovan "Officer." *Perhaps,* Ivy thought, *to keep guests from worrying about a maid continually being checked on by the police.* And the young police woman often came before she began her shift, dressed in casual clothes. Ivy suspected Officer Donovan was attempting to develop a trusting relationship with her in the hope of catching "Luke."

"I'm finishing the beds," Ivy said, emerging into the hall. "Okay if she comes upstairs?" Ivy disliked sitting across a table from Donovan, as if they were in an interrogation room.

"No problem," Donovan replied from below. "I've always wanted a peek in the rooms." She climbed the steps quickly, looking as she always did, dark hair pulled back in a low ponytail and curved sunglasses up on her head. "Oh! Homey!" she said, entering the room called *Apple Time*. "Homey and pretty."

"This is one of my favorites," Ivy replied as the policewoman took in the stenciled borders, apple-red quilt, and bedside tables made of old apple bins. Donovan chose to sit in a rocking chair with a needlepoint cushion. "One day I'm going to have a house with rooms like this."

Ivy nodded and spread a clean bed pad over the mattress, anchoring it at the corners.

"So, I have some news," Donovan said. "Luke's moved on."

Ivy was shaking out the bottom sheet and stopped, letting the cotton float slowly down to the bed. For a moment, her heart had stopped. "Moved on—where?"

"Off the Cape. He may be out of Massachusetts by now."

Ivy wanted him to be safe, but . . . "How do you know?"

"He dropped his cell phone at a service plaza stop. It was found by the cleaning staff about 5 a.m."

"Where?" Ivy knew she'd asked the question too fast, with too much interest, but she couldn't help it.

"On the Massachusetts Turnpike. Ludlow. The bad news is he could have hitched a ride going anywhere from there, north or south on Route 84, or west to the New York Thruway." Donovan paused, studying Ivy. "The good news is that he's probably far away from you by now."

Ivy turned her back, pretending to be focused on making the bed.

"Ivy."

She yanked on the final, tight corner of the sheet. "Yes?"

"Criminals who are lone wolves often run out of money and helpful strangers. It's not unusual for them to return to the last person who assisted them. I want you to be cautious in the next several weeks."

"All right." Ivy positioned the top sheet so it hung evenly on each side.

"He's dangerous."

"Right," Ivy said, tossing a summer blanket over the top sheet.

"Very dangerous."

"I know."

Donovan stood up and took hold of the blanket edge, facing Ivy across the bed, not letting go till Ivy looked up. "Listen to me, Ivy. Even if you don't yet believe that Luke is a murderer, you can't ignore the viciousness of the fight he was in. You saw his condition in the hospital. One way or the other, Luke is part of a violent world. Don't get caught in the crossfire."

"That's good advice."

"Yeah," Donovan muttered. "If only you would take it."

They finished the bed and Donovan left.

Half an hour later, passing through the garden that lay between the inn and the cottage, Ivy saw Beth and Will sitting on the yard swing. Beth held an open sketchpad in her lap, but she didn't seem interested in it. Will sketched on another spiral pad. Ivy longed for the way it used to be, so easy between the three of them. She had loved watching them, their heads bent together, laughing and creating, totally lost in the world of their graphic novel. Couldn't Will see it—the distance Beth was keeping from everything that used to matter to her?

"Hi," Ivy said.

Although Beth refused to acknowledge her, Will looked up. Having been the one to go to the police about the stranger they called "Guy," he would have recognized Rosemary Donovan. Ivy fought her leftover anger and said what Will already knew: "Officer Donovan came by to see me."

"Did she?"

"She thinks Luke's left the Cape. They found his cell phone at a rest stop on the Mass Pike."

Will nodded without speaking, without showing any

emotion. Ivy would have preferred anger to Will's coolness and apparent indifference. She felt entirely alone. Turning away, she headed toward the cottage, where she scooped up her music books.

She had put off practicing piano for more than a week. It had been too much to face Father John, the priest who had allowed her to use the piano in his church and then helped her friend "Guy" find a job with one of his parishioners. Recommending the services of a murderer to one of his parishioners: That couldn't look good on a priest's résumé. She wouldn't blame him if he decided not to unlock his church for a girl with friends like that.

Fifteen minutes later, while Ivy was speaking to the rectory's housekeeper, Father John emerged from his office. "Ivy. I've missed you. Are you here to practice?"

"Yes."

"I'll walk you to the church. I want to show off my latest rose, Glamis Castle."

The priest led Ivy to a garden plot enclosed by a picket fence. Stopping inside the gate, he turned to face her.

"How are you doing?" he asked.

"Okay."

"A hard week, I think."

"Yes."

"Kip was asking about you."

Ivy nodded. "He was so nice, giving Luke a job and a

place to live, lending him the phone and motorbike."

"Kip and his wife were very fond of him and as stunned as I was to hear—"

"I apologize for not telling you about the hospital situation and all. I—I should have, but I trusted him."

"And you don't anymore?"

Ivy bit her lip.

"I saw no evil in him," the priest said. "Nor did Kip. We saw only a hard and honest worker. Kip said Luke left everything behind, including his pay. We were both hoping that the police had gotten it wrong, and he would be back."

"Me too," Ivy said, relieved that someone else saw what she saw, the person beneath the surface. It was less lonely knowing that the goodness in Tristan was apparent to someone who didn't know the true story. It was a relief not to have to pretend to be horrified by her connection with Luke.

"Thank you," Ivy said gratefully.

Father John pointed out a bush that shimmered with white, cabbagelike roses, then walked Ivy to the church door and unlocked it. Inside the church, Ivy sat down at the piano and began to play, losing herself in the music. She didn't want to think about what it had been like to be here with Tristan.

An hour later she stretched, and all the thoughts she had blocked out came rushing in. She gazed at the large stained glass window above the altar: Dark blues and greens showed a boat tossing in a storm, with Jesus extending his hand toward Peter, inviting him to cross the roiling waters. *A test of faith*, Ivy thought.

She heard voices outside the church. Father John entered, followed by a man with a huge arrangement of summer flowers.

"We have a wedding in an hour and a half," the priest told Ivy. "But keep playing. It makes my work light."

As more flowers were brought in and Father John set the altar and side tables for the celebration, Ivy played music she knew well, steering clear of any piece she associated with Tristan. The florist left, and a minute later, when Ivy paused to select another piece, she heard Father John exclaim with surprise.

He stood at the back of the church, his hands resting on the edge of a large marble bowl on a pedestal. A baptismal font, Ivy realized, and she watched the priest reach in and retrieve something small enough to be held in the palm of his hand.

He walked down the aisle toward her, looking both delighted and puzzled, his wet hand outstretched. "It's a penny. A very shiny penny."

Ivy studied it. "I guess a child dropped it in. My brother Philip was always asking for pennies to toss in the mall fountain."

"Perhaps," the priest replied, sounding unconvinced.

That's when Ivy noticed his glasses: Water had splashed on one lens. She quickly rose from the piano bench and walked back to the baptismal font. Reaching into the water, she retrieved a second copper penny. "Were there two in here?"

"Two?" Father John repeated, puzzled.

A penny under water—*a sign from Tristan?* Had he gotten inside the church and left it for her? But the splashed water—this had just happened. . . . Ivy's throat tightened. Tristan couldn't come himself, she realized, so he had sent Lacey with his good-bye.

She glanced around the church. Its small side windows shone with stained-glass angels, white dresses and wings against jewel-colored backgrounds. One of the dresses shimmered purple. *Lacey?* Ivy called silently.

The violet hue disappeared, then shimmered in a window behind Father John. Knowing that a believer would see Lacey's glow, Ivy guessed that the angel wanted to stay hidden from the priest. Ivy joined him at the front of the church. When he held out his hand, she gave him the second penny, smiled, and shrugged. Believer or not, she couldn't imagine him buying her explanation.

"I'll put them in the poor box," he said.

Ivy wanted to stop him. She'd trade a billion pennies for these two. Tristan was thinking of her; he loved her. That made these two pennies priceless. But all she could say was "Good idea."

"The doors are unlocked for early wedding guests," he told her. "Leave when you like—and come back soon," he added.

After the heavy wood door closed behind the priest, Ivy glanced around. "Lacey, you still here?" There was no response. She couldn't see the angel's glow, but knew it would be easy for her to hide.

"If you're here, please talk to me. I need to know where Tristan's gone. Is he all right? Please tell me he's safe. Please talk, just for a minute."

Still there was no answer.

"Bad-tempered angel," Ivy muttered, gathering her books together and sliding the piano cover over the keys. Thirty feet away, a heavy book slammed to the ground. Ivy whirled around.

"Okay, okay, I get it. You left the pennies because Tristan begged you to. You're not here for me."

Ivy crossed the altar and crouched down to pick up the large Bible. Her eyes fell upon words printed in black and red, initial letters laced with gold:

BUT RUTH REPLIED, DO NOT URGE ME TO LEAVE YOU OR TO TURN BACK FROM YOU.

WHERE YOU GO I WILL GO, AND WHERE YOU STAY I WILL STAY.

Ivy began to cry. The fear and pain that had been building inside her for nine days spilled over. She would have gone where he'd gone, stayed wherever he stayed,

56

if only Tristan had let her, if only he had asked her to go with him.

At last she stood up. Setting the Bible back on the side table, she saw that its gold-edged pages weren't lying flat. Afraid that a page was curled up and damaged, she quickly opened the book. Wedged into the beginning of the Book of Ruth was a coin. Although it was stamped with the shape of an angel, like the one Philip had given to "Guy" weeks ago, this coin appeared to be real gold.

Ivy dropped it in the poor box as she left.

"You're a piece of work, Lacey," she said, laughing through her tears.

Eight

"WHERE HAVE YOU BEEN?"

Tristan ignored Lacey's question and wearily dropped to the ground behind a barricade of broken pine branches. The need to be constantly vigilant had been more exhausting than the actual trek, and he had walked for miles.

"Around," he finally replied, lying back on the soft bed of needles and closing his eyes.

"This is no time to rest," the angel said.

"It's dark—seems like a real good time to me."

"Okay, grumpy, just thought you'd want to be on the lookout for your hot date."

Tristan sat up. "Ivy? You saw her?"

"Sure. I dropped off some change, just like you asked. Now we'll see how smart she is."

"What do you mean?"

The purple mist twirled in front of him. "I left Ivy a clue. We'll see if she figures it out."

"Lacey, this isn't a game— "

"It is to me," the angel shot back. "It has to be," she added with a touch of wistfulness. "Anyway, I've got to get going—I have other clients, ones who appreciate me. You know, I used up an awful lot of energy, changing a chunk of a candlestick into a gold coin."

"What candlestick?"

"The big fat one near the baptismal font at St. Peter's."

"You took a piece of their candlestick?" Tristan asked, struggling to make sense of what Lacey was saying.

"Just a little doodad on it." She moved closer for a moment. "You don't think I can create a gold coin out of nothing, do you? *Creating* is the job of Number One Director. Unlike you, I don't go around trying to take over His productions."

Tristan, still puzzled but understanding at least *that* message, shook his head and let his breath out slowly.

"Stay awake, Tristan. And keep an eye on the pond," Lacey advised him. "The chick might be smarter than she looks."

———

IVY TOSSED AND TURNED. AFTER THE PREVIOUS night's party, Kelsey and Dhanya had gone to bed early. Beth had followed, and Ivy had hoped to catch up on sleep but couldn't stop wondering where Tristan was. Without Lacey's help, she'd never find him.

A soft mew at the living room window was followed by a fierce shaking of the screen. Ivy rose from the sofa to let in Dusty. Since realizing that Gregory's power was growing stronger, Ivy hadn't been able to sleep in her bed, just two feet away from Beth, without waking up at every stirring in the night. After everyone upstairs was asleep, she crept down to the living room sofa. The huge Maine coon had discovered this and was dropping by every night now, looking for some attention.

Ivy sat down, petting Dusty and thinking. Something wasn't right in what she'd heard today from Donovan. If Tristan still had a phone, why hadn't he called her to say he was okay? If he was being cautious, worrying that his call might be tracked by the police, he probably wouldn't have been careless and dropped it at a rest stop. And how would they know it was his? The phone had been purchased in Kip's name.

So maybe the phone in police custody had belonged to the real Luke. The real Luke had died four weeks ago, but Ivy supposed it was possible that the phone had been kicked under something at the rest stop accidentally. In any case, its discovery appeared to convince the police that their fugitive was off the Cape.

What if he wasn't? Ivy wondered. Why had Lacey visited her? A flame of hope flickered in Ivy's heart. She rose and quietly slid open a drawer in the living room desk, where tourist information was kept. Turning on a small lamp, she studied a brochure with a map of Nickerson State Park. If Tristan had returned there, what part of the large, wooded area would he choose as his safe haven?

Her breath caught. She had heard of Flax and Cliff Ponds, where the beaches and boats were, but had never noticed the small dab of blue that lay west of Cliff: Ruth Pond. *"Where you go I will go, and where you stay I will stay."*

Ivy reached for her car keys. A few minutes later she left the inn, just as she had the night she drove back to Race Point Beach after Tristan's memorial, feeling drawn to a place; only this time, she had reason to hope Tristan would be waiting for her.

In the middle of the night, the state park was closed except to campers. Ivy checked the map, looking for a place to leave her car outside the park. She was beginning to regret her distinctive white Beetle. She did not want to leave it too close to a gate by Ruth Pond, like a flag for anyone wanting to find Luke, but the crescent moon didn't shed much light and she didn't want to use the small flashlight she had brought unless absolutely necessary. She ended up on a road off of 6A, about a mile from where a paved road crossed over a hiking trail that led to Ruth Pond. She felt almost giddy walking down the empty road outside the park at two thirty in the morning. She felt like spreading her arms and singing. Then a car passed, slowing when it was behind her, as if the driver were taking a second look. She sobered quickly.

She glanced over her shoulder, but the car had disappeared around a corner. A second car went by, slowing like the first. There was no time for her to duck out of sight. *No big deal*, Ivy told herself; she would do the same thing if she came upon a girl walking alone in the middle of the night. Still, she was relieved when she reached the wooded footpath.

Fifty feet down the path, despite the fact that her eyes were well adjusted to the darkness, Ivy couldn't see where she was going. The nearest campsite was a little over a quarter mile away. She reluctantly turned on her flashlight, hoping the woods were dense enough to prevent someone from seeing the moving beam. She focused it on the ground, just in front of her feet, wrapping her fingers around its head, trying to filter and soften the light.

Behind her a branch cracked. Ivy flicked off her light, turned, and looked toward the clearing where the trail crossed the paved road. The darkness enveloping her was lighter toward the clearing, like black velvet brushed the wrong way, but she could see nothing distinctly. Chiding herself for being skittish, she continued on.

She had planned to count her steps as a way of keeping track of how far she'd gone, but they were stumbling strides at odd lengths, so there was no point. She knew there was a place where the trail divided into three paths. The two paths to the right traveled close to the pond's edge. The one to the left eventually looped around the pond but veered away from its shore. If Tristan had sent the message via Lacey, wouldn't he stay close to the pond? Even so, he'd be hidden, Ivy reasoned, so she would have to be seen—she would have to make herself obvious, if they were to connect.

A crisp splintering of wood followed by a trampling of brush made her whirl around. She raised the flashlight's beam to a point fifty feet behind her, striping the trees, making a kind of optical illusion in which it was hard to distinguish solid tree trunk from space between. She lowered the beam a notch, which succeeded only in tangling the light in fallen branches and brush.

Ivy reminded herself that animals made noise—they weren't all as stealthy as cats. She continued on. The walk to the fork seemed endless, and she wondered if she had missed it. She went twenty feet farther, then raised her flashlight. There it was: the trail marker! Breathing a sigh of relief, she chose the middle route, which tracked closest to the water.

63

Under the crescent moon, the pond lay perfectly still, a surface of polished ebony. If Tristan were here, how could she get his attention? Hiding and calling to him would be safer for her, but silently letting herself be seen would be safer for him. Ivy ducked under branches, walked through waist-high reeds, and waded into the pond.

AFTER LACEY LEFT, TRISTAN HADN'T BEEN ABLE TO keep his eyes open. The route between the hospital and Nickerson was about twenty miles each way, a long hike to make in one day. With the park's campsites clustered around three ponds, Cliff, Little Cliff, and Flax, he had settled at Ruth's Pond several days ago. The woods here were his refuge, wrapping him in gentle night. He fell asleep and dreamed.

In his dream he was lying on the porch of an old house, watching Ivy wade into a pond. She swam for a long time, unaware of him, sending ripples of gold over the sapphire surface. He watched her with wonder, the way she had come to love the water. After a while she turned on her back and floated.

He longed to go to her, gaze down at her face, and touch the tips of her floating hair. He knew how it would look, spreading out from her face like rays of the sun.

Then he heard her speak, her voice so close to him that he heard it inside him: *It's such a great feeling, floating on a pond, a circle of trees around you, the sun sparkling at the tips of your fingers and toes.* Her words had once been his, when he'd taught her to swim.

He yearned to hold her. All he wanted was to kiss her one more time. He waded in. He reached for her, but as he brought her close, he felt himself being pulled under.

"Ivy!"

"Tristan? Tristan, where are you?"

"Ivy!"

His own heaviness drew him down into the darkness. The surface of the water, rising over his head, became his sky. Submerged tree limbs entangled him. He fought to get back to her.

"Ivy!"

"Tristan? Are you here?"

He jolted awake. Sharp-scented pine branches surrounded the place where he was lying. Lifting his head, looking toward a clearing, he saw a thin moon hanging high in the sky. Tristan rose to his feet and saw someone wading in Ruth Pond. As she moved, the silver light made bright circles in the water.

"Ivy," he called softly.

She turned around, searching for him among the trees, then hurried in the direction of his voice. When he emerged from the pines, he saw her stop and look uncertain. He laughed, remembering his beard and shorn hair.

Then she laughed and rushed to him. "Oh God! It's really you."

He held her tight, burying his face in her hair. To see her, to touch her, to hear her—were those the longings of a fallen angel? He didn't care; he *needed* these things.

She clung to him. "How I have missed you!"

"Every minute," he said. "Every day."

"I thought you had left."

"I couldn't bear to."

Then she turned in his arms, glancing over her shoulder. "We have to be careful. Someone might see us."

"No one's around," he told her. All that mattered was being with her. Being with her made him reckless.

"But out in the open like this—"

Reluctantly he released her, then led her to the pine brush where he had been sleeping. Kneeling down, he tried to make a soft place for her to sit. When he glanced up, she was smiling.

"Thanks for fluffing the pine needles," she teased, "but I plan to use you for a pillow."

Tristan stood up and kissed her, not touching her with his hands, holding her only with a long and pure kiss, until she melted against him. When they sat, he propped himself against a tree trunk and pulled her to him. She laid her cheek against his chest.

For a long time they didn't speak. He was happy just to

hear her breathing, just to feel a strand of her hair tumble over his wrist.

"If we could stop time," he said, "or wind it back . . ."

She raised her head. "We don't need to, Tristan. The miracle is that we've been given another chance to be together."

It was the second time today the word *miracle* had been used. Were Andy and Ivy right, or was Lacey? Was being in Luke's body a miracle or punishment?

"I've been trying to figure something out," Ivy said, and told him about Donovan's visit and the recovery of the cell phone. "What happened to the one Kip lent you?"

"I gave it back. I left it in the shed with his other things."

"So the phone found at the highway rest stop must have belonged to the real Luke. Donovan talked as if it were proof that you had left the Cape. But Luke would have stopped using it before he died, four weeks ago or more. You'd think they'd check on whether calls had been made from it in the last several days."

"Someone might have used it. It could even have been taken and recently used by the person who killed Luke."

Ivy sat all the way up. "I wish we knew what happened the night you were found on the beach. If I could get my hands on the police report—"

"You don't think they'd be a little suspicious when you asked for it? Ivy, I think the best strategy for you is to pretend you want nothing to do with me."

"Then maybe the medical report. If I could talk to Andy—"

"I already did."

Tristan recounted his conversation from earlier that day, and Ivy listened intently.

"A drug that doesn't leave a chemical trace," she repeated slowly. "Then the attack was premeditated."

"Yes."

"Tristan, please be careful!"

"I will, I am," he said soothingly.

"If the murderer has followed the news, then he believes that Luke has survived. What if he comes back for you? He tried it once, he'll try—"

"I don't think he'd risk it. He would know the police are hot on my trail. Why risk being caught for murder, when he could leave his revenge to the law?"

Tristan studied Ivy's face, trying to discern if she believed that line of reasoning. In his gut, he didn't. His experience with Gregory had taught him that murderers, even those who began with careful plans, didn't think through all the consequences, not even consequences to themselves. Once Gregory had started killing, he couldn't stop.

"How's Beth?" Tristan asked, deliberately changing the subject. "Do you still think Gregory is haunting her?"

"I think she . . . is struggling. She's pulling away from everyone but Will, and Will won't talk about the change in her. It's like he's in denial."

Tristan sensed that there was more and waited patiently, but Ivy simply shook her head. "I can't reach Beth. The best I can do is try to win back Will's trust in me, then get him to help her."

Tristan suspected that Ivy wasn't telling him everything that worried her, but then, he wasn't telling Ivy his worst fears. Using his own brand of denial, he pushed all thoughts of danger out of his mind. And really, for him, there was only one kind of danger, because death was defined just one way: separation from Ivy. Right now he had her with him, and that was the only thing that mattered.

Nine

"NO, I'M BEACHING WITH IVY," DHANYA ANNOUNCED
Friday afternoon.

Ivy, who was pulling a T-shirt over her bikini, glanced
up, as surprised as Kelsey by this announcement. Beth and
Will were meeting on the beach closest to the inn, and Ivy
had planned to join them, even if she sat with them for just
a few minutes before taking a walk along the surf. She was
snatching every available opportunity to mend her relationship with Will and prove she could be trusted. It would take
both of them to fight Gregory.

"But we're supposed to go to Chatham," Kelsey objected.

"We're going tonight and tomorrow night," Dhanya replied. "Isn't that enough?"

"Are you mad at me?"

"Kelsey, just because I don't spend every waking moment with you doesn't mean I'm mad at you."

"So you didn't mind me flirting with Max two nights ago."

Dhanya frowned, trying to remember the moment. "Why would I mind? Besides, if you were flirting with Max, you were also flirting with everyone on Bryan's hockey team."

"Of course I was!"

They both laughed, and Dhanya turned to Ivy. "Ready?"

"Yeah. Let me grab my book."

A few minutes later Ivy and Dhanya crossed the garden, circled the outside of the inn, and stopped at the top of the stairway leading down the bluff to the beach. The view was breathtaking: the broad dunes, the sweep of flat white beach, and the glimmering blue of the sea beyond. To the north, the ocean slipped around a sandy point, creating an inlet where lobstermen and pleasure-boaters anchored.

Halfway down the fifty-two steps, Beth and Will sat on facing benches on a landing. Will leaned over a sketch-pad, his hand moving quickly. Beth sat quietly, showing no interest in Will's drawings or the binder that lay open next to her.

When Ivy and Dhanya were a few steps above them, Beth suddenly looked up, as if they had been sneaking up on her. "Why are you following me?" she demanded.

"Excuse me?" Dhanya replied.

"Not you. Ivy. Why are you following me?"

Will lifted his head, his expression speculative as he looked from Beth to Ivy.

"I'm going to the beach with Dhanya."

"But I'm here," Beth protested.

Dhanya glanced sideways at Ivy, shook her head, then said, "It's a big beach, Beth."

"And you don't have to sit with us. I can see you're busy with the novel," Ivy added, trying to sound calm and understanding as she led Dhanya past Beth and Will.

"She's getting weirder and weirder," Dhanya remarked, when they reached the end of a narrow boardwalk that connected to a path through the dunes.

"She's not herself, that's for sure."

They trudged across the warm sand.

"Kelsey warned me that her cousin was strange, but I thought she meant her own definition of strange, meaning anyone who doesn't play sports, party hard, and chase guys."

They spread their towels a distance from the other beachgoers, most of whom were guests staying at the Seabright.

"What's wrong with Beth?" Dhanya asked bluntly.

"I don't really know."

Feeling alone in her fear for Beth, Ivy wished she could confide in Dhanya. But Dhanya wasn't likely to believe her—and if she did, she'd probably freak out. As graceful and composed as Dhanya seemed on first meeting, people and experiences that ran beyond her expectations rattled her and were usually rejected. Max, for instance.

Ivy and Dhanya had just opened their paperbacks to read when Will and Beth joined them, placing their towels on the other side of Dhanya, away from Ivy. Ivy pretended not to notice. "How are the new adventures coming?" she asked.

They were creating a graphic novel at the request of her brother, Philip, a series of adventures for Lacey and Ella the Cat Angel.

In response to her question, Beth stared out at the ocean.

"This batch is taking place on Cape Cod, right?" Ivy persisted, banking on Will's politeness.

He nodded. "Philip wanted pirates."

"Why, shiver me timbers!" Ivy replied, and he smiled a little.

Dhanya put down her book. "Can we see your sketches?"

"I'm still working on settings more than the action. We, uh, have some writing to do," he said with a glance toward Beth.

Beth had started blocking after the séance—the first sign, Ivy now realized, that something was taking over her mind.

"But see what you think of these," Will continued, opening the sketchpad to his most recent sketches and handing it to Dhanya. Dhanya shared it with Ivy.

"The church with the bell tower," Ivy said. "It's terrific, Will."

"It looks abandoned," Dhanya said.

"It is."

"Will always gives an atmosphere to his buildings," Ivy told Dhanya.

She flipped the page.

"Ella." Ivy smiled. "Ella was my cat," she explained to Dhanya.

"The one Gregory killed?"

Beth looked over her shoulder at them.

"Yes. She's looking quite pleased with herself, Will, walking along the back of the church pew."

"Like she owns the place," Will said. "I think we're going to make it her and Lacey's home on the Cape." He leaned toward them and turned the page: Ella sat in the bell tower.

"As high as the birds," Ivy observed. "Ella really is in cat heaven!"

"The details are awesome," Dhanya said as they flipped more pages and studied interior scenes of the church.

"Yes, they are," Ivy said thoughtfully. She hadn't teased

Will since they'd broken up and wondered how he'd react. "You know I thought the church's windows had panes of opaque glass—meaning you can't see into the church from the outside."

Will smiled a little.

"There's something you should know about Will," Ivy said to Dhanya. "He's an upstanding, law-abiding citizen, except when it comes to getting a closer look at something he wants to draw."

"The latch on one of the basement windows is broken," Will explained.

"Oh, a personal invitation!" Ivy teased.

"In the basement you can see the original stone that is the base of the bell tower," he went on enthusiastically, "and a piece of coiled rope. It must have run up to the bell."

"Did you get into the tower?" Ivy asked.

"There's no stairway to it. On the main floor of the church, there's a trapdoor in the ceiling, right below the tower, and a ladder that goes up to it. Maybe they rang the bell from the basement."

"'Ask not for whom the bell tolls,'" Beth said, moving her head slowly till her eyes met Ivy's. "'It tolls for thee.'"

Dhanya gave Ivy a *see-what-I-mean* look. Will acted as if he hadn't heard Beth.

He sees the change in her, Ivy thought, *but he can't admit it.*

Still, she was making progress. She had received the first smile from him in weeks, and though Dhanya had made the request, he'd been willing to share his drawings and interest in the church with Ivy. They looked at a few more drawings, then she and Dhanya returned to their reading and Will to his sketching.

The sun on Ivy's back made her drowsy. Short of sleep from the night before, she quickly drifted off. Sometime later, she was awakened by voices and laughter.

Ivy lifted her head, and Kelsey remarked, "Get enough rest? You'd think you were the one out late partying."

"Maybe she is and we don't know it," Chase said, laying down a card. The two of them, Bryan, and Max were playing on a picnic blanket spread next to Ivy. Will was sketching and Dhanya reading. Beth was gone.

"You'd go to someone else's party and not mine?" Max asked.

"Maxie, sometimes *you're* not at your own parties," Bryan pointed out.

"I'm there." Max studied his cards then laid one down. "I take breaks, that's all."

Bryan dropped a card on top of Max's. "Bad move, Max."

"Bad move, Bryan," Kelsey said triumphantly, placing a card on his.

Chase laughed and threw down his hand. "She cheats."

"She *wins*," Kelsey corrected him. "Maybe if you paid

more attention to the game, *you'd* win." She turned over his cards. "You were dealt a better hand than me. You should have taken me."

"I compete only when it matters," Chase said, tipping back his bottle of green tea and taking a long sip.

"Like at Max's party?" Kelsey baited him. "I couldn't believe it when you bet Stefan all that money that you could beat him at pool. What were you *thinking*?"

"He got under my skin," Chase said. "Is that guy on steroids or something?"

Bryan leaned back, resting on his elbows. "All hockey goalies are crazy."

"It was more than that," Dhanya said, looking up from her book. "He looked kind of scary."

Bryan grinned. "You ought to see him during the season, when he's all banged up."

"Why does he call you 'Top'?" Dhanya asked.

"It's a nickname. I'm good at spinning away from defenders."

"You know where your teammate's from, don't you?" Chase remarked, then paused and slowly screwed on the top of his bottle, waiting to make sure he had everyone's attention.

Will wore a poker face, but Ivy could see from the way his pencil dug into the paper that Chase had gotten to him.

"The same hood as Luke McKenna."

"Really?" said Max. "He told you that?"

"He was bragging and started talking about the rink at River Gardens. I know the hood—it has some blue-collar types and a lot of lowlifes, a lot of drugs," Chase said with a dismissive flick of his hand. "My dad has a few clients there."

"Your dad sells drugs?" Will responded, and everyone laughed but Chase.

"He's a criminal defense attorney," Chase replied coolly.

The same neighborhood, Ivy thought, *and the same age.* It was a sobering reminder of how many visitors to the Cape might recognize "Luke" if she and Tristan got careless.

The conversation moved on to other people who'd attended the recent party.

"If you can tear yourself away from your Gatsby parties, I'm having some people over on Saturday night," Chase said. "Some friends who have ski homes near ours at Jackson Hole. You'd like them."

"What are Gatsby parties?" Bryan asked.

"Parties like those thrown in the Fitzgerald novel," Will guessed.

Chase nodded. "*The Great Gatsby.* Rich guy with all kinds of toys tries desperately to win a girl, letting people get drunk at his expense."

Ivy figured this plot summary was a putdown of Max.

"Sounds good to me!" Kelsey said enthusiastically.

"Chase's party or Gatsby's?" Bryan asked.

"Gatsby's, of course," Kelsey replied, lifting her auburn hair from her shoulders and waving it about, making her ponytail a fan.

"I'd like to come, Chase," Dhanya said.

"Me too," Max chimed in quickly. "Since we're both going, why don't I pick you up, Dhanya?"

Dhanya blinked, caught by surprise. "Well, uh, I did have plans with Ivy tomorrow night."

This was news to Ivy—and it was pretty lame. But Chase nodded, not seeming to recognize a rejection of his offer. "Great. I'll bring the other car. It's got room."

"And Will and Beth," Dhanya added.

Will stopped sketching. Kelsey rolled her eyes at Dhanya's contrived excuses. Ivy figured that somewhere in the Moyers' fleet of cars there was one big enough for all of them, but Max had caught on. His tan became tinged with pink.

"So," Will said, loudly enough to draw attention from Kelsey's grimace and Chase's smug smile, "since it's easier to keep plans sort of the same, the four of us will meet you there, Max."

"And Max will be my date," Bryan added.

"What about me?" Kelsey demanded.

"I thought you preferred Gatsby parties," Bryan teased. "But you can bum a ride with us if you want."

Ivy listened to the banter for a little longer, then stood up and walked to the ocean's edge, letting the wind blow away the group's conversation and laughter. It seemed as if it would be forever until that night, when she'd see Tristan again.

They both knew they were taking a chance by meeting. It would be easier to take precautions if they knew who had threatened them. Had Gregory learned that Tristan was inside Luke's body? If Gregory knew, would he openly attack Tristan or lie in wait for a vulnerable moment? Maybe Gregory wouldn't have to do anything but help Luke's enemies. To kill the body that was now Tristan's would be just as good as killing her.

But who were Luke's enemies? If Andy was right, someone or maybe several someones out there had planned a successful murder—though they didn't know how successful they'd been. Would they try something else just as effective? Was she going to lead Luke's enemies directly to Tristan?

A light touch on Ivy's elbow startled her.

"Hey."

"Bryan—hi." Turning, she caught her long hair as it whipped around in her face. "Going in the water?"

"No. Hanging out," he said with a jaunty half-smile.

Not this again, Ivy thought, recalling the night he had flirted with her at the skating rink. He'd denied it was an attempt to make Kelsey jealous, but getting a rise out of each other was their favorite sport.

Bryan moved closer to Ivy and faced the beach—so he

could enjoy Kelsey's reactions, Ivy thought. "Bryan, isn't there another big party going on tonight?"

"Yeah, a couple houses down from Max's. Want to come?"

"No. I want you to wait till then and find some party girl to make Kelsey jealous. You should remember this from college: Roommates are off-limits."

His green eyes sparkled with laughter, then suddenly grew serious. "Here's the deal," he said. "I'm going to smile while we talk and touch your hand, like the great flirt I am—"

"Please *don't*."

"But it's all for show."

"No kidding!"

"Because there's something I need to talk about, and it's hard to get the time to do that with you alone."

Ivy had begun to turn away, but turned back. "What do you mean?"

"It's about Luke."

Now he had her full attention.

"We were friends."

Ivy stared at him with amazement. "Friends!"

Bryan barely nodded, then said, "You're looking kind of intense. I'm going to tilt my head and smile at you as if fascinated—"

Ivy grimaced.

"Good thing *you're* not facing the beach," Bryan added, laughing.

"You know Luke? Why did you wait till now to tell me?" All this time, Bryan had known facts that she and Tristan had desperately needed.

"Because I'm a coward."

Ivy studied him. "I don't think so."

"Really, I am. The pressure's off now. Luke's gone. I don't have to figure out what's right, what's wrong. I don't have to decide whether to help him again."

"You helped him before?"

"I told you, he was my friend."

"A close one?"

Bryan glanced over Ivy's shoulder, checking out the others, then said, "We grew up together. Yeah, in that hood Chase speaks so highly of. I knew it would come out sooner or later. Luke and I skated together. His mother was an alcoholic, drank herself to death. His father was gone all of his life—who knows where. Luke spent a lot of time at our house."

Bryan took a deep breath and let it out slowly. "It's really hard for me to believe that everything a person knows about his life can be erased—that everything we did together is suddenly gone."

Ivy remained quiet.

"But I guess it's better for Luke that way."

"Better?" she asked sharply. "Not knowing how to defend himself or who to fear?"

"The truth is, Luke didn't know that even when he remembered everything," Bryan said. "Mind if we walk a little? I know Kelsey's body language—she's thinking about joining us. But she's got too much pride to chase us."

They walked silently for several minutes, Ivy watching the frothy surf roll over her feet, trying to work out what this discovery meant.

"Luke was a good person," Bryan said at last. "He'd do anything to help out a friend. But he was a bad judge of character, and when you grow up in a tough area where survival is the first order of business, you have to know your friends from your enemies."

"Did he have many enemies?"

Bryan stopped to watch a gull wheel and drop toward the water. "You only need one. But no—most people liked Luke, and those who didn't just blew him off."

"What was his relationship with Corinne?"

"He was totally in love with her." Bryan shook his head and continued walking. "She played him for a fool."

"That's hard to deal with, but unless you're the posses-sive, abusive type, you don't usually murder the person who breaks up with you," Ivy said. "Was he abusive?"

"No. But Luke's feelings always ran strong—you must have seen that yourself. At times his passion made him a brilliant hockey player; other times it destroyed his game. He couldn't harness his feelings. And like a lot of guys, the way he played his sport was the way he lived his life. When he drank, he had even less control."

"Was he drinking the night she died?"

"Yes."

"So how did you help him?" Ivy asked.

"I pretended to cooperate with the police by giving them a tiny piece of accurate info. Then I gave them enough fake leads to send them rushing in the wrong direction, allowing Luke time to escape. I drove him a hundred miles or so and gave him some cash. The police were pretty ticked, but they chalked it up to me being a stupid hockey player from a bad hood—to being a lowlife, as Chase puts it, ultimately loyal to another lowlife."

Ivy's hair kept blowing in her face; she turned her head as she tossed it back. "Kelsey's coming."

"Is she? So I guess Luke isn't the only poor judge of what a girl will or won't do," Bryan replied with a wry smile. "Ivy, no one on the Cape but my uncle and Stefan—the guy Chase was talking about—knows my connection to Luke, and I want to keep it that way."

"Okay." It was in Tristan's best interest to keep things quiet. And she thought it better to let Bryan assume "Luke" had fled the Cape until she and Tristan had thought things through.

"I've told you all this for a reason," Bryan continued. "I know my friend. If Luke has feelings for you, he'll come back, even if it means risking his life."

Ivy worked hard to keep her face neutral.

"If you need my help, you know where I—"

"Well, hello," Kelsey interrupted. "Feeling all energized, Ivy?"

Ivy took a step back from both Kelsey and Bryan. "Actually, I'm dragging," she replied. "I was just heading back to my beach towel."

Ivy walked away quickly—too quickly, she realized, for someone who was supposed to be tired. Reaching her towel, she glanced up the beach and saw Kelsey pushing Bryan toward the water and Bryan pushing back. He was laughing—she was not.

When Ivy sat down, Dhanya gazed at her with obvious curiosity. The conversation must have looked like a flirtation to more than just Kelsey.

"I wish Bryan wouldn't tease Kelsey that way," Ivy said.

"Yeah," Dhanya replied a bit faintly as if unconvinced that it was just Bryan's game.

Ivy glanced toward Will. He met her eyes with the coolness she'd seen for the last several weeks. Whatever trust she had earned from Will earlier in the afternoon had just been lost. One step forward, one step back.

Ten

"BRYAN!" TRISTAN EXCLAIMED. "NICE OF HIM TO SAY something now that I've finally figured out who I'm supposed to be."

"That was my first reaction," Ivy replied. "But then I reminded myself that at least he kept your secret. It was Will, not Bryan, who told the police where you were."

Tristan wanted to pace. He wanted to snap branches in half and kick stones. He was starting to feel like a caged animal, but it was ten thirty at night and campers were still awake. On a night lit only by a slender peel of the moon, most people weren't taking hikes, so they were relatively safe. But this morning, a child, bored by fishing, had wandered away from his family and found Tristan asleep. Later in the afternoon, in search of attention, the child had returned. It wouldn't be long before the kid was boasting about his new friend.

"The first time Bryan would have actually seen you was the night of the carnival," Ivy went on, "the night before the police came for you. Until then, he'd only heard of you as someone named Guy."

"Can we trust him?"

"I've been thinking about that," Ivy said. "He's torn between his friendship and what he thinks is the right thing to do." Ivy recounted everything that Bryan had told her. "I think we should wait a little longer before I tell him you're here."

"Still, he knows the things I need to know," Tristan pointed out.

"Things that I can find out without revealing anything," Ivy replied. "He knows I fell in love with you—with Luke. My curiosity will seem natural to him."

Tristan studied Ivy. Her amazing dark-gold hair was completely hidden by a tightly wrapped bandana. And she had come from a different direction tonight, her shoes muddy from walking the edge of the pond rather than following the bike trail. She was as worried as he was that the police—and Luke's enemies—would find out where he was.

"What? What is it?" Ivy asked.

Tristan flexed his hands. "I don't know. . . . Just the feeling of being watched."

Ivy bit her lip.

"You feel it too," he guessed.

"Last night I did, yes." She took a deep breath. "Tristan, I think you need to leave the park. I think you need to leave the Cape."

"No!"

"You need to get far away, Tristan."

He held her by the shoulders. "I'm not leaving as long as Gregory is here."

"Just for a while," she said. "When I've learned a little more about Luke and who his enemies are—"

"No."

"Tonight I can drive you somewhere off the Cape, to the other side of the canal," Ivy rushed on. "Tomorrow night, I'll leave earlier and drive you farther." Her eyes glistened with tears. "Next week, Mom, Philip, and Andrew are going to California, but no one at the inn knows that. I'll ask if I can go home for a few days. We'll stop there, get provisions, then I'll drive you miles away."

Tristan took her face gently in his hands. "Listen to me, love. Between here and 'miles away' there are bridges and tolls—there are cameras everywhere. Officer Donovan warned you that I'd come back, and she'll check on you. If the police find you've left the Cape, they'll check your home, then put out a bulletin."

Tears ran down Ivy's cheeks. He pressed his cheek against hers, as if he could stop them.

"Tristan, if Luke's murderer finds you, I—I couldn't survive having you die twice."

"And if Gregory destroys your life, how could I survive that?"

She buried her face in his shoulder.

"Let's think it through. There must be a place. Is there another park on the Cape?"

"The national park or any place farther along the Cape is too open, and going in the other direction. . . . The church!"

He almost laughed, but afraid he'd hurt her feelings, said gently, "I don't think Father John's going to welcome me back."

"Another church, a small one, about three miles from here. A group is raising money to restore it as a community arts center, but the grass is long, and no one seems to be around. One of the basement windows can be opened—Will was there the other day taking pictures."

"What if Will comes back?"

"You could fix the window with the broken latch, put a piece of wood in it so he can't open it. If someone unlocked the front door and entered that way, you would probably hear it and have time to escape through the basement."

"Can you give me directions?"

"I'll drive you," she said.

"Better for me to walk there later tonight."

She began to shake her head.

"Ivy, we don't want a little white Volkswagen to be seen near the church."

She nodded solemnly, then looked into his eyes.

They had had so little time together, he thought, for sharing the simple happiness of walking side by side, exploring a summer night, and being in each other's arms. It would have been better for her if she had never loved him.

"I don't know what you're thinking, but it's wrong," Ivy said, then held him tightly until they both knew it was time to part.

WHEN IVY ARRIVED HOME FRIDAY NIGHT, ONLY DUSTY was there to greet her. Hoping to find out more about Luke's life so she could figure out who might want him dead, Ivy opened her laptop on the kitchen table and typed in "River Gardens Providence." A map of the neighborhood came up and, after studying it for several minutes, she sent it to her cell phone. A survey of the other Google entries revealed a hair salon, barbershop, two liquor stores, several bars, and an elementary and middle school that bore the neighborhood's name. But most of the entries were articles she had read a week ago about the death of Corinne Santori.

Two photos ran with the articles, both showing a striking nineteen-year-old girl with dark hair and dark eyes. According to the articles, she and Luke McKenna had gone through school together, but Luke had dropped out at sixteen. Friends said they were secretly engaged, until Corinne ended the relationship in February, two months before she was murdered.

Ivy was amazed that Luke and Corinne had stayed together as long as they did. Having finished high school, Corinne attended art school to study photography, had a job in a camera shop, and had gotten her own apartment, away from River Gardens. But Luke appeared to be trapped in a downward spiral with underage drinking, two DUIs, and an assault outside a bar on his record, although charges for the latter were dropped. Maybe Corinne had felt sorry for him, Ivy reasoned. Or maybe she had been afraid of the violent streak in him, too afraid to break it off.

The cottage's screen door banged back and Ivy quickly clicked out of her search and into her e-mail. "Hey," she called out.

There was no response. Dusty, who had been snoozing on one of the kitchen chairs, stood up and looked toward the living room, nose twitching.

"Beth? Dhanya? Kelsey?" Ivy guessed aloud.

Footsteps, which Ivy recognized as Beth's, stopped at the entrance to the kitchen. Ivy saw the cat's tail switch and his pupils grow into round black mirrors. She turned toward Beth but could not see what had drawn such a wary reaction. Ella had been aware of Tristan when he was an angel. Could Dusty sense Gregory?

"I was just going to make some popcorn," Ivy said, hoping to lure Beth into a conversation. "Sit down—save me from eating it all."

"I'm not hungry."

"Well, then just keep me company," Ivy suggested lightly.

Beth continued toward the stairs.

"Beth!" Ivy stood up and caught her friend by the arm. "You're not yourself. You don't speak or act like yourself. Do you understand?" She tried to look in her eyes, but Beth turned her head away. "Something has happened to you. Gregory is haunting you."

"That's ridiculous," Beth replied. "It's you he wants. Gregory is haunting *you*." She pulled away from Ivy and hurried up the steps.

Ivy gazed after her for a moment, then returned to the kitchen table, feeling uneasy. Dusty stood at the edge of the table, the thick fur along his spine bristling. "What do you see?" Ivy asked softly. "Has he grown strong enough for you to see him now?"

She hunched in front of her laptop, not knowing how she could stop Gregory, wondering what would satisfy his desire for revenge. Lacey had been right—he wanted revenge—and he was already getting it, bit by bit, destroying someone Ivy loved.

She feared that Beth would have to do something extreme before Will would recognize what they were dealing with. Would Beth be too far gone by then? There must be a way to get through to her. "Angels, help me. Guide me. Show me!"

Ivy stared at the list of e-mails on her screen—Philip, Mom, Andrew, Philip again, Suzanne.

Suzanne. Two weeks earlier she had written to Beth saying that she was having dreams of Gregory. Ivy clicked on the new message:

IVY, I MISS U. WISH U WERE HERE.

Wish you were with me, Ivy thought.

IS BETH OK? YESTERDAY GOT A STRANGE MSG FROM HER ABOUT
A DREAM SHE HAD. SCARED ME.

Ivy glanced at the clock—12:28 p.m. In Italy, 6:28 a.m. WHAT WAS THE DREAM? she typed, sending the message as an IM. Then she rose, fixed herself a glass of ice water, and paced the kitchen. Dusty sat on the stones at the edge of the hearth, looking up the cottage's steep stairway.

Wake up, Suzanne. Wake up, Ivy thought.

A soft beep drew her back to her screen.

DO YOU KNOW WHAT TIME IT IS HERE?!?! GIRL WITH SNAKE COILED AROUND HER NECK, CHOKING HER.

Ivy frowned, then, sitting down again, typed: PROBLY ABT PROVIDENCE GIRL STRANGLED BY EX. EX WAS HIDING ON CAPE.

Ivy didn't know how much Suzanne knew about the Luke story and was debating what to add when a low growl from Dusty caught her attention. Ivy sent the message as it was, then crept to the steps, listening intently for movement above.

Soft steps, lighter than Beth's usual tread, crossed the floor to Kelsey and Dhanya's side. Ivy thought she heard a bureau drawer slide open and closed. She sniffed for the scent of burning candles and wished she had thrown out all of them as well as Dhanya's Ouija board. The first week they were on the Cape, when Kelsey and Dhanya had wanted to play with the board, Beth had objected to the use of cranberry candles, saying they needed white ones to attract only good spirits. Now Beth kept one dark red votive on the night table between her and Ivy's beds.

Hearing Beth return to the side of the room they shared, Ivy tiptoed up several steps and inhaled a sulfurous smell; Beth had lit a match.

"Beth?"

Ivy climbed the remaining steps and, reaching the landing, saw Beth lying back in bed, eyes closed, the candle flickering inside its crimson glass. Ivy's angel statue, pushed to the edge of the night table, looked ghostly in the wavering light.

Although Beth didn't move, Ivy knew she couldn't have fallen asleep that fast. She crossed the room and sat on her bed across from her friend. Beth's face was still, but not peaceful—a death mask. Tristan's goodness, trapped in a body of a killer, and Gregory's evil, wrapped in the body of the sweetest person Ivy knew—there were so many ways for a person to die, Ivy thought, so many ways to lose a person you love.

The amethyst necklace Ivy and Will had given Beth for her eighteenth birthday lay sparkling next to the candle. Beth hadn't worn it for several days, maybe a week. Ivy touched the stone with one finger, then leaned over to extinguish the votive flame.

"What're you doing?" Beth asked sharply.

Ivy straightened up. "I was going to blow out your candle. It's not safe to leave it burning while you sleep."

"It's in a glass."

"Even so, if you turned in your sleep suddenly, you could knock it over. Or a sheet could blow on top of it and catch fire."

Beth's only reaction was to shrug, then roll on her side, away from Ivy. The candlelight danced, making Beth a dark shadow huddled against the wall.

"Beth, I have a question for you. I found glass in my shoe. How did that happen?"

Beth kept her back to Ivy. "You put it there."

"*I* put it there! That makes no sense. Why would I cut myself?"

"To get attention," Beth replied, and added in a singsong voice: "No more Will. No more Tristan. Poor Ivy needs everyone's attention."

Ivy drew back. Was Gregory controlling Beth's words? Or did Beth, her mind twisted by Gregory's presence, actually believe what she was saying?

"That's a lie," Ivy said.

"That's a lie," Beth repeated back.

"Beth, look at me!"

Beth turned over suddenly, swinging her arm as she did, and knocked over the candle. It rolled across the night table.

Ivy snatched it, singeing the tips of her fingers, then blew out the flame. "I don't know how to get through to you, Beth. I don't know how!"

Beth met Ivy's gaze, her eyes coldly glittering though there was no light in the room to reflect in them. Struggling to keep her hand steady, Ivy carried the votive down to the kitchen.

She sat down shakily. A message had come back from Suzanne.

IVY, THE GIRL BEING CHOKED WAS YOU.

Eleven

TRISTAN LIFTED HIS HEAD, STILL HALF ASLEEP, NOT
sure what time it was or why he was lying in somebody's
attic. He rolled over. High above him was a square of light—
daylight, he thought—illuminating a ladder with flat wooden
steps that led to the bright opening. He sat up. There was
enough light to see support beams forming giant upright
Xs against the walls of the all-timber room. A thick piece of
rope hung from the ceiling, its frayed tail ending about ten
feet above the floor. He was in a bell tower in the church Ivy
had told him about.

Before Ivy had left the park the night before, she had

given him a clean blanket, flashlight, and spare bottle of water, items from her car's emergency kit. Tristan had waited till the night sky began to lighten to hike to the church, arriving just before the sun rose, glad for the morning's heavy mist. The house closest to the church, facing Route 6A, was small and hidden from the church by a screen of trees. The frame house across Wharf Lane, also shielded by trees, was large enough to be an inn, but dilapidated, with just one car in the rutted driveway. Directly across 6A, another old structure had been converted to a gallery, which, according to its sign, closed at six o'clock each evening. Still, Tristan had been cautious as he crept along the side of the church, trying each window till he found the one with the broken latch.

With one side of the basement brightened by aboveground windows, the area had been light enough for him to find his way to a stairway without turning on his flashlight. The steps led to the altar end of the church's main floor. At the opposite end he'd found the ladder to the trapdoor. Standing at the top of the ladder to the tower room, he had finally turned on his flashlight, looking around, hoping not to find a pair of beady eyes looking back.

The room had been cleaner than he'd expected—or maybe the long hike to the hospital the day before and his shortage of sleep since had made it seem that way. He had thrown down his bedroll, put the clean blanket from Ivy on top, and, feeling more secure than he had for the last eleven nights, slept soundly.

Slept for how long? He peered down into the shadowy vestibule below him, then squinted up at the square of light above his head. Standing up, he tested the ladder to the belfry, grasping the steps from underneath to see if they would hold his weight, then climbed them. The upper ones were more weather-beaten than the lower, and he stretched out and grabbed the end of the rope in case the wood splintered. But the steps held, and the air at the top was fresh and cool.

After pulling himself onto the floor of the open belfry, Tristan kept his head below the sills so he wouldn't be seen from the street, and studied the massive bronze bell and its wheel. A thick rope ran along the lip of the wheel, then rolled over a pulley before disappearing through a hole in the floor. Tristan laughed at himself: If he'd fallen from the ladder and grasped the rope, he would have rung the bell.

Each side of the square belfry had a pair of large windows making a Gothic arch that framed the sky, dark blue on one side, streaky orange opposite it. He's slept twelve hours! Tristan could hear the soft *whoosh* of traffic from the main road and slowly raised his head above the sill to peer through a row of decorative metal spikes. The churchyard with its stone path and overgrown bushes lay undisturbed, as if all the summer vacationers had agreed to walk around its edges.

Tristan returned to the room where he had slept and descended the ladder to the main level of the small church. Its windows, leaded-glass in a diamond pattern with pastel-colored panes, shielded him from the outside, but let in enough light for him to delineate the Gothic ribs of the building. Sitting in a pew, memories from a lifetime ago flooded Tristan's mind. His toy action heroes had scaled a lot of pews in the hospital chapel while he'd waited for his dad to finish up paperwork in the chaplain's office. His mother would finally show up with "Dr. Teddy Ann," the bear who made evening rounds with her, stuffed in a lab-coat pocket.

Because of his mother's medical practice, he had grown up knowing that children and teens died. And he had always assumed that his father, Reverend Carruthers, would be there to pray with people who were scared and worried and grieving. It had never occurred to him that their own safe and happy circle might be broken. He wondered how his parents were doing. He longed to hear their voices again and to hug them as unselfconsciously as he had when he was a child.

Tristan sat for a long time as dusky shadows filled up the corners and height of the church. Ivy was supposed to leave a care package for him at the beach up the road, a kid's backpack with Philip's name scrawled on it, stuffed with food. He was waiting for nightfall.

When it was almost dark, he descended the turning stairway to the basement, wanting a glimpse of it before the light completely faded. The windows in the basement were clear and curtainless, so he stood with his back against the wall, surveying the room. In addition to old tables and chairs, it contained some of the church's "memories": a children's puppet theater, tarnished Christmas decorations, and rusted fans on tall poles for warm summer Sundays.

Tristan memorized the layout so he could reenter the church in total darkness and find his way. Suddenly, he couldn't wait any longer to get outside. It was dark enough, he told himself as he walked to the window with the broken latch. He froze. Someone stood at the edge of the church lawn, gazing at the church. Beth.

She stood as still as a stone figure in a cemetery. While she was too far away for him to see her eyes, he knew by the lift of her chin that she was looking upward, staring at the bell tower. He couldn't see Gregory in her, but the unnatural way she held herself, her unrelenting gaze at the place where he had climbed, was creepy. Could Gregory sense that he, Tristan, had been in the tower?

No, of course not, he told himself. If Gregory could perceive him, Beth would be focused on the basement.

But that left the question of why exactly Beth was there.

Twelve

"DO YOU MIND DRIVING TO THE PARTY?" WILL ASKED
Ivy Saturday evening. She and Dhanya met him outside the
cottage, Dhanya walking like a robot, the polish on her toenails and fingernails still drying.

"You're not going to Chase's?"

"Beth has my car," Will replied.

"Beth! You lent it to her?" Ivy exclaimed. *Open your
eyes, Will,* she wanted to say. *Beth's not connecting with
people. She's hostile. She shouldn't be driving around alone.*

Beth's dream haunted Ivy—not because she thought it

was one of her prophetic visions; more likely, it expressed Beth's fear that "Luke" would strangle Ivy as he had Corinne. But what if *Beth* believed it was prophetic and acted on that belief? What if she attempted to hunt him down to "save" Ivy? What if the dream was created by Gregory—seeded by him as he prowled her mind—the beginning of a dangerous and demonic plan?

"Look, if you don't want to drive, I'll call Bryan," Will said, his voice growing edgy. Dhanya looked from one to the other.

"No, c'mon," Ivy replied. "I'm just worried about Beth."

Ivy realized that Will wasn't looking forward to this party any more than she was. She wished they had gotten off to a better start this evening. She'd hoped that an uncomfortable party among people they didn't know would make Will her ally, if only for the evening, and she could make progress toward talking to him about Beth.

They followed 6A west to Chase's house, which took them past Tristan's hideout. When Will turned in his seat to look at the church, Ivy got nervous. She reminded herself that Will was the one who'd first noticed it.

"Okay, keep an eye out for Toby's Landing," she said.

"There," Will replied almost immediately, and she turned off 6A, following the road to another one marked PRIVATE. Chase's was the last of three widely spaced homes facing Cape Cod Bay. The shingled home rose before them, its center portion anchored by two large gambrels that faced the driveway, each one several windows wide.

"It's perfect," Dhanya said as she stood on the cobbled drive, gazing at the old home. "If I lived on Cape Cod, this is the exact house I would buy."

"You could probably get it for five mil," Will told her.

Dhanya was unfazed by the price tag. "Max's house costs more than that, but there's no comparison. I hope it has trellises with climbing roses and a bench under an old arbor. This is the way a house on Cape Cod *should* look!"

"Except of course, for the tiny homes that are actually called 'Cape Cods,'" Will remarked.

Ivy laughed, but Dhanya was too impressed to pay attention to Will's wry comment. "Chase said his father is a famous defense attorney," she went on.

"Yes, we heard," Ivy replied as they walked to the front door.

"Which tells you that crime pays—at least for somebody," Will said.

"No, most of their money was inherited from his grandfather. Not that Chase's father doesn't earn a lot of money. His mother runs a gallery selling fine art during the summer, but Chase says it's not about money. She's fulfilling herself."

Ivy and Will exchanged glances, and for a moment it felt like old times, when an unspoken thought passed between them: Poor Max, thwarted in his effort to drive Dhanya to the party, was on his way to heartbreak. He might have a huge house and a lot of "toys" but Ivy didn't see how he, with his bargain-chain father could compete with this tasteful, justice-seeking, self-fulfilled family.

Chase answered the door, then gestured and stepped aside, allowing them to appreciate the dark-paneled hall, the carved staircase with its mysterious alcove halfway up, and a gallery's worth of art. Will, surrounded by painted canvases, could no longer act disdainful. When Ivy and Dhanya followed Chase to a porch off the back of the house, Will stayed behind to look at the art.

Chase introduced Ivy and Dhanya to his friends, a dozen guys and girls from various states who had grown up skiing together at Jackson Hole. His friends didn't appear too interested in talking to the newcomers, but that was natural, Ivy thought, for a group enjoying a reunion. They were dressed casually in designer labels—the kind about which Suzanne had educated Ivy.

"Don't sit down till you've snagged something to drink," Chase said, leading Dhanya by the hand. He looked over his shoulder and beckoned to Ivy to follow them to a table of refreshments at the end of the porch. It looked like one of the college-faculty spreads put on by her mother and Andrew: chilled wine, imported beer, Perrier, fancy kabobs, and smaller hors d'oeuvres. The layout told Ivy that Chase's parents had approved the alcohol.

After Dhanya chose a Perrier, Chase steered her toward a guy and girl who were deep in conversation. Ivy stayed by the table. Will entered the room, looked around at the strangers, hesitating, then joined Ivy. "You know you're at a classy party," he observed, "when you need utensils to pick up the snacks."

"I sure could use a handful of chips right now. How's the fine art?" she asked, borrowing Dhanya's term for the kind of gallery Chase's mother ran.

"I have to admit, some of it's really good," Will said.

Ivy nodded. "And I have to admit this place is beautiful—so close to the water."

The lawn beyond the porch dropped down slightly to the beach. It was a warm, humid night, and the stars looked soft enough to melt over the calm expanse of bay.

"It would be real nice to set up an easel here," Will said, his voice wistful.

Ivy was about to ask Will if he wanted to walk to the water's edge when a pretty raven-haired girl, whose back had been to them, turned around. "Do you paint?"

"Yeah. Do you?"

Will and the girl quickly got into a discussion of art. Realizing that she had missed her chance, Ivy drifted on and ended up talking with a brother and sister from Chicago. She had started to enjoy their conversation about college—the guy had finished freshman year as a music major and his sister was the same age as Ivy—when Bryan, Kelsey, and Max stepped onto the porch.

Bryan was wearing cargo shorts and one of his college team shirts; Kelsey showed as much skin as possible in short shorts, a glittery tube top, and heels that would have pitched anyone less athletic flat on her face. Perhaps Max's two preppy shirts, which he had worn several times for Dhanya's sake, were in the wash. Tonight he wore faded jeans and one of his many bright tropical prints.

"Well," said the girl talking with Ivy, "looks like the entertainment has arrived!"

"A trio!" The guy eyed Kelsey. "Why don't you ever dress that way?" he teased his sister.

"Stop staring, Brett. That's what the girl wants."

"Then I'm glad to give it to her," he replied.

"The girl is my roommate, Kelsey," Ivy interjected. "And Max and Bryan are new friends we've met on the Cape."

"Does one of them play bongo drums?" Brett joked.

"No, a steel drum," his sister observed, "if you're referring to the Caribbean clubber." She turned to Ivy. "But I'm sure they're nice."

"They are." Ivy replied. Deciding it would be a waste of politeness to excuse herself, she simply walked away, joining Max and Bryan, who were parked at the food table. Max tried one thing after another, picking them up with his fingers rather than the toothpicks. Bryan studied the selection of beer. Kelsey was quickly stolen from Bryan's side by two guys who'd turned almost giddy at the sight of her. Bryan watched her walk off with them, then winked at Ivy.

"Next time," Bryan said to Max, "all of us should wear tube tops. Did you see the way people stared when we walked in?"

Max looked down at his shirt. "I like this outfit."

"And I like *you*, Max, for liking it," Bryan said. "I gave you bad advice when I told you to wear the button-down for Dhanya."

Max gazed across the porch at Dhanya, who was standing close to Chase, talking to another couple. The four of them were so perfectly matched, they looked as if they had double-dated for years and would one day be in each other's weddings. *Boring*, Ivy thought, surprising herself that she preferred—and was even growing fond of—Max.

"You're your own man, Max," Bryan went on, "not part of the herd. Don't you think so?" he asked two girls who had approached the table to get something to eat. They looked at Bryan, then Max, and giggled.

"The rest of these guys here—they're wearing a uniform. This guy," Bryan went on, clapping Max on the shoulder, "he likes to experiment with color. Don't tell me you girls want a guy with no imagination or sense of fun! How romantic is that?"

The girls looked at each other. The taller one shook her

head at the shorter, dismissing Bryan, but he continued. "You like catamarans—you like flying across the ocean like you've got wings? Or do you like cigarette boats that race past Chatham at ninety miles per hour? Maybe you're into yachts. Max has them all—take your choice. *And* he's his own man."

Max started to blush.

Ivy watched with amazement as Max's endearing bit of shyness, along with his boat résumé and suggestion of wealth, drew the girls in. They introduced themselves, the shorter girl seeming especially interested.

The taller girl turned to Bryan. "Are you dating anyone?" she asked bluntly.

"Yeah," he said, putting his arm around Ivy.

Ivy choked on her drink.

"Whoa! Careful. You okay, babe?" Bryan asked solicitously. "Come on."

Choking and laughing, Ivy allowed him to lead her into the house. "What was that all about?" she asked when they were out of earshot.

"Maxie. He's a good guy and deserves a girl," Bryan said. "Not one of them, but they'll do for now. I had to do that, Ivy. Otherwise he'll wander around and make puppy eyes at Dhanya all night, which'll be a real turn-off to her. I wish he'd get over her."

"It would be better if he did," Ivy agreed, and added with a sigh, "But you love who you love."

Bryan tilted his head to one side, studying her. The room's lighting softened his features. "You miss him."

"Yeah. A lot." Her voice sounded funny. It was hard to disguise the intensity of her feelings when talking with someone who also cared about "Luke."

"You're afraid something will happen to him," Bryan guessed.

"Yes, and that I won't be able to do anything about it."

Bryan rested his hand lightly on her shoulder. "That's the problem with Luke. You want to fix things for him, but in the end you can't. He has to do it for himself, especially the drinking part, which is where he always gets in trouble."

Ivy nodded, feeling more in control of her emotions now because they were talking about the real Luke, not Tristan. "Thanks. Thanks for understanding."

"You know what you need? Solid food," Bryan said. "I saw the last kabob get picked up out there. I'm looking for the kitchen." Bryan studied the three doors that appeared to lead to other rooms. "My built-in divining rod—it's very sensitive to food—says Door Number Two. Join me?"

Ivy wondered what Chase's parents would say if they discovered Bryan and her raiding their kitchen; after a moment of indecision, she nodded and followed him, hoping for the chance to ask some questions. Bryan's divining rod was spot-on, taking them to a kitchen worthy of Martha

Stewart: a square room with two cooking ranges, a granite-topped island, and a chandelier of copper-bottomed pots. There was a bouquet of daisies, a few of them tumbling toward their reflections in the dark, polished surface of the island. A ceramic pot with small sunflowers graced an open hearth. Bryan stood in front of a gigantic stainless-steel refrigerator.

"See anything good?" Ivy asked.

He turned around, grinning and holding up a container. "Leftovers—looks like steak. Want some?"

She shook her head.

Bryan continued with his exploration, opening and closing drawers, lifting lids. At last he said, "I've discovered what's wrong with Chase. His diet lacks junk food. There isn't one piece of decent junk food in this fridge. But the steak will do."

He closed the door, then lifted the lid of the container, peering down at its contents. "Meat like this shouldn't be mauled. . . . Knife and fork," he murmured, surveying the large number of kitchen drawers, finding what he wanted on the second try, then setting the silverware and container on the center island.

"What if someone is counting on that for a midnight snack?" Ivy asked as he cut into the meat.

"What if several people have been counting on it," he replied, "and no one admits they ate it? That would be a scene." He stuck his fork in a piece, raised it halfway up to his mouth, then paused. "You look very disapproving."

"I am disapproving."

Bryan popped the piece into his mouth. "Filet mignon," he said, then sighed and closed the container. "You sure know how to ruin a guy's appetite."

Ivy laughed at him and he smiled back. Returning the meat to the refrigerator, he went back to searching the drawers and returned to the island with a bunch of grapes. "There are plenty more in there," he said, "so don't frown at me."

"All right. Listen, Bryan, I have some questions."

He sat down on a tall chair and pulled out the one next to him. "Obviously you didn't follow me here to raid the refrigerator. I figured you wanted to talk about something— like Luke."

Ivy sat down and wrapped her feet around a chair rung. "Luke was really in love with Corinne, even after she dumped him, right?"

"Yes. God, yes!"

"From what I read about Corinne, she was going to art school and had her own apartment and a job. Luke didn't make it through eleventh grade. They seemed kind of a strange match."

"No stranger than Luke and *you*," Bryan said, dropping a grape in his mouth. "What draws you to him?"

Ivy thought quickly—Tristan, not Luke, had drawn her. She tried to remember how Bryan had characterized Luke the last time they talked. And she was careful to speak in the past tense. "I guess I saw a kind of need in him. On the surface he seemed strong, but underneath he was vulnerable—almost lost."

"Exactly. Luke only had his mom, who'd do just about anything for a drink. She couldn't take care of herself, much less him. No schedule, no real meals, no clean clothes from the time he was a little kid. Growing up, he hung around our house—I told you that. My parents laid down some rules and fed him. It helped. But after a while, I guess it gets weird hanging with your friend's parents. Then he found Corinne. She was very sure of herself and was glad to order him around like a parent."

"You didn't like her," Ivy guessed.

"I admired her. Corinne's own home life was no picnic. Her mom ended up with the prince of evil stepdads, at best a jerk, at worst . . . " Bryan shrugged and didn't finish the statement. "But Corinne was like a good athlete, disciplined and ambitious. You know the old saying, 'What doesn't kill you makes you stronger'? That girl had steel in her, and Luke was drawn to it."

"And she was drawn to his need, his vulnerability," Ivy filled in.

"Aren't all girls?"

Ivy grimaced.

Bryan shrugged. "Maybe not. Anyway, what was between them worked for a while, until Corinne cashed in her ticket. You need to understand, Ivy, everyone in River Gardens is looking for their ticket out. Hers was her photography. Mine was hockey."

"And Luke—"

"Could have had one in hockey. He had more raw talent than me, but there were things he just couldn't overcome."

Bryan pushed the grapes toward Ivy and she plucked off two.

"Who were his enemies?" she asked.

"Luke didn't have any *real* enemies."

"But in an article I read he was charged with assault and—"

"Those charges were dropped," Bryan said sharply. "Sorry, didn't mean to jump on you. It's just that, after Corinne died, reporters started digging around for old stories, you know, something to show that the justice system and social workers should have seen trouble coming. They made something out of nothing. Everyone in River Gardens knew he had a drinking problem and steered clear when necessary. When sober, he was a good friend, the best. The person who he got in a fight with—just a bar brawl—was passing through and acting stupid."

"And yet," Ivy said, "a few weeks ago someone beat him up—"

"Yeah, I see where you're headed. If the news accounts were accurate, that was more than a scuffle."

"He was left for dead!" Ivy said. "He was unconscious. If the tide had washed over him, he would have drowned."

Bryan drummed his fingers against the shiny granite countertop. "He must have gotten help from someone in the stretch between me and you. He had to eat. He probably stole. Maybe he made an enemy while on the lam."

Ivy sat back. She hadn't considered that possibility. She could search out every detail of Luke's life in River Gardens and still not find out who wanted to kill him.

"Do you know where he went after he left Providence?" she asked. "How far did you drive him?"

"I left him off in New York. He and I are city kids— he'd never make it hiding in the mountains of Vermont. Manhattan was a good a place to get lost in a crowd."

And an impossible place for her and Tristan to trace Luke's path, Ivy thought. But he had ended up close to his roots, and she had to start somewhere.

"After Corinne's murder, how did the people in River Gardens see Luke? Did they turn against him?"

"I don't know for sure," Bryan replied. "It was April, and I was at school when the news broke. I went home for the funeral, of course, but everyone was still in shock. The weekend after, I went home again, but that time I was just getting Luke out of there, not hanging out with old friends."

"If someone from River Gardens recognized him, would they go the police?"

Bryan pushed away the grapes and leaned forward on his arms, thinking. "Maybe. If the police offered a decent reward, I know a few who would. I just hope Luke stays far away from Providence."

"People travel all over in the summer," Ivy continued. "A lot come here. There was the girl at the carnival—"

"Alicia Crowley? She'd never turn on him. Alicia had a major crush on Luke going back to River Gardens Middle. She left our high school at the beginning of senior year— her parents beat it out of the neighborhood as soon as they could. Anyway, I always thought she was in love with Luke. I know she could never hurt him, not like Corinne. "

"Do you think he killed Corinne?" Ivy asked bluntly.

Elbows on the table, head bowed, Bryan was silent for a long time, then shook his head. "I don't see how the Luke *I knew* could have."

Ivy's heart skipped a beat. Did she dare to hope? Or was this just a wish fueled by Bryan's loyalty and her own desperation?

It didn't matter—she couldn't stop hoping. What if someone else had killed Corinne? What if she and Tristan could prove Luke was innocent? Then they would be free to live and love in the open. That's all she was asking for—a chance to love as they would have, if Gregory hadn't destroyed their life together.

If this hope was real, they needed to find Luke's enemy to protect Tristan, and Corinne's enemy to free him. Which meant Ivy had to learn everything she could about Corinne as well as Luke. And the place to start was the third person in their unhappy love triangle—Alicia Crowley.

Thirteen

"EXCUSE ME FOR INTERRUPTING," KELSEY SAID sharply.

Bryan quickly raised his head and Ivy turned on her stool. They had been sitting silently, their heads close together, Ivy debating whether to ask for Bryan's help in locating Alicia.

Kelsey strode across the kitchen, bearing down on Ivy. "When Will told me you were with Bryan, he didn't mention you were having an intimate conversation."

"We were just talking," Ivy replied mildly.

"That's how it starts."

"C'mon, Kelsey," Bryan said in a teasing voice. "Don't you know roommates are off limits? That's what Ivy told me."

Kelsey took the bait: "So *you* were hoping—"

"No, no." He reached for her hands and pulled her close. "I was just waiting to see when you'd get tired of Tweedle Dee and Tweedle Dum."

Ivy slid off her stool, eager to get away before she got sucked into another round of their romantic game. "Where's Will?"

"Trying to reach Beth," Kelsey replied, leaning provocatively against Bryan. "He's wasting the whole party texting. The girl he was talking to gave up and stalked off."

To Ivy this was good news; it meant Will realized there was a reason to worry. She headed back to the party. After being sidetracked on the porch by Max and the girl who'd been lured by his expensive boats, Ivy found Will standing alone at the end of the yard. He looked at his phone, punched something in, then slipped it in his pocket. She walked toward him quickly.

"Did you hear from Beth?"

Will swung around. "No."

"I'm worried, Will."

"And you think I'm not?"

The thin peel of moon and stars had melted away completely. Heat lightning flashed in the distance.

"I know for a fact that you are," she assured him. "With your car, she could be anywhere and—"

"You're blaming me for lending my car?"

Ivy hesitated, then answered honestly. "A little. I know you meant well, but I don't think you realize—"

"I'm not stupid! I can see she's not acting like herself."

Ivy remained silent in the face of his defensiveness, hoping they could get past it and really talk about Beth.

"You know," Will continued, "when people go through rough times and act a little different than they used to, their true friends stick around and listen."

"The problem is, Beth won't let me," Ivy replied, and took a step closer.

The edge of the lawn gave way to a short slope of rocks with four steps down to the beach. Will descended the steps, keeping a distance between him and Ivy.

"Beth has pulled away from me and nearly everyone else," Ivy continued. "You saw her at the fireworks."

"She doesn't like Chase," Will said as if that explained it all.

"You saw how she was yesterday, when Dhanya and I came down to the beach," Ivy persisted, joining Will at the bottom of the steps. "And with the guests at the inn—you've seen how different she is from when we started the job—how cold she's become."

"She's tired."

"You're making excuses, Will! Why can't you face it? Something is very wrong with Beth, and simply listening to her is not going to help." At the bottom of the steps a path led through a meadow of sea grass to the open sand. Will strode down the path. Ivy watched him for a minute, then followed slowly, trying to give him the space he needed, but determined to get to the issue of Gregory.

"Will, on Wednesday, Beth left broken glass in my shoe."

He turned toward Ivy.

"You remember what Gregory did to Ella and me last summer," Ivy continued. "It's a warning."

"Beth claims you put glass in *her* shoe."

"I heard her tell you that, but she was either lying or confused."

"You heard her? How?"

Ivy bit her lip.

"You were eavesdropping," Will said, his voice accusatory. "You were sneaking around under my window."

Ivy tried to explain: "I was coming over to tell you about the glass and got there just after she did."

Will shook his head. "I think you're both crazy."

"You can think what you want about me," Ivy replied, "and a lot of your anger, I admit, I've earned. But right now we're talking about Beth, and I want you to listen hard— for her sake. Gregory has come back. He slipped inside her mind the night of the séance and is using her to get at me.

I don't how to help her, how to get rid of him, how to bring back the Beth you and I love. The only thing I know for sure is that I need your help. Gregory is getting stronger."

For a moment Will just stared at her. In the distance a flash of lightning outlined clouds over the bay. After a long pause, thunder rumbled.

"Think about it, Will," Ivy said. Then she left him alone, hoping he'd figure it out sooner rather than later. For Beth's sake.

SHORTLY AFTER, WITH A STORM APPROACHING, THE party moved inside. Claiming she had a headache, Ivy made arrangements for Dhanya and Will to get a ride home, then headed to her car. The storm broke quickly, a smattering of fat raindrops on her windshield suddenly turning into a downpour. Peering through the torrent, watching the road ahead appear and disappear as images of it were wiped off by the rubber blades, Ivy couldn't see the church as she drove past. "Be safe, Tristan," she murmured and continued on to the cottage.

She planned to start her search for Alicia Crowley as soon as she arrived home. Hopefully, Alicia had posted enough information on Facebook to allow Ivy to get in touch with her. She could friend Alicia, but she didn't want to leave an electronic trail for the police or anyone else who might be searching for "Luke." A face-to-face meeting would work best.

Arriving at the inn's lot, Ivy saw that Will's car was still missing, but just inside the cottage door she found a pair of Beth's shoes that she didn't remember seeing earlier. The canvas shoes were coated with a damp and gritty mix of sand and soil, like the kind found on the grassy marshland of bayside beaches.

Ivy slipped off her own shoes, soaked from the downpour, and placed them next to Beth's. Dusty emerged from the kitchen, mewing a greeting.

"You stayed nice and dry," Ivy said, petting him. "Treats for you, tea for me."

In the kitchen, Ivy knelt by the cat for a moment as he purred and crunched on his treats. After grabbing a raspberry iced tea from the fridge, she sat down at the kitchen table, eager to get started on her research. She lifted the lid of her laptop, surprised she had left the computer on. The dark screen leaped into life with a photo: She looked into the angry eyes of Gregory.

TRISTAN WAS SWIMMING, OR MAYBE HE WAS FLYING— the luminous water was as light as air, and his being could move however he willed it. There was just one rule: He couldn't look back.

He did, and he saw Ivy. Amazed, he turned quickly and flew toward her. She was farther away than he first thought. To reach her, he had to use all the strength and grace given to him. As he did, the ethereal lightness around him changed. It darkened to a sea and grew heavy with salt and sand. He became aware of his limbs and the way they dragged him down. He heard murmurings from the depths of the sea—menacing, barely human voices. Their voices overlapped, wave after wave washing over him.

The dark voices grew louder, making it hard to think. Every sense except his hearing dimmed. "Ivy?" he cried out. "Ivy! Where are you?"

Tristan awoke, his clothes damp, a trickle of water on his cheek. He sat up quickly and was relieved to find himself in a familiar place, the church tower, and grateful that he heard only the wind high above him. Realizing that rainwater was coming through the open trapdoor, he climbed the ladder.

Quietly, so quietly that at first he thought it was the whine of the wind, the voices began to murmur again. He hurried to the top, reached through the opening, and pulled down the heavy door, slamming it closed. The sound stopped. Taking a deep breath, steadying himself, he backed down the ladder, feeling for each rung, having no light to guide him.

When he reached the bottom, he searched for his flashlight. He thought it was in his backpack, but he couldn't find it in the darkness. Ivy had left him a wristwatch with a face that glowed. Where was it? As his mind darted from thought to thought, the sound of the voices came again. They were barely audible, rising between the words of his thoughts. But they grew loud, as loud as his thoughts, then louder still.

Tristan held his hands to his ears, but he couldn't muffle the voices. Scrabbling over the rough wood floor on hands and knees, searching for his backpack, he found the edge of the trapdoor and pulled it up. He climbed down the ladder to the church.

For a moment he thought he had escaped the voices. All he heard was the wind rattling the leaded-glass windows. The rain had eased and the sky had lightened. It was almost dawn, he realized, then froze. In the gray light a shadow shaped like a dark wing swooped past a window. *A tree branch*, he told himself, *a branch dragging leaves, nothing more.*

Then the voices started again. He knew this wasn't a dream. He was fully awake and he could hear them, though not the words. It was maddening the way they grew increasingly loud but no more clear.

"Leave me alone!" Tristan cried out.

They seemed to draw energy from his anger, but he couldn't help himself, and cried out again. "Leave me!" A tide of voices rushed toward him. He dropped to his knees. "Help me, God. I don't understand what's happening to me. Lacey, Lacey I need you."

Fourteen

SUNDAY AFTERNOON, WITH THE CAPE WASHED TO A sparkle from the previous night's storms and her work done at the inn, Ivy set out for a farm stand on a road that ran between 6A and the highway.

Last night, after being spooked by the unexpected image of Gregory's face gazing at her from her laptop screen, Ivy had figured out how the "haunting" had occurred. Someone—Beth—had connected Ivy's screen saver to a file that contained only photographs of Gregory. When Ivy saw that the new file had been created from her family photos, carefully cropped and enlarged, it felt as personal and creepy as having things in her bureau drawer rooted through.

Doing her best to shake off that feeling, she'd done a search for Alicia Crowley and discovered that Luke's old friend was spending her summer working at her grandparents' farm stand on Cape Cod. Alicia's Facebook page had a link to the business's website.

Arriving at Crowleys' Farm Stand at three thirty on Sunday afternoon, Ivy squeezed onto its sandy lot next to cars packed for a return to the mainland. The white building had an overhanging roof that invited you into its coolness. Risers across the building's front supported buckets of bright flowers, baskets brimming with colorful vegetables and fruit, and bunches of herbs. A chalkboard next to the building's screen door promised breads, pies, jams, cheeses, and comb honey inside. *Bread* was crossed out, the words *more tomorrow* scrawled next to it; Ivy guessed that it would be worth coming back for.

A white-haired man with sunglasses looped around his neck helped customers outside. Ivy found Alicia inside, working a cashbox. A woman with silver hair was standing with hands on hips, listening to a customer and nodding pleasantly—*Alicia's grandmother*, Ivy thought. She figured the farm stand was like Aunt Cindy's inn, the kind of place people came to back year after year.

Picking up a handbasket, waiting for a chance to approach Alicia, Ivy selected a jar of strawberry jam and a wedge of cheese, thinking she could add them to Tristan's stock. Between customers, Alicia glanced at her, then looked back a second time as if Ivy looked vaguely familiar.

Ivy wandered outside, added a pint of blueberries to her basket, and brushed her fingers against fragrant bundles of rosemary, marjoram, and sage. After ten minutes of going in and out, she gave up trying to catch Alicia alone and got in line to pay.

"Hi, Alicia," she said, placing her purchases on the wood table.

"Hi." Alicia's dark hair was pulled up on her head, tendrils curling away from a clasp decorated with wampum beads. Her hazel eyes held a puzzled look as if she couldn't quite place Ivy.

"I saw you at Strawberry Days. I was with a friend. A really good friend."

Alicia suddenly remembered—Ivy saw it in the widening of her eyes. She looked past Ivy toward her grandmother, who was busy with a customer. "Oh! How is . . . he?"

"Okay. I know I said I'd call you," Ivy went on, taking a chance, hoping Alicia would play along. "But things have been really busy at the inn—hardly getting any time off."

Alicia nodded slightly.

"It's awesome finding someone else who's going to

URI," Ivy added, glad she had memorized Alicia's Facebook page. "Maybe we could get together, go on an ice-cream run or something."

Alicia took Ivy's money and quickly calculated her change. "I'm due a break. Give me five minutes. Do you like snowballs?"

"Love them."

"They sell them down the road."

Ivy put her purchases in her car. A few minutes later, she met Alicia at the edge of the lot.

Alicia pointed the way and said nothing more until they were well out of earshot of the farm stand. "How is Luke? How is he *really*?"

"The last time I saw him, scared."

"Where is he?"

"Hiding." Although Bryan had said Alicia would never betray Luke, Ivy didn't want to give out information that Alicia might unwittingly pass on to the wrong person.

"When did you last see him?" Alicia asked.

"When the police tried to arrest him, the night after you ran into him at the carnival."

Alicia turned to her. "I didn't tell them anything!"

Ivy nodded. "I know."

"I read the news articles," Alicia said. "I've always been afraid he'd end up hurt, lying in the middle of nowhere, with no who cared about him there to help."

"Alicia, who would have beaten up Luke that way?"

"I have no idea."

Ivy wondered if Alicia was being as cautious as she was in admitting what she knew.

"But as his close friend, you must've known who his enemies were." Ivy stopped so that Alicia would stop, wanting to look at the girl's face and read whether she was being truthful.

A small pucker formed above each dark eyebrow. "I didn't think he had any real enemies."

Ivy sighed and continued walking. "That's what Bryan said."

They had reached the snowball stand and spoke no more about Luke till they sat down at a rough-planked table, away from others who were crunching on the syrupy ice.

"Bryan Sweeny gave you my name," Alicia guessed. "He was best friends with Luke. I don't know this for sure, but I think he helped Luke escape."

Ivy spooned up a mouthful of frozen emerald chips. "He did."

"I didn't."

"You didn't . . . ?"

"Help." Alicia's voice shook. "I didn't know what to do. I thought that if I talked to the police, I'd make him look guiltier." She chopped at her snowball with her plastic spoon, but didn't eat any.

"What was it like, his relationship to Corinne?" Ivy asked.

"Even before Corinne broke it off, there were big problems between them. I hated the way she treated him. When she finally dumped him, he was devastated. She hurt him badly." Alicia shook her head. "I found it so hard to believe."

"That he would love her, or that he would kill her?"

"Both."

Ivy watched a dribble of pink syrup run over Alicia's fingers.

"I couldn't understand why he loved her," Alicia went on, "but knowing how much he did, I couldn't believe he'd kill her."

"What if he didn't?" Ivy asked.

Alicia stared at her. "*Didn't kill her?* What did he tell you? Does he remember that night?" Her words were quick with hope.

"He doesn't remember anything," Ivy said. "But both you and Bryan, two people who knew him better than anyone, can't believe he killed her."

"I was with Luke the night Corinne died."

"You were?" Ivy hadn't seen that in any of the accounts. "I thought he was home alone and drinking."

"He was drinking," Alicia acknowledged.

"Drunk?"

"He was getting there when I arrived, but he wasn't when I left him." Alicia paused, eating several spoonfuls of her melting snowball. "You see, we were always friends. When my family moved away from River Gardens two years ago, my parents forbade me to go back. They'd been trying for years to get enough money to get out of there and put me and my younger sisters in a better school. But I found ways to sneak back, and then, last fall, when I moved into my college dorm, it was easy to slip away and see him. We had always talked. He listened to me, and I listened to him."

Alicia blinked and turned her face away. Ivy suspected that Bryan was right: Alicia had been in love with Luke. "Luke was lucky to have you."

Alicia pressed her lips together and nodded, her face still averted from Ivy. Ivy waited quietly, wishing she knew her well enough to hug her.

"Sorry," Alicia murmured.

"It's okay," Ivy assured her and stirred the spearmint slush in her cup. When Alicia faced her again, Ivy asked, "Doing all right?"

"Yeah." Alicia took a deep breath, then said, "The night Corinne died, Luke called me early in the afternoon. He was really down. I talked to him again at five. I had a paper due, but I knew he needed me. I picked up subs on the way and made strong coffee when I got there.

We talked and talked. I thought we were getting some-where, that he was starting to accept that he and Corinne weren't meant to be.

"Then good old Corinne sent him a text. I swear, if she had been within reach, *I* would have strangled her. But she was at Four Winds Farm, Corinne and Luke's romantic meeting place. It's an orchard outside of Providence—closed through the winter.

"So Corinne wanted him back?" Ivy asked.

Alicia shrugged. "She just said she wanted to see him. He told me he wasn't meeting her—he wasn't even going to reply. He thanked me for helping him. I thought he was going to be all right. We watched TV for an hour, and at eleven o'clock, I went back to the dorm to work on my paper."

"So the text came in around ten?"

"Just after," she said. "Just after *Law & Order* began." Her eyes filled with tears. "There was a lot of alcohol in the apartment—there always was, except when he ran out of money—but I thought he was going to be all right." Tears ran down her cheeks.

"The next day I heard that Corinne had been strangled at Four Winds, and the police were searching for Luke. It took them two days to catch up with me and ask questions. I told them nothing. Anything I might say—him drinking and getting a text from her—would have made it worse for him.

And they had already made up their minds. 'No reason to flee if you're not guilty,' they kept telling me."

Ivy leaned forward on her elbows. "Murderers aren't the only people who have reasons to flee."

"I want to believe that. In my heart I do. But maybe I'm being naïve." Alicia shook her head, then glanced at her watch. "I have to get back."

As they walked to the farm stand, she gave Ivy the names of people who knew Corinne and Luke, as well as tips on approaching them.

"Corinne's gran thought she could do no wrong, but she also had a huge soft spot for Luke. Corinne's mother is a real head case—used to compete with Corinne, dressed like she was a teenager. The stepfather's name is Hank Tynan. He works for a sedan service—picks up executive types and drives them places. If you talk to him, do it when other people are around. He has a temper. Corinne told Luke that her stepfather used to hit her. She could have been making it up, but even before I heard that, I didn't trust the man. There's something about the way he looks at you. He and Luke never got along."

"Thanks for the heads-up."

Before parting, they exchanged contact information.

"One more thing," Alicia called, after Ivy had already started across the lot to her car.

Ivy turned around. When Alicia didn't continue, Ivy walked back to her.

"If you talk to Luke, would you tell him I'd like to see him?" Alicia asked.

Ivy hesitated.

"Just one more time," Alicia said quietly, her eyes pleading with Ivy. "Just one more time."

Fifteen

TRISTAN LAY BACK ALONG THE LENGTH OF THE PEW, hands behind his head, staring upward, his eyes tracing the gothic lines of the church's ceiling. The voices he'd heard at dawn had stopped after he had called to Lacey and prayed. But he had a bad feeling it wasn't as easy as that.

He looked at his watch, now fastened securely around his wrist. Four ten p.m. It had been almost twelve hours since he'd called to Lacey, and she still hadn't come. For a moment he worried that something bad had happened to her. Then he worried that she'd miraculously accomplished her mission and gone on to the Light without saying good-bye.

"Stop sighing."

At the sound of her voice, Tristan quickly sat up.

Lacey, in the traditional pose of Buddha, wearing a rosary necklace, earlocks, and kufi, gazed back at him from the front of the church.

"Interdenominational," she said. "What do you think?"

"Impressive."

She studied him for a long minute, then unfolded her legs and jumped to her feet. "You're not grouchy, are you? I came as soon as I could."

He stood up slowly. "It's no big deal."

She walked closer, peering up into his face. "Oh, really. *Lacey, Lacey, I need you!* I was sure that was you sounding totally desperate, but I guess I'd better check on my other clients." She faded to a purple mist and drifted past him.

"Lacey, wait! I do need you. . . . I'm . . . kind of on edge."

This time she materialized as herself. "Guess what? I can now maintain my physical form for fifteen minutes."

"Great," he muttered.

"And I can add props as you just saw. I constantly amaze myself."

"And God as well, I imagine."

Lacey surveyed the church. "Some hideout you found! Who'd expect to find an angel here?"

"I hide in the bell tower," he told her.

"Bell tower?" Her dark eyes shone. "Awesome. Ever see *The Hunchback of Notre Dame*?" She raised one shoulder and began to limp. "Of course, you remember what happened to Quasimodo when he became totally obsessed with a woman. He—"

Tristan was losing patience: "Lacey, I'm hearing voices."

She straightened up. "Now?"

"When I called you. And I've heard them before. The first time I was asleep and thought they were part of a dream. But today I was awake and they kept getting louder, so loud I couldn't think."

She looked intrigued. "What were they saying?"

"They were angry and excited, hundreds of voices talking at the same time. I couldn't understand the words."

Lacey raised an eyebrow.

"They were like the voices the night Gregory died."

Lacey took a step back.

"Is it because of him?" Tristan asked. "Is he one of them?"

"Don't know."

"Can you hear or see Gregory?"

"When I look in Beth's eyes, I see darkness, a kind of restless darkness, like smoke."

"How do you know that the darkness is Gregory?"

Lacey thought for a moment. "It's hard to explain. It's

like recognizing people in a dream, even if they look different in everyday life. You just know."

"When Gregory looks out through Beth's eyes, what does he see?"

"Opportunities."

To hurt Ivy, Tristan thought, *to kill her and separate them once more.* "Does he see you?"

"He never acts like he does," Lacey replied.

"He must be aware of me."

Lacey grimaced. "You flatter yourself, Tristan. Do you think that some kind of celestial trumpet sounded to announce your return? I had no idea you were back until Ivy told me. If you're lucky, Gregory still hasn't figured it out."

Tristan paced the front of the church, then sat down and drummed his fingers on the back of a pew. "So then Gregory doesn't leave Beth's mind—he doesn't roam at all?"

"I suppose he *could.* . . . You remember how it was when you came back the first time. You were most powerful when you were working through Will and Beth, when you slipped inside their minds, but you were limited by what they saw and thought. It was dangerous for you when you stole into Eric's drug-fried mind. He was vulnerable to you, but you were vulnerable to him and his drugs as well. Whatever happened to Eric when you were inside would've also happened to you."

Tristan nodded. "Good, that's good. At least, while Gregory is in her mind, he won't do anything to hurt Beth."

Lacey laughed harshly. "Since when has self-destruction stopped him? Since when has self-destruction stopped anybody who is obsessed with something—or *someone*."

Tristan barely listened, his mind racing ahead. "So maybe I've come back in Luke's body to remain hidden from Gregory. And I'm back with the mission of saving Ivy from him."

Lacey pointed her finger at Tristan. "Your mission is to save *yourself* from *Ivy*."

"That's what you think. I disagree," he said calmly.

Lacey threw up her hands. "Listen to me, Tristan! Ivy was a dead girl. Crash, smash, dead! *Exit Ivy*. You had no right to give her another entrance."

"And the person who drove her off the road that night, you're saying that person had the right to kill her," he replied angrily, "but I didn't have the right to bring her back?"

"Neither of you had the right."

"And this is what you've learned during your three years of fooling around and failing to find your own mission."

Lacey glared at him, then strode down the church aisle, turning back when she reached the door. All of this was for effect, since she could have disappeared whenever she wanted.

"Maybe I've never read the big script," she said, "and maybe Number One Director has never consulted with me, but I can tell you what I see from the audience: an angel, who has lost his powers, is occupying the body of a murderer, and he hears the voices of demons getting closer and closer. You made a big mistake, Tristan. Now it's time to save yourself."

SHORTLY AFTER IVY LEFT ALICIA AT THE FARM STAND, she found a convenient place to pull off the road and write down everything Luke's friend had told her. Then she drove on to St. Peter's Church, where she spent the rest of the afternoon practicing piano and working on the summer assignments. Playing the piano always seemed to help her think things through.

By the time she returned the church key to the rectory, she realized there were two items she hadn't seen in the online news stories: an estimated time of death and the time at which the body was found. In the news reports Ivy remembered, Corinne's death had been noted as occurring "late on the night of April 14." If Alicia had left Luke's at eleven o'clock, depending on how long it took to drive to Four Winds, he would have had just a small window of time to commit the murder and leave by midnight.

After dinner in Chatham, Ivy arrived back at the cottage just as Kelsey and Dhanya were headed out. When they had left, Ivy walked back to the kitchen stairs and called up to Beth. The floor creaked, but Beth didn't reply. After several attempts, Ivy gave up and opened her laptop. For a moment she held her breath, but her usual screensaver came up.

Checking the file in which she had copied news reports about Corinne's death, Ivy wondered if the police had withheld information while interviewing possible suspects. None of the early stories mentioned the circumstances of the crime's discovery; but a recent one, written after "Luke" had been found on the Cape, named the person who had discovered Corinne's body: James Oberg.

Ivy searched Facebook without luck, but found a number for James P. Oberg in a phone book for metropolitan Providence. She quickly placed the call. The voice on the answering machine sounded old but strong. *Slightly belligerent*, she thought. Ivy hung up and debated whether to leave a message. Deciding that old people were likely to be annoyed by repeated calls in which a caller did not identify herself, she called a second time and left a name: "This is Abbie Danner, a journalism intern with the *Cape Cod Times*. I have a few questions to ask for an article I'm writing." She gave her cell phone number, explaining it would be the easiest way to reach her.

That done, Ivy located Luke's neighborhood and Four Winds Farm on Mapquest: The fastest driving route took forty minutes. Even allowing for empty roads and the possibility of speeding, Luke's window of opportunity was getting very narrow!

Ivy researched Hank Tynan, Tony Millwood, and every Facebook friend and person mentioned on Corinne's page, collecting the information on a thumb drive. She was especially interested in Tony Millwood, Corinne's confidant. According to Alicia, it had been a love-hate relationship, and Tony had become increasingly angry and resentful of the way in which Corinne used him.

Corinne had posted plenty of her photography and other works of art; some were still on her art-school site, and Ivy studied it, trying to read Corinne's personality and interests in the work she'd left behind.

Two hours later, she stretched and stood up. A demanding meow caught her attention; Dusty peered through the screen in the back door.

"Aren't you supposed to be earning a living, protecting the garden from hungry critters?"

Dusty lifted a paw, about to claw the screen. "No, no," Ivy said, quickly opening the door. She filled a bowl with fresh water and set it down on the floor. "No treats. This morning Aunt Cindy lectured us about you. You're getting too fat and lazy with everyone feeding you."

Dusty stared down at the water, then looked up at her as if to say "You can't be serious."

"Sorry." After fixing herself some ice water, Ivy sat back down in front of her computer, calling up a map of Providence and using the zoom to study the streets of River

Gardens. When she looked up, Dusty was sitting on the kitchen table with his paw in her glass, about to scoop up a drink of water, true to his Maine coon breed.

"Hey, do I go drinking out of your water bowl?" Ivy asked, laughing.

The cat purred, obviously in the mood for company. As she typed, he rubbed her wrist with his cheek, then squeezed under her arm, trying to fit his large body on her lap. Twenty pounds flopped down on her legs. Ivy scratched the thick ruff of fur around Dusty's neck, then combed her fingers through his heavy coat. Beneath her hand, the cat's body suddenly tensed. He switched his tail hard against her hip, then sat up, gazing at the stairway next to the kitchen hearth.

"What is it?" Ivy whispered.

Dusty lifted his chin, his eyes drawn up to the ceiling. He appeared to be tracking something from the corner where Beth slept to the top of the stairway, and back again. His ears were sharper than Ivy's—she hadn't picked up a sound.

Dusty leaped off Ivy's lap, walked cautiously to the base of the steps, and stared upward, tail lashing. Ivy rose quietly and tiptoed to the stairway. She debated whether to call to Beth again, then decided not to warn her and crept up the steps.

The room was dark except for a crimson glimmer at one

end. Beth had lit the candle again. As Ivy stole toward her, she saw that Beth was lying in her bed, eyes closed, her body still as death. Sitting down on the bed across from Beth, Ivy studied her friend's face, then out of the corner of her eye saw something sparkling.

Beth's amethyst pendant glittered in the quivering candlelight. Its silver chain had been looped over the knob on Ivy's headboard, then looped again at the other end—fashioned into a noose. Ivy's china angel hung by her neck.

In a mental flash, Ivy saw herself in Beth's dream, a snake of rope coiled around her neck. She began to shake. She reached to free the angel, then quickly pulled back her hand as Beth's eyes flipped open. They were pools of black, her pupils nearly rimless, the candle's flame reflected in them. The tiny smile that played on her lips wasn't Beth's. It belonged to a dark soul lying in wait for Ivy.

Ivy made herself calm. "Untie the knot."

Beth glanced toward the strangled angel then down at the crimson candle. She didn't speak, but Ivy had seen it—a slight contraction of the delicate skin beneath Beth's eyes: She had winced. For a moment, Beth's own soul had shrunk from what she saw.

Hopeful, Ivy pressed on. "Look at what you have done."

Beth refused, keeping her eyes on the flickering votive.

Ivy reached out and placed her fingers beneath Beth's chin, lifting it. Beth clawed at Ivy's hand, knocking it away, but Ivy kept her gaze on Beth's face and saw it again: the flinch, the sign that something of her friend Beth was still present.

"Take it down."

Beth shut her eyes. Ivy saw the tension in Beth's throat. She wanted to hold Beth's face gently in her hands, but when she leaned toward her, Beth quickly turned away. Ivy lifted the chain from the bedpost and laid the necklace and statue in Beth's lap. "Free her."

Beth's hands were knuckles of stone. Still, Ivy pushed on, seeing that, small as the opening was, something was allowing her to get through to Beth. "You can do it. You can fight him, Beth."

Beth turned her head and gazed down at the amethyst in her lap. A tiny blue vein pulsed in her temple.

"I'm here," Ivy said. "You and I, together we're stronger than him."

Beth touched the purple stone with one finger.

"That amethyst was Will's and my gift to you—a sign. Our love is stronger than all his hate."

Beth's fingers opened, then closed around the stone. "I can't stop him, Ivy. He will hurt you. He will use me to get his revenge. Stay away from me."

"I won't stay away! I won't let him have you!"

"It's too late. It's no use."

Ivy untied the knot at the end of the necklace, freeing the

angel, then slipped the silver chain over Beth's head. Was it possible that the purple stone made Beth stronger, allowing Beth to break through the hold that Gregory had on her mind? Ivy remembered how, in the weeks that followed the séance, Beth had held on to the amethyst and warned her that Gregory was here. "Don't take this off, Beth. Don't forget that Will and I are with you. We'll find a way out of this, I promise you. Don't take it off."

"I'm tired."

Ivy looked into Beth's eyes. They were rimmed with azure now, but the votive's flame still shone in their darkness. The circles beneath her eyes looked like bruises.

"So tired," she said softly.

"Sleep now. Lie back. I'll stay with you."

"No, Ivy, not with me! He wants to destroy you."

Ivy blew out the candle. "Hush. Lie back. I'll stay with you till Dhanya and Kelsey come home."

Even after Ivy's roommates returned, she lay on her bed across from Beth's, her mind at work. Making plans, telling herself there were things she could do, was the only way to keep back the terror. Tomorrow she would urge Suzanne to e-mail Will about Beth's dreams. If he heard these things from someone else who knew and cared about Beth, he might finally listen. Together they could battle Gregory. Then she'd tell Tristan what she had learned from Alicia, and she'd talk to the man who found Corinne. . . .

Make me strong, Ivy prayed. She was stronger than the darkness that was ignorance. She was stronger than the darkness that was evil itself. She would find the way for all of them.

Sixteen

FOR TRISTAN, THE ISOLATION WAS WORSE THAN THE fear. When he was in the hospital, he had thought it was the absence of memory that drew him under waves of despair. Now he knew better. It was how Ivy's absence made him feel: exiled. Maybe that's why he was hearing the demon voices; maybe that's what hell was, he thought, the state of exile from Ivy.

Then he heard a melody. Someone was standing outside the church, whistling. Tristan stood in the foyer close to the ladder, ready to climb to safety, but suddenly found himself humming along with the cheerful whistler. The song was from *Carousel*, the music Ivy played for him.

He rushed to the stairway that led to the basement. It was Monday afternoon, the basement lit with sun, exposing him to whoever might peer in the clear windows. It was stupid—dangerous—he knew it. And then he saw her, sitting in the tall grass by the window, whistling. Stupid, dangerous—and she knew it. They would take the chance anyway.

Tristan hurried to the window, tapped on it and removed the wood block. At first he thought she hadn't heard him; she glanced around so casually, looking as if she were daydreaming. Then she scooted to the window, slid it open the same time as he, and climbed through into his arms.

"Steps," he said as she pulled the backpack through. He shut the window, replaced the block, and followed her. They made it only to the landing halfway up the steps. Safe in the bent arm of the stairway, they clung to each other. He covered her face with kisses.

"Missed you."

"Missed *you*!"

"Love you."

"Need you!"

Her hair tumbled over his face and hands. He lost himself in her smell, her touch, and her voice. The sweetness with which she kissed him went straight to his soul. If he was fallen, he thought, Ivy was the grace sent to him, redeeming him.

"Tristan," she said. "I missed you so much. I shouldn't have come in the daylight, but—"

He silenced her with a kiss.

"It never gets easier, being away from you."

"I know." He held her against him and gently stroked her cheek. "I will always want you with me."

"I was worried about you during the storm Saturday night. But you look fine."

He decided not to tell her about the voices he had heard. There was no reason for her to fear something that was happening only to him.

"No big leaks?"

"Not after I thought to close the door to the bell platform."

She smiled and walked around the main floor of the church, tracing its carved wood and remnants of delicate stenciling with her finger. Then they sat together on one of the long wood benches. Watching the light of the milky glass play over the contours of Ivy's face, Tristan wondered if he would ever get over the simple wonder of looking at her.

"I have some new information about Luke," Ivy said, and told him about her conversation with Bryan on Saturday night and yesterday's meeting with Alicia.

"Then Luke may actually be innocent. . . ."

"He *is* innocent. I just know it!"

"Slow down, Ivy. Let's not celebrate too soon," Tristan warned, but his heart lightened in spite of his attempt to be cautious.

Ivy recounted her information about the man who had found Corinne's body, then checked her cell phone. "Still no response. But reporters are supposed to be persistent," she added, pulling up James Oberg's number and trying it again.

Her eyes brightened. "Yes, hi. This is Abbie Danner." She held the phone away from her a little so Tristan could hear.

"The college girl who left a message earlier," the man was saying.

"That's right. I'm working on an article about the death of Corinne Santori."

"Been done," he told her.

"Yes, but as you may know, Luke McKenna was spotted a few weeks ago in Orleans, and the police have renewed their search for him. Here on the Cape there is a constant turnover of summer people, so not everyone read the previous article."

"Reprint it," the man replied.

"I'm an intern, sir. I'm writing my own piece. I aim to impress."

He laughed. "All right, just one question. This'd better not take long."

"Would you describe for my readers how and when you found the body?"

"I was walking my dog—our usual route. We were three quarters the way around Four Winds. Rufus had just done his business, and we were hurrying back. We're always back for the news."

Tristan and Ivy exchanged glances. Alicia had been with Luke till the end of *Law & Order*—eleven o'clock.

"TV news? The local news?"

"Only one I watch."

Ivy squeezed Tristan's hand, trying to control her excitement.

"At eleven p.m.? There wasn't any delay, like for a baseball game or something? Was it on at eleven p.m. that night?"

"Why else would we've been hurrying? But then Rufus started sniffing, started acting like a damned bloodhound, and found the girl in a clump of bushes."

"So when did you call the police?"

"When we got home. Eleven ten. Wake-up Forecast comes on at eleven ten. I hate the way they string out the weather nowadays."

"Thank you. Thank you, Mr. Oberg. You've been very helpful."

Ivy put down the phone and gazed at Tristan, her eyes luminous. "Last night I went on Mapquest and checked the driving time between Luke's and Four Winds. Forty minutes! There's no way Luke could have done it, if the body was found and reported by 11:10. We know for sure now, and we've got his alibi!"

It felt as if shackles had been removed from Tristan's hands and feet. He rested his forehead against Ivy's. Was she thinking the same thing as he? If they could convince the police that Luke was innocent, he and Ivy would be given back their life together.

"I'll see Alicia as soon as I can," Ivy went on, "and ask her to go to the police."

Tristan smiled, then saw the glow in Ivy's face disappear. "You don't think she'll do it," he guessed.

"I'm positive she will, no matter how much trouble it makes for her. That's the kind of person she is. But there's something else we have to think about. Alicia asked me to tell Luke that she'd like to see him. 'Just one more time'— she said it twice—she was begging me. She was his close friend to the end, and even more, I think she was in love with him."

Tristan ran his hand over the smooth grain of the old wood bench. "So you're wondering if it's right to ask her help in clearing the name of someone she falsely believes is alive."

"She'd want to clear Luke's name, no matter what. What I'm not sure of is whether you should see her and try to tell her the truth."

"If we don't tell her I'm someone else, we'll be deceiving her," Tristan said.

"I know. And deceiving is always wrong, isn't it? But Tristan, after you died, I would have done anything to see you just one more time—to see you as you looked in our life together. When I finally heard your voice inside me, it helped so much. It helped even when I had to let go of you again." Ivy reached for his hand. "But that was really you. What if I learned later that it was someone else who had taken on your voice? Would the moments of happiness and comfort have been worth the lie?"

Ivy rose, then walked up one aisle and down the other.

"If Alicia was close to Luke, she might realize I'm not him," Tristan pointed out.

"But she believes you've had amnesia, so that would account for things you don't know or remember. The awful irony is, the closer a person has been to Luke, the more believable you will seem, because that person will recognize all the details they knew about Luke's appearance and voice. You even have the Rhode Island accent. It's just your way of thinking that might seem different. And all that Luke had been through would explain that difference."

Tristan walked to the front of the church and sat on the altar step. The world outside the windows, muted by the stained glass, lacked color and definition. Inside the building, light flowed into shadow. Tristan longed for the boundaries of an ordinary life. Ever since Lacey had claimed that he'd fallen when he'd saved Ivy, the line between right and wrong seemed murky.

"The problem is, Alicia saw you once on the Cape," Ivy went on, "and her eyes have convinced her that Luke is alive. No matter what we said, who would believe in an imposter angel?

"Of course, I could tell her that Luke is far away now, and that he couldn't risk being in contact with anyone who was part of his life. But," she added, "it would kill me, after all we've been through, if you chose to leave me without saying a word."

"*Anything* would be better than thinking you didn't say good-bye to me," Tristan agreed, reaching for Ivy as she passed him, pulling her down next to him. "So there's our answer."

TRISTAN SHOWED IVY HIS "LOFT," THE ROOM IN THE tower directly above the church vestibule, and invited her up to his "deck," the sun-washed floor that supported the bell, beneath the tower's steeple. They sat together, enjoying the warmth, gazing up at the framed patches of sky, then Ivy departed for Crowleys' Farm Stand.

Hours later, just after dark, she returned and whistled a song from *Carousel*. When Tristan joined her, they walked to the lot where she had parked her car.

"I haven't told Alicia anything yet—we only had time to set up where we were meeting—but when I asked for a place where no one would see us, I saw the hope in her eyes."

Tristan nodded solemnly.

"She jogs every night on the beach, so her grandparents won't think anything of her going out. Here's the map she gave me."

Tristan studied it. "It's close by. Why don't we just walk from the beach by the church?"

"We'd have to go past Chase's house to get to the salt marshes. It's safer to go to the town beach further down and work our way back."

The lot for the beach was empty when they arrived. They moved silently across the crescent of beach and turned east. The shore softened beneath their feet, its deep sand giving way to marshes of long grass. Streams of water ran in from the bay. Kayaks and canoes had been dragged onto the grass, their long curves shining with the night's dampness. Alicia had told Ivy that there were just a few houses here, set far back from the water's edge, behind the marshes and clusters of trees. Closer to shore, they were supposed to look for a woodshed used for storing boats.

They rounded a point and Tristan saw her, a slender figure separating from the gray mass of a boathouse, moving tentatively at first, then coming toward them quickly. She stopped a foot away.

"Luke," she said softly.

For a moment Tristan regretted his decision to come. He didn't know how to make his voice respond with the same intense emotion as hers. So he said nothing and reached out his hand. Alicia took it, holding it gently. She lifted it to her cheek and he felt her tears running over his fingers.

"I'm so sorry," he said, words that were true. He put his arms around her, his heart aching for her pain.

"Call when you want me," Ivy said quietly, and walked a distance down the beach.

Alicia lifted Tristan's baseball cap and laughed at his raggedly cut hair. With a light finger, she touched his beard. "You look—you look good," she said.

On this moonless night, Tristan knew that physical sight would tell a person nothing, but he also knew from watching Ivy in the dark, how love gave you sight not dependent on moon or stars.

"You look . . . . cared for."

He nodded. "I've been lucky. Alicia, thank you for all the time you've spent listening to me, caring about me. Thank you for all you have given me." It was what Luke might have said to her, if he had known all that Tristan knew now.

"You look better than ever," she went on. "I am really grateful to Ivy."

Tristan remembered, after his death, the pain of watching Will take care of Ivy. More than anything he had wanted

Ivy to be comforted and loved. Even so, helplessly watching someone else take care of her had been for him a kind of agony. His heart went out to Alicia.

"I didn't know you at the carnival," he told her. "I wasn't trying to put you off. I had amnesia."

"I know. And now?"

"I've been remembering—slowly."

"So all that we shared . . . most of it's gone?" She looked in his eyes. "Yes, I can see it is." Her voice shook.

"But I am continually remembering more," Tristan said quickly, no longer trying to tell a selective truth or even a truth Luke might have spoken, wanting only to ease her pain.

"So maybe in time," Alicia said.

"In time, yes." His eyes burned.

Alicia touched his cheek with one hand, as if she would catch a tear before it fell. "You're in love with Ivy, aren't you." It was a statement, not a question. "I'm glad for you, Luke. I'm glad you love someone who will be good to you. You deserve that."

Tristan felt humbled in the face of such unselfish love.

"It's okay. Really. It makes me happy seeing you happy. But there's something I have to say, because I promised myself that if I ever saw you again, I would. I fell in love with you a long time ago. I love you still. I will always love you."

Tristan bowed his head. "I'm so sorry that I'm hurting you like this."

She put her hand on his shoulder, trying to comfort him. He pulled her close to him. For a moment, he felt her pain so intensely there seemed no barrier between her soul and his.

"Thank you," she said quietly, "for coming, for listening. And you know what I always say—"

He would have given anything to be able to guess and say it back to her.

She laughed. "Okay, remember it from now on: Endings are beginnings, and beginnings are ours to turn into something good."

IVY HAD RETRACED SOME OF HER STEPS, WANTING to give Alicia time alone with "Luke." She had stopped at what she considered calling distance and studied the shoreline around her. At night the salt marsh had its own beauty, with its glistening grass, satin water, and deceptive stillness. Life teemed beneath its surface, but in the darkness, the only hint was its pungent smell, which Ivy liked. The marsh's calm accentuated the smallest sound. When Ivy heard movement, she turned quickly toward the trees. Birds had been disturbed from their night roost. She saw a light. It disappeared, but she was sure she had seen it for a half second.

There were houses behind the trees, she reminded herself, then strained to decipher the reassuring outline of a building. Even if there was no house there, people took walks, she reasoned; people walked dogs and brought flashlights with them. She and Tristan would have, if they didn't have to worry about being seen. She continued to gaze toward the trees, until she heard Alicia calling her.

When Ivy rejoined Tristan, Alicia touched her lightly on the arm. "Thanks, Ivy."

"Sure."

"Luke told me you found out something important."

"Yes. Yes, I should've noticed it before," Ivy replied. "None of the articles written at the time of Corinne's death gave an estimated time of death or information on how the body was discovered. But a recent one listed the name of the man who first called the police. He found her when he was walking his dog—*before* the eleven o'clock news."

Alicia looked from Ivy to Tristan. "He's sure of that?"

"He told Ivy that he made the phone call at ten minutes after eleven," Tristan said, "when a regular part of the news came on."

"The police must have a record of the time," Ivy added.

"So the only thing they don't know is that Luke and I were together until the end of *Law & Order*, and he could never have gotten there in time. Do you think they'll believe me?" Alicia asked. "I'll give a sworn statement, but you know what they're going to say—why didn't I tell them before?"

Ivy nodded. "There's an officer named Rosemary

Donovan, part of Orleans Police. She questioned me the night they arrested Luke. I think she'd understand that you were afraid you'd make things worse for him."

"Rosemary Donovan," Alicia repeated. "I'll call her tomorrow."

Alicia and Ivy agreed to meet in the same place the next night. Ivy hugged Alicia good-bye, and Tristan did the same, letting go of her gently after she let go of him. Then Ivy and Tristan headed west, and Alicia east.

Tristan stopped suddenly. "Alicia," he called, his voice sounding husky with emotion.

She turned around.

"Endings are beginnings," he said, "and beginnings are ours to turn into something good."

In the darkness Ivy couldn't see Alicia's face, but she saw her lift her fingers to her lips, then gracefully reach outward, tossing Luke a kiss.

Seventeen

TUESDAY AFTERNOON, WHEN WORK WAS OVER, IVY checked for texts and e-mails, but the only messages she had received were from Philip and her mother, who were flying with Andrew to California to visit friends. Alicia had promised to contact Ivy after she spoke to the police. Ivy guessed she was tied up with work at her grandparents' stand; even so, Ivy was getting increasingly nervous.

Suzanne still hadn't responded to the request Ivy had texted yesterday. Sitting on the swing outside the cottage, Ivy sent her a second message, pleading with her to contact

Will and tell him about her strange communications from Beth. Time was running out. Ivy believed that she and Will were strong enough to fight Gregory now, but she didn't know how long that would last.

She had just tapped send when Beth emerged from the cottage carrying a basket of dirty laundry.

"Hey, how was your day off?" Ivy asked.

Beth acted as if she hadn't heard her.

"Beth? Did you enjoy your day off?"

She kept walking. Ivy leaned forward on the swing, trying to see if there was a glint of silver around Beth's neck. Arriving home late from the meeting with Alicia, she hadn't seen Beth last night, and Beth had been alone for the last seven hours. Ivy checked inside the cottage for the necklace; not finding it, she walked quickly to the inn's laundry room.

The washer was filling and the old dryer noisily tumbling clothes. When Ivy touched Beth's arm, she jumped, then swung around. "Why are you sneaking up on me?"

"I wasn't. I was just coming to talk."

"Leave me alone." Beth turned back to the washer, and started stuffing clothes into it. Her neck was bare, shining with small beads of sweat

"Beth, where's your amethyst?"

"I don't know what you're talking about."

"You need to keep the amethyst with you. You need to wear it."

Beth didn't respond. She leaned over the washer so Ivy couldn't see her face.

"It was a gift from Will and me. I think it helps you. We talked about this. Remember?"

"You're lying."

"I have no reason to lie to you. Where did you put it?"

"I threw it away."

Ivy's stomach tightened. "Why?"

"The water wanted it."

"The water! The ocean?"

"I was walking last night, and the water asked for it," Beth said, her voice matter-of-fact. "I threw it down to the water."

"Where? Here?"

"How would I know? It was dark. It's gone."

"Oh, Beth," Ivy said, resting her hand on her friend's arm.

Beth yanked her arm away. "Get away from me!"

Footsteps in the hall silenced both of them. Ivy waited till the guest had passed, then left the inn, deep in thought. If her hunch was right, Gregory had realized the power of the amethyst and had told Beth to get rid of it. It was likely that Beth had gone no farther than the inn's beach. But jewelry didn't float like a shell—it wouldn't wash up on the sand. Perhaps if the tide had been high when Beth threw the necklace . . .

Walking through the garden, head down, Ivy didn't

see Bryan sitting on the cottage step until she was a few feet away from him. He was leaning forward, staring at the ground, hands clasped tightly.

"Hey, what are you doing here? Kelsey said she was meeting you at Max's place."

He raised his head. The usual mischief in his eyes was gone, and the absence of his smile made his face seem older, leaner. His broad shoulders were hunched forward.

"Bryan, what's wrong?"

"You haven't . . . heard," he said, sounding uncertain, searching her face. "Sit down." He made room for her on the step. "You remember we talked about Alicia Crowley, the girl who was close to Luke. . . . She's dead."

"What?" Ivy leaped to her feet. "When? How? That can't be!"

Bryan reached up for Ivy's hand and after a moment, pulled her down next to him. "They found her body two hours ago."

"Oh, God."

"They'd been looking for her since last night. I thought you'd hear it on the news or from one of your guests."

"Since last night." Ivy's stomach was a knot.

"She's been living and working with her grandparents this summer, here on the Cape, that's what they said on the radio. My uncle has the news blaring every morning at six a.m."

Despite the warm day, Ivy felt cold all over.

"Last night she went out for a jog. She didn't come back."

"Oh, God!"

"I know what you're thinking," Bryan said, "but it's not possible. There's no way Luke would do that to her, not the Luke I know."

"Do what? She was murdered?" Ivy began to shake.

"In the news, they're calling it a suspicious death."

Ivy struggled to think clearly. "What does that mean?"

He started to speak, then hesitated. "Anything that's not natural. Murder. Or suicide."

"Suicide! It couldn't be!"

Bryan looked at her curiously.

Ivy caught herself. She hadn't told Bryan that she had contacted Alicia, and she needed to think it through before she did. "I—I guess I just can't imagine doing that."

"They found her in the canal. Below the railroad bridge."

Ivy shut her eyes. Was she to blame for this? No, Alicia went jogging every night. She could have run into the wrong person on any given night.

But the light Ivy had seen in the trees—should she have paid more attention? How do you tell a murderer from an innocent person walking a dog?

"The railroad bridge," Ivy repeated, the details starting to sink in. "The one suspended high over the canal?

But that—" She caught herself again. It wasn't anywhere near where Alicia had met them, but Bryan hadn't told her where Alicia jogged. "It just seems impossible."

They were silent for a long time. Ivy gazed at the garden, watching a butterfly dance among the white phlox. "Her parents and her grandparents. I feel so sorry for them."

"I'm worried about Luke, how he'll react if he hears about it."

"Do you think the police will try to link it to him?"

"It would be convenient, wouldn't it?" Bryan replied. "Another girl he was close to, dead. But I'm pretty sure her family doesn't know she stayed in touch with him after they left River Gardens. So at least they won't be pressing for it."

"When they tried to arrest Luke," Ivy recalled, "I told the police that a girl at the carnival recognized him. But I didn't know her name then."

"They might come around with a photo of Alicia and ask you if she was the one."

Ivy nodded.

"Ivy, it would be better for Luke if they don't make that connection."

"I know."

"Can you lie?" Bryan asked.

In the last year, Ivy had told herself she was merely *faking* it to survive, and merely faking it to help "Luke," but she had to face it, she was lying and getting good at it. "If I have to."

"If Luke hears about this, he may come back, even at his own risk," Bryan added. "He'll be really upset, probably at himself. If he returns, he'll contact you. Just giving you a heads-up."

One way or another, Ivy thought, she might need Bryan's help. She pulled out her cell phone. "Give me your number."

TRISTAN STARED AT IVY IN DISBELIEF.

"Dead?"

In the bell tower's dim light, he saw Ivy blinking back tears.

"How?"

She told him in gulps. He didn't know that he was crying until Ivy wiped the tears from his face.

"I can't believe it."

"I can't believe it was suicide," Ivy said, and buried her head in his shoulder.

He listened to her breathe, felt the warmth of her body, reveled in her scent and closeness, and then felt guilty for rejoicing in the way Ivy was alive to him, while Alicia was dead. The sudden nearness of death made him cling to every physical sensation that meant life.

"I'm late because Officer Donovan stopped by to show

me a picture and ask if Alicia was the girl who recognized you at the Strawberry Festival."

"What did you tell her?"

"I lied." Ivy pulled back to look at him. "Tristan, did Alicia die because of us?"

"No! How can you even think that?"

"But what if the person who killed Corinne has been watching me? What if the killer needed to make sure that Luke never had an alibi? Last night, while you were talking to her, I saw a light. Someone was in the trees beyond the marshes, where I was standing. I told myself it was just somebody out on a walk."

"Of course. Why would you think any differently?"

"It's like Eric," Ivy went on, her voice quivering. "Last year, when Eric asked me to meet him, he was going to tell me about Gregory—he was going to help me—and Gregory killed him before he could. It's the same thing all over again."

Tristan felt her shiver. "What?" he asked, pulling Ivy close again.

"It's strange that they found her beneath the railroad bridge."

Tristan thought for a moment. "You mean because of Gregory's . . . *affection* for trains and bridges. Would he have the strength to throw her off?"

"The physical strength? I don't know. Maybe not. It's just creepy."

"How's Beth?"

Ivy told him about the amethyst. "She said the water wanted it, that she threw it 'down to the water.' Oh my God, I was thinking she meant the ocean. But what if she was at—"

"The canal? There's no way, Ivy," he said. "With or without the pendant, Beth isn't capable of killing."

"With Gregory inside her, she is capable of hurting. She put broken glass in my shoe."

Tristan stared at her. "You didn't tell me that!"

"And sometimes," Ivy pressed on, "someone who means only to hurt or warn can go too far."

"Ivy, I want you to stay with me tonight."

"You know I can't do that."

He held her by the shoulders. "You can if you choose to."

"And tomorrow night?" she asked. "And the night after that?" She shook her head. "We can hide from the police. And if there is someone who wants you dead, we can hide you from that person, too. But Gregory will find me wherever I am. Gregory isn't stopped by walls."

"Ivy, if he's gaining power over Beth—"

"Then I had better deal with him now, before he gains any more."

Eighteen

THE FEAR ON TRISTAN'S FACE WHEN IVY LEFT HIM that night stayed with her even after she turned out the living room light. Arriving home, she had been glad to find Dusty waiting for her on the cottage step. Given the cat's increasing wariness around Beth, his willingness to curl up with Ivy on the living room sofa reassured her. Ivy clicked on a nightlight and fell asleep listening to Dusty's heavy purr. But sleep opened the door to dreams, and each of her dreams ended the same way.

She dreamed of Alicia, turning one last time to toss

"Luke" a kiss before she disappeared into the darkness; of Will, driving off fast in his car, as he did the night he and Ivy had broken up—disappearing into the darkness; of Beth, yanking away the hand Ivy had reached for and slipping under a sea of darkness.

Something in the darkness lay in wait for Ivy. Though she couldn't see it, she sensed it moving, as if its secret motion riffled the air between them. It crept slowly toward her, draining all sound from the night; absolute silence signaled its nearness. It reached toward her.

The pressure on her ribs was light at first, no more than a cat resting on her. The cat leaped off, and something came down hard on her chest. Jolted awake, Ivy opened her eyes. The small bit of light she saw immediately disappeared. *Who's there?* she cried out, but as in a dream, she couldn't make a sound. She felt the rough texture of the sofa's weave and the crevice between its cushions pressing against the back of her arms, and she knew it wasn't a dream. Then she tasted the dry fibers of a pillow being held against her nose and mouth. She couldn't breathe!

Terrified, Ivy clawed at the hands pushing the pillow against her face, then wrenched her head to one side, trying to get free of it. The pillow momentarily slipped, and Ivy gulped air, but the attacker came back at her, pressing down harder. The weight on Ivy's chest increased, crushing her lungs, squeezing out her breath.

Her arms still free, Ivy clawed at the weight on her chest. Realizing her attacker was kneeling on her, and feeling fabric give way to skin, she scratched wildly, digging her nails in deep. The attacker pulled back for a moment. Ivy couldn't see the attacker's face, but the dim nightlight caught the texture and swing of her hair.

"Beth!" she gasped, and for a split second was too stunned to fight.

The bruising weight had convinced her it was a guy. Even now Ivy's mind refused to believe it, and she reached up to push back the curtain of hair. As she caught hold of the soft strands, Beth's hand grasped Ivy's with brutal strength. Ivy stared up at the face of her friend: her eyes had grown completely black, her pupils unnaturally dilated. It was like looking into the abyss of hell. Gregory's hell.

Ivy started to fight again, struggling to push Beth off. *Angels, help me*, she prayed. Her arms began to tingle and the tingling rose to her skull. Her body ached for oxygen.

Suddenly Beth fell backward, and the pillow was knocked away. Ivy arched her back, gasping for breath, then caved against the sofa cushions. A hand rested on her chest, rising and falling with each hard breath. When her breaths grew even, another hand gently pushed back the hair that had tumbled over her face. He leaned forward.

"Will." She began to cough.

"Shh. Catch your breath."

"Ivy? Beth?" Dhanya called from upstairs. "Are you down there?"

Will turned quickly and Ivy followed his glance toward Beth. She was slumped in a chair, eyes closed.

"Are you okay?" he whispered to Ivy.

She nodded. Physically she was fine.

"Is everything all right?" Dhanya called down again, sounding uncertain.

"Yes." Ivy struggled to keep her voice from quavering. "Fine," she replied and started to cough. Hearing Dhanya on the steps, Ivy rose from the sofa and hurried toward the kitchen. Out of the corner of her eye, she saw Will pick up Beth and carry her toward the front door.

Ivy met Dhanya at the bottom of the kitchen stairway. "Beth couldn't sleep, that's all."

"That doesn't mean the rest of us have to stay awake!" Kelsey hollered from above.

"Go back to bed," Ivy said quietly to Dhanya. "I'll keep Beth company."

"Something's really wrong with her," Dhanya said.

"I know. I'll stay with her. She's almost asleep now. Go back to bed."

"You're sure you're okay?"

Ivy wasn't sure; inside she was still shaking. If Will hadn't been there, she would have told Dhanya everything.

"Yes. G'night."

Ivy returned to the living room, then slipped out the front door. Will had disappeared with Beth. For a minute Ivy didn't know where to look, then a soft whistle drew her attention. She followed the path to the parking lot, glad Will was thinking more clearly than she, getting Beth away from the others.

When Beth came to, would she remember anything? Would she try again? Ivy couldn't get out of her head the moment of looking up and seeing Beth's hair swinging down over her face. She couldn't block out the dark hatred and misery she had seen in Beth's eyes. It wasn't Beth—but it *was*. Ivy's rib cage still felt the pressure of Beth's knees; her heart felt broken in two.

When Ivy reached Will, she saw he had laid Beth in the grass beside his car. Ivy dropped to her knees next to him. "How is she?"

"Breathing. Her pulse is normal. But she didn't respond when I tried to wake her."

"We should take her to the ER."

Will glanced up at Ivy. "Who would we ask to see—an exorcist? Oh, God, Ivy! I didn't believe you. You tried to tell me, and I wouldn't believe it. I could hardly believe even when I was watching her try to kill you!" Trembling, Will reached for Ivy's hands. "I'm so sorry."

Ivy rested her forehead against his.

"God help me," he said. "God help us."

For a few minutes they simply held onto each other, then Ivy spoke. "I keep telling myself that it was Gregory, not Beth, suffocating me."

Will shook his head. "At this point, what's the difference?"

"It makes a difference, Will, it has to! Gregory is in her mind, the way Tristan once slipped inside yours. He's trying to take over, but we can still reach her."

"Tristan never controlled me like that."

"No," Ivy admitted, "but Gregory doesn't have complete control. He's not stronger than the two of us, not yet."

Then she told him about the amethyst. "I've been thinking about it since the other night. When this started, whenever Beth would warn me that Gregory was back, she played with the necklace. I thought it was just a habit, but now I think the stone gave her the strength to fight him."

"*Gave*—you mean for a while, but no longer?"

"It's gone." Ivy gazed down at Beth. "She told me that the water wanted the amethyst and she threw it down to it. Gregory must have figured out its power when I did."

"We can't let him have her."

"He's using her. It's me he wants."

"He should have used me instead!" Will exclaimed. "He should have used anyone but Beth. She's too gentle, too vulnerable—"

"Which is why he chose her. When he first came back,

his powers were weak. He is growing in strength, but together we are still stronger than him."

Will pressed his lips together as if he were struggling to believe in Ivy's strand of hope.

"When I needed you tonight, you came. How did you know to come, Will? Did Lacey tell you?"

"Lacey's still around?"

Ivy nodded. "Philip kept in touch with her. I called to her when"—Ivy caught herself; telling Will about Tristan would needlessly confuse things—"when I first noticed something wasn't right with Beth. I thought maybe Lacey called you to help me."

"No." He sat back on the grass, leaning against his car. "I've been worried about Beth—you know that. At first I thought Chase was pushing her too hard, and that she found Kelsey and Dhanya annoying. And I told myself she was right to be mad at you, but deep down, I was afraid something more was going on." He gazed at Beth, his brown eyes troubled. "At work, with guests, she was okay for a while, then I saw her withdrawing from them, too. Aunt Cindy noticed. She said she was worried about both of you.

"When I was out tonight, I saw Beth walking toward the steps that go down to the beach. I followed her. She stopped at the top for a long time, her lips moving, saying nothing. When I called to her, she acted as if she couldn't hear me. I stood next to her, but she wouldn't look at me. I turned her toward me, then asked her who she was talking to.

"'The water,' Beth said. I knew things had gone too far. It was already eleven o'clock, so I decided I'd talk to you tomorrow.

"An hour later, I couldn't sleep and heard an e-mail come in—Suzanne. She forwarded the e-mails Beth had sent her. After I read them, I ran to the cottage. I didn't think about what I was doing—why I was running—I just had to find you and Beth."

Sheer luck? Ivy wondered. Too much had happened in her life to believe in sheer luck.

"I guess everything I'd been denying suddenly became clear to me, including how I was putting both Beth and you in danger."

Ivy took Will's hand and he squeezed hers hard. She rested her other hand in Beth's open palm, then felt Beth's fingers curl over hers. Ivy fought the urge to pull back and swallowed hard, as if she could keep the fear from rising in her.

"Beth? Wake up," Will said. "You're with Ivy and me. You're safe, Beth."

Her eyes opened. She clung to Ivy's hand and stared up at Will.

"Is he gone?" Will asked. "Did Gregory leave you?"

Beth turned to Ivy without answering. Ivy saw the lighter

ring of blue in her friend's eyes; the darkness had lessened, but it had not disappeared. "He's retreating," Ivy said.

"No, he's resting and waiting." Beth's voice shook. "He's winning."

"We won't let him," Will said.

Beth lifted her hand and touched Ivy's mouth. Ivy steeled herself—wouldn't let herself shrink back.

"Was it real?" Beth asked.

"Was *what* real?" Ivy replied.

Beth shuddered. "I wanted it to be a nightmare, but it wasn't. I did it—I tried to suffocate you."

"*Gregory* tried."

Beth sat up. "If you hadn't been there to stop me," she said to Will, "I would have killed her."

He put his arm around her.

"Ivy, if ever I hurt you, I couldn't live with myself!"

"You're not going to hurt me."

"When this started, I didn't understand what was going on," Beth continued. "If I had known enough to run away—"

"No!" Ivy said sharply. "When Gregory was alive, his strategy was to isolate and control. Beth, think about it, think how he managed me . . . Suzanne . . . Eric. Don't let him separate you from us. Our strength is in our love for one another."

Beth looked from one to the other. The color that had just come into her cheeks vanished again.

"Lie down," Ivy told her. "You're exhausted."

Will put his arms around Beth and eased her back on the grass. He took off his shirt and laid it under her head, then stroked her cheek. His tenderness brought tears to Ivy's eyes. She wiped them before he could notice.

When Beth was peaceful again, Will gestured to Ivy and she followed him to a place beneath the trees, where they could keep an eye on Beth.

"As long as Gregory is in her mind, you're still in danger," he said in a quiet voice. "And Beth's not the only one who's exhausted. Why don't you go home for a few days, stay safe with your family, and get some rest."

Ivy shook her head. "We should stay together."

"And wait for this to happen again?" he argued.

Ivy gazed at Beth, lying pale in the grass. How much more could her friend endure?

If I left, Ivy wondered, *would Gregory follow me and leave Beth alone?* "Let me think about it," she said aloud.

Both Will and Ivy wanted to stay with Beth till morning. Will nudged Beth awake and helped her to her feet. "I'll get blankets," Ivy said.

"We'll meet you behind the dunes," Will replied.

Ten minutes later they spread them in a warm hollow between the bluff and dunes, about thirty feet from the steps, out of view from the inn. Ivy set her cell phone to awaken them for work. She hoped none of the inn's guests would be out for a dawn stroll, but knew that "camping under the stars" would be more acceptable to Aunt Cindy than Will sleeping at the girls' cottage or Beth staying in his room.

Beth was already asleep again. Will lay down next to her, and Ivy next to him. She was the last to drift into a fitful sleep, and she awoke before the others.

Sitting up, feeling the morning's damp chill, she hugged her knees to her chest. On one side of them the dunes looked like pale and rounded hills against an orange sky. On the other, the bank of dark vegetation gradually assumed the leafy outlines of shrubs and dwarfed trees. As the sky brightened, Ivy's gaze fell upon the end of the narrow boardwalk extending from the bluff's stairway to the dunes. "Dusty."

She rose to her feet, and the cat, tail held high, turned circles on the walkway, meowing when she was close enough to pet him.

"Some watch-cat you are, cutting out when things get rough."

Dusty rubbed his cheek against her hand and trotted toward the steps.

"I'm not in danger now, thank you."

The cat waited for her at the bottom of the steep stairway, his back to her, his nose pointed upward and tail waving lightly. Ivy glanced toward the landing, halfway up the steps.

"Looking for me?" Lacey asked.

"Actually . . . yes." Ivy climbed the stairs, arriving at the facing benches just as Dusty leaped into Lacey's lap.

"Good boy," Lacey said, running her purple-painted nails through the cat's orange fur. "You know, when Ella was alive, it took all my energy just to materialize the tips of my fingers so I could pet her."

"Ella liked you and Tristan."

"She was partial to Tristan," Lacey replied. "But then, aren't we all?"

Lacey looked as Ivy had seen her the last time, dressed in a tank top and ripped jeans. Her blunt cut bangs blew in the wind.

Ivy sat down opposite her. "Lacey—"

"'*I need your help*,'" Lacey interrupted. "You know, if I had a feather for every time you've said that, I'd be—"

"An angel?"

"A cockatoo. So what is it this time?" Lacey asked.

"Beth, Will, and I need your help."

"The radio especially." *Radio* was Lacey's term for a natural medium, a person open to spirits from the other side. "She's getting mostly one channel now. Gregory's."

"Can you help her?" Ivy asked. "Can you slip inside Beth?"

"What? Do you think I'm crazy?" Lacey exclaimed

"Or inside me," Ivy said, "and help Will and me expel Gregory."

"The way you talk, chick, you'd think it was as easy as

voting him off the island." She spread her hands as if holding up a title. "I can see it: *Soul Survivor,* Heaven's newest reality show."

Ivy grimaced.

"I've been making some inquiries about the situation," Lacey went on. "A demon is expelled from this world if the person he's occupying dies. Of course, if the demon realizes what's going on, he'll slip out before his doom is sealed and find another host."

Ivy shook her head. "There must be some other way to get rid of Gregory."

"Well, then, you figure it out. I have other clients who appreciate me and— "

"Beth tried to kill me last night."

Lacey blinked. "Excuse me?"

"Afterward she passed out, but when she came to, Will and I could communicate with her. The only other time I could get through to Beth was when she was holding a pendant we'd given her. Could it have special power?"

Lacey sat back against the bench, thinking. "No more power than you and Will have. And no less either. Must work kind of like saints' relics—as an extension of the strength in you and Will. She shouldn't take it off."

"It's gone."

"A pendant, you said. With an amethyst? Look anything like this?" Lacey asked, holding it up.

"Where did you find it?" Ivy cried, both stunned and relieved.

Lacey flicked her head. "At the bottom of the steps."

Beth had said the water wanted it, and Will had seen Beth standing at the top of the stairway, talking to "the water." This was as far as she had been able to throw it.

Dangling from Lacey's fingers, the purple stone caught pink fire from the rising sun, then the angel dropped it in Ivy's hand. Ivy's fingers closed around it.

They sat quietly for several minutes, watching the sun edge above the horizon.

"I'm glad to have this back. Still, Will and I could really use your help watching over Beth."

"Like I told you, if I had a feather for every time you've said to me—"

"So maybe I'm your mission," Ivy suggested mischievously.

Lacey stared at her. "Only if Number One Director has a rotten sense of humor."

Ivy shrugged. "Anyway, Will thinks I should go home for a few days."

"Your family's gone. I saw Philip just before they left."

"I know. I was thinking of going to Providence." Ivy felt Lacey's sharp eyes probing her.

"Have you told that to Will?" Lacey asked. "Have you mentioned to him that you're still seeing 'Killer Luke' and that he's really Tristan?"

"For Will to believe that Luke is dead and Tristan is occupying him is too much to ask right now. I don't want to push for too much too soon. He needs to trust me fully so we can fight Gregory."

"Trust you fully and be partially in the dark," Lacey remarked.

"Yeah. It's the best I can do."

The sun was up. Ivy reached in her pocket and turned off her alarm. "I have to go, Lacey. Aunt Cindy will be making coffee, and we've got to slip past her."

Lacey looked over her shoulder. "I might be able to arrange a distraction. Just for my own amusement," she added quickly. "Not because it would help you."

"Of course not," Ivy replied. "You're the best, Lacey."

Nineteen

"EVERYTHING OKAY?" AUNT CINDY ASKED IVY THE next afternoon.

Ivy's packing had been interrupted by another visit from Rosemary Donovan.

"Yes, thanks," Ivy replied, carrying her overnight bag and a shopping bag filled with treats through the cottage's screen door.

Aunt Cindy, gardening in the large plot between the cottage and inn, rose from her knees and peeled off her gloves. "Ms. Donovan seemed concerned."

"She was a little." Ivy set her bags on the swing. "The girl they found in the canal, Alicia Crowley, was once a close friend of Luke. Officer Donovan is afraid he might be back on the Cape."

She had come to warn Ivy as well as to show her the photo of Alicia for a second time. But there was no need to do that: Alicia's picture was all over the news.

"Then I'm doubly glad you're leaving!" Aunt Cindy said, tucking strands of faded red hair behind one ear. "And when you come back, I'm going to persuade Beth to go home for a few days. My agreement with your parents was to treat you like independent college students, not little campers, but the two of you are looking a bit too much like college kids—I think you've been burning the candle at both ends."

"We probably do need some sleep," Ivy replied. "Thanks for the time off. See you Sunday."

"Drive safe!"

"And thanks again for the homemade goodies," Ivy said, holding up the bag stuffed with Aunt Cindy's bread, jam, and cookies.

As she walked the path to her car, Ivy remembered her stepfather saying her mother's love brought out the best in him. So what did it mean when the person you loved brought out the liar in you?

But what choice did she have? Ivy asked herself. When fighting for someone's life and freedom, when those things had been unfairly taken away, right and wrong seemed to get mixed up.

"Hello, Ivy."

Lost in thought, she hadn't seen Chase getting out of his small black Porsche.

"Hey, Chase. Looking for Dhanya? She went with Kelsey to Chatham."

"Did she? I guess we got our wires crossed."

"A half hour ago," Ivy said, continuing to her car.

"Let me help you with that," Chase said, reaching for Ivy's overnight bag.

"Thanks, but I got it."

For a moment, both their fingers wrapped around its handle and pulled. Swallowing her irritation, Ivy let go.

"Where are you going?" he asked.

"Home."

"Nice," he said. "For how long?"

"A few days."

"Is everything all right?"

Instead of carrying the luggage to her car, Chase stood still, boxing in Ivy. She made a wide pass around him and unlocked the VW. "Just taking a break," she said, holding out her hand for the bag, then tossing it in the trunk.

"I thought maybe you and Will weren't getting along."

"We get along fine," Ivy lied.

"It didn't look like it at my party."

She walked around to the other side of her car to put the food up front by the air conditioning. Chase's habit of showing up unexpectedly and talking about things that weren't his business felt invasive.

"You left my party early," he continued.

"I had a headache. I tried to find you, but you were busy. Dhanya was supposed to tell you."

Chase rested an elbow on the roof of her little car. He was "gorgeous," as Beth had once observed. With his dark curly hair and gray eyes, he needed only a heavy sweater, boots, and a backdrop of Irish headlands to be a travel ad. But he didn't read social signals very well.

"Sorry, Chase, I've really got to go," Ivy told him, opening the door, forcing him to step quickly out of the way.

"The girl who killed herself," he said suddenly, "Alicia Crowley. She was the one at the carnival, the girl who recognized Luke, wasn't she?"

If this was bait to keep her talking, he had succeeded. Ivy stood with the door hanging open. "Yes."

"Do you think her death had anything to do with Luke?"

Ivy kept her voice light, trying to sound innocently surprised by the question. "How would I know?"

"Female intuition."

She grimaced.

"She wasn't strangled," Chase volunteered. "That must be a relief to you."

"Not much of a relief to *her*," Ivy snapped. She was getting angry.

"And there was no obvious sign of violence on her body, no sign of a struggle," he added.

Ivy frowned. "How do you know that?" Donovan had refused to give Ivy any details about the investigation, saying the police would make a public statement when they thought the time was right.

"My dad has friends in law enforcement."

"I thought he was a lawyer in Providence."

"He is. His legal counsel is sought all over. He knows everybody."

Was Chase showing off again, demonstrating his knowledge of things no one else knew and his family's many connections, or was he really looking for information about "Luke"?

Ivy dismissed the latter idea. She suspected that Chase had an enormous need for attention. As soon as he perceived himself as "rejected," whether by Beth's backing away or Ivy leaving his party early, he acted like a child seeking to win back attention however he could.

"Well, it sounds as if your dad knows a lot more than I do," Ivy replied, getting into her car, slipping her key into the ignition. "Keep me posted. And if I were you, Chase," she added, "I'd get down to Chatham. I'm sure Dhanya is waiting for you."

TUESDAY NIGHT, AN HOUR AFTER DARK, WHEN Tristan was emerging from the church basement, he heard someone whistling. Stepping back inside the window, he listened intently: the song from *Carousel*. Ivy had come to the church again. He whistled back and waited impatiently, barely able to see the dark-cloaked figure slip out from a stand of cedar.

Ivy handed a knapsack through the window, then climbed into his arms. With the window still open, they didn't say a word, but he couldn't wait—he pushed back her hood and covered her face with kisses. The feel of her arms around his back, holding on as if nothing could ever make her let go eased his mind and heart.

After a few minutes he softly closed the window and replaced the block of wood, then picked up the sack and led the way upstairs, a path he could now traverse in total darkness. After so many hours alone in the church, he could tell where he was by sound, from the slightest creak made by the pressure of his foot to the miniscule heating and cooling noises of wood, glass, and metal. He knew, too, the smells, and was as sure as a cat in the dark.

"You shouldn't have come," he said softly. "But you came! You shouldn't have, but—"

"Make up your mind!" They were standing in the altar area, he holding her, she burying her laughter in his chest. He tugged on her hood. "Nice cloak. I wasn't sure if it was a stray princess or a vampire climbing through the window."

"I picked it up in Providence today. You can find anything there. I have some things to show you, Tristan. Can we go to the tower?"

Again he led her though the dark church, and when they reached the ladder, placed her hands on either side of it. "The trapdoor's open." He followed her up the ladder, then reached effortlessly for the flashlight, which he had learned to leave in the same place. Ivy had brought a second light and turned it on. Then she removed her cloak.

Tristan blinked, unsure what to say. He didn't want to hurt her feelings, if this was some new trend. He'd never understood fashion and makeup. To him, the simpler the better—he wanted to see the real girl. As his old friend Gary used to say: What's better than naked?

"Wow," he said.

Ivy smiled and turned around. "I'd do a runway walk, but I'd probably fall through the trapdoor."

She was wearing leggings that were sheer as stockings and colored with hearts, roses, and skulls, looking almost like tattoos. Her booties were open-toed thongs, and her toenails were painted different colors. He pointed to her feet. "Are they, uh, comfortable?"

"Sure."

He fished for something else to say. . . . "Lacey likes tank tops."

Ivy was wearing a black one, but it was the long vest she wore over it that he couldn't stop looking at. It was loosely woven from shiny ribbons and pieces of glass, fragments that appeared to be recycled from beer bottles.

"I hope they filed that glass smooth." The moment he spoke, he regretted it. He sounded like his father.

Ivy burst out laughing. "You hate my outfit."

"No, no, I think it's . . . really interesting."

"Do I look like an art student?"

"An art student," he repeated, mystified.

"One who might have gone to school with Corinne?"

"Oh . . . *Ivy—*?"

"Wait till you see the makeup!"

"You've been spending too much time with Lacey. Ivy, what are you up to?"

"A little research in Providence. I want to start with Tony Millwood, the guy Alicia said was Corinne's longtime confidante."

"Alicia also said that Corinne took advantage of him, and he became angry and resentful."

"Exactly. Resentful people feel the need to talk, to voice all those things that infuriate them."

"Things like the way new friends—art students—replace old friends like him?" Tristan pointed out.

"There's a possibility he'll refuse to talk to me," Ivy conceded. "But on the school website there were student pages with links. Some of Corinne's stuff is still there, including a photo essay on a body shop. Which means I now have a believable reason to show up at his shop and ask questions, a reason that should flatter him. "

But refusal to talk was the least of Tristan's concerns. "Ivy, we're looking for a murderer. Everyone in Corinne's life, especially someone she made angry and resentful, is a suspect."

"I'll be fine. With two girls dead from the same neighborhood, only a lunatic would go after a third," Ivy reasoned.

"Just how sane do you think a murderer is?"

"It will be daytime," she argued, "with people around. And if you go to Providence with me, you won't be far away." Ivy took his hands in hers. "Tristan, the police are not going to ask the questions that need to be asked. It's too easy for them to blame everything on Luke. If we don't dig for the truth, no one else will."

Tristan withdrew his hands and walked a tight circle around the tower.

"We owe it to Alicia," she said.

Tristan stopped in his tracks. He didn't need the reminder.

"I heard that there were no external signs of a struggle," Ivy said. "If nothing odd is found in the autopsy, the authorities are going to call it a suicide. Andy thought that a paralyzing drug that leaves no chemical trace was used on Luke. If it was used on Alicia, she couldn't have put up a struggle as she was dumped in the water. I think that Alicia died—that she was murdered—the same way as Luke."

"These are just theories," Tristan said, not because he thought Ivy was wrong, but because he hated the idea that Alicia had been drawn into the murderer's web by trying to help them save himself from Luke's fate.

"Okay, but there is one indisputable fact," Ivy said. "Alicia wanted to clear Luke's name."

"Because she thought *her Luke* was alive. We can't be sure she would have met with us if she had known Luke was dead."

Ivy squeezed shut her eyes, but the tears still fell. Tristan felt powerless to comfort her because he couldn't comfort himself. Alicia was dead—they had asked her to help them, and now she was dead.

At last Ivy said, "All I know is, at this moment, you are alive. And we need to pick up where our search left off."

Twenty

"HEY. GEMMA," TRISTAN SAID SOFTLY. "COME ON, sleepyhead."

Ivy took her time opening her eyes, wanting to hold onto this moment of being wrapped in Tristan's arms, safe in the bell tower. She felt his breath on her cheek, then his finger tenderly tracing her lips.

"In an hour it will be dawn. You didn't even hear your cell phone go off." His finger followed the soft line of her eyebrow. "You've got makeup to do," he teased. "I'll hold the flashlight and mirror. You turn yourself into Gemma the art student."

Ivy's response was to press her face between his neck and shoulder.

"Playing possum?" he asked, but his voice shook, and Ivy knew he was making small jokes to ease the pain of ending their precious time alone.

Last night, before falling asleep, they had studied maps of Providence and its neighborhood of River Gardens as well as street views Ivy had printed from Google Earth, trying to become familiar enough with the area to find their way around without calling attention to themselves. They had plotted out where they would park and memorized escape routes in case things got rough. They also reviewed the info Ivy had mined from social networks and websites—anything to do with life in the neighborhood and at the schools Corinne and Luke had attended. Ivy planned to do as much of the interviewing as possible. They had argued over the pros and cons of "Luke" showing up at Corinne's old house. Did Corinne's grandmother still have a soft spot for him?

During her shopping spree in Providence, Ivy had purchased a cell phone for Tristan, to be used only in extreme emergencies, since they wanted to leave no electronic trace of their actions. She had already turned off the GPS in their phones. They were as prepared as they could be.

As Ivy sped along the Mid-Cape Highway, she caught Tristan peeking at her and grinning.

"If your eyelashes were any longer, you could use them for paintbrushes," he said.

Ivy batted them. "This is what a lot of girls wear."

"Maybe, but I like your curly blond ones."

Arriving in Providence, they drove a distance beyond the city, following Route 1 along the coast, gradually merging with the morning rush. They didn't want to show up in River Gardens until they could blend into the neighborhood bustle rather than appear as unfamiliar figures on a near-empty street.

After a fast-food breakfast, Ivy left Tristan and the car at the edge of River Gardens and walked several blocks to Tony's. The streets were lined with wood frame homes, bungalows and three-story houses; many of the taller ones had several mailboxes, indicating they were divided into flats. Rusty chain-link fences and spans of electric wires knotted together the streets. The small lawns were like worn carpets, with patches of pebbles and dirt showing through.

Tony's home and business was at an intersection, the bungalow facing one street and the entrance to a large, paved backyard facing the other. A cinderblock building behind the house had two bays, and the garage door was open in one of them. Inside the open bay someone worked on a car with a whining power tool. Someone else must have been at work in the closed bay, for fumes were pouring out of an exhaust fan high in the wall. The sign on the door said PAINTING. STAY OUT.

The paved lot between house and business, which held two damaged cars, was surprisingly orderly in its piles of stuff: cans and drums of chemicals, coiled hoses, twisted metal, and swept-up shards of fiberglass and cracked lights. A rack with a new windshield stood near a car bearing a mesmerizing web of fractured glass. In the photo essay, it was the twisted metal and broken glass that had drawn Corinne as a photographer.

Ivy was staring at the web of glass when she heard a door open in the painting bay. A person wearing a hooded visor with a breathing apparatus studied her for a long moment, having the intimidating advantage of being able to see her face while she could not see his. The painter ducked back into the building for a moment, then reappeared, having disposed of his headgear and gloves, and walked across the lot toward her.

"Help you?"

"Yeah, hi. I'm Gemma. I'm looking for Tony."

"You found him."

"Do you have a few minutes?" she asked.

"Depends."

Tony's long hair was light brown and pulled back in an elastic band; his eyes were dark blue and intense. He was the same height as Ivy and, as far as she could tell, slender in build. His jumpsuit with its many brilliant colors looked more like an artist's smock than industrial overalls; Ivy assumed he did custom painting—perhaps cars tattooed with skulls and orange flames—as well as repair work.

"I was a friend of Corinne's."

If he hadn't been sweating, Ivy wouldn't have seen the change in him: the tightening of his jaw and the muscles in his neck.

"I went to art school with her."

"Three cheers for you."

His voice said *who cares*, but his eyes, which were glued to her, betrayed him.

"We have a gallery at school. We're doing an exhibition in October and each entry needs an artist's statement. I volunteered to do Corinne's for *Carscape*, her photo essay."

"That was done before art school."

"Was it? Oh, well, nobody'll know but us. I was hoping you could fill in some background, tell me how you came to know her, how she came to photograph this place, something about the time she spent shooting pictures here, all that kind of stuff. The more personal the better. We want people looking at the art to have a sense of the person behind it."

"Anything I have to say, you don't want to print."

"So tell me a few things, and we'll see," Ivy said lightly.

He gazed at her as if she was an idiot who hadn't caught on to his anger and his buzz-off message.

"Lots of artists are controversial," she went on. "It makes them interesting."

"Tony?" someone called from the house.

A woman, who appeared to be in her twenties, stood on the back step, gave Ivy the once over, then moved swiftly toward them as if she had seen something she didn't like. *Older sister*, Ivy thought; she had the same hair and eyes, though she was heavier than Tony.

"Who are you?" the young woman demanded.

"Gemma Schumann," Ivy said, holding out her hand.

The woman didn't shake it.

"Are you Tony's sister?" Ivy asked.

"Does it matter?"

"Gemma was an art school friend of Corinne's," Tony told the woman.

What had been instinctive wariness now settled into confirmed distaste: "I have nothing to say to her snotty art friends. I don't know why you waste your time, Tony."

"So I guess," Ivy said quickly, "Corinne was as *popular* at home as she was at school."

The young woman smirked. "You tell me. Was she a manipulative bitch? A world-class snitch? That's the Corinne we all knew and loved."

Before Ivy could think of a response that would elicit

enough trust or anger to draw more information, the woman turned on her heel and stalked back to the house.

"So . . . so it wasn't just the pressure of school that made Corinne the way she was," Ivy baited Tony.

He didn't reply.

"At art school, things can get competitive—cutthroat." She saw Tony's hand flex. "So I figured it was a school thing. . . ." She shrugged. "Anyway, that doesn't make Corinne any less of an artist."

He snorted.

"Is that what made you friends?" Ivy asked. "You're an artist, aren't you? Cars are your canvas. Was it a love of images that drew you together?"

"Corinne used images to hurt."

Hurt—how? Ivy wanted to ask. Aloud she said, "Well, art is often provocative. It is a form of social conscience. I can think of several famous photographers who—"

"Corinne had no social whatever. She didn't care about issues, much less about other people!" His hands were shaking. As if suddenly aware that she had noticed, he shoved them in his pockets.

"Okay, so it was art for art's sake." Ivy was pulling out every cliché she could think of to keep him talking.

"Corinne loved power, not art. For her, a photographic image was power over others. She destroyed, not created."

Ivy wondered if Corinne's photos had hurt or angered

someone enough to attack her. "She liked to post her photos on the Internet. Did she get some people upset?"

Tony eyed Ivy suspiciously for a moment. *Perhaps a school friend should know that,* Ivy thought. She was afraid she had blown her chance with him.

He glanced toward the house, then shrugged. "Doesn't matter. She's dead now."

"Can I see what you're working on?" Ivy asked, hoping that, like most artists and musicians, he liked an audience. "Is it a custom paint job?"

Without replying, he started toward the closed car bay and Ivy followed, hoping this was an unspoken invitation.

Leaning over, he yanked up the garage door. "The fumes will kill you," he warned.

"Wow! It's incredible!" She didn't have to fake admiration. With every quarter-inch covered with shapes and colors, details that must have taken months to paint, he had created a car writhing with snakes. Coiling, undulating, and intertwining bodies, burning eyes and yawning mouths—the details were beautiful, the whole work horrific.

"Do you copy designs from different sources?"

"Sometimes, but this one came from my dreams."

Ivy was glad she didn't have *his* dreams and wondered what generated them, but made no further comment, instead inquiring about the kinds of paint he used. While she knew nothing about pearls, metal flakes, and chameleon pigments, she knew the kind of questions to ask from listening to Will talk about his artistic media. At last she attempted to shift their conversation back to Corinne.

"Did Corinne ever help you design or paint a car?"

Tony studied Ivy so intensely, she felt as if he were scraping the makeup off her face. "You really didn't know her, did you?"

"You mean know her well? She was in two of my classes, and, well, I guess everybody kind of puts on an act at school," Ivy replied, trying to sound casual.

"She made fun of this kind of work. She called it 'Redneck Fantasy.'"

"I see."

"She hated River Gardens—she was on her way up, she kept saying. Had a job at a mall, her own place, and art professors. She was just too good for the rest of us dummies who couldn't figure out how to get out of here." His voice was as bitter as the smell of the paint.

"So I guess she didn't have any friends left here."

"No real ones. Corinne watched out for only one person, herself."

"Apparently she didn't watch out enough," Ivy remarked.

He cast a sidelong look then made a motion to pull down the overhead door. She stepped back quickly.

"No one who knew Corinne blames Luke," he said.

"Because . . ." Ivy hesitated. "They don't think he killed her?"

"Because she got what she deserved."

"I see."

A long silence followed.

Ivy pulled a small notebook from her pocket. "Maybe for the exhibition I could use your earlier quote, 'For Corinne, image was power.'"

"Sure," he said, "along with my other quote: 'She's dead now.'"

Turning his back on Ivy, he walked toward the house, where the woman with the same hair and eyes was watching from a window.

Twenty-one

"HEY, BABE, NEED A LIFT?" TRISTAN ASKED, SITTING IN the driver's seat, sunglasses on, baseball cap pulled down, making a joke to disguise the fact that he had sat with his eyes trained on the entrance to the store lot for the last thirty minutes, nervously waiting for Ivy's return.

"I already have a boyfriend," Ivy replied, then leaned down to peer in the window. "But you are kind of cute with that beard and all. Oh, why not?"

She scooted around the car and slipped into the passenger seat.

Tristan grasped her hand, intertwining his fingers with hers for a moment, then said, "Security has cruised by twice. I'm going to take off, then we can talk."

Ivy waited till they were weaving through streets beyond the boundaries of the neighborhood, before recounting her conversation with Tony.

"So what do you think?" she asked at last.

Tristan shook his head in disbelief. "Makes you wonder what Luke saw in Corinne."

"Tony saw it, too," Ivy pointed out. "Remember, Alicia had said he was once Corinne's confidante. I don't know if she betrayed him in some way or just tossed him aside on her way out of River Gardens, but he's pretty bitter."

"Bitter enough to kill her?"

"Perhaps. The woman who seemed like an older sister definitely wanted me off the premises."

Tristan slowed for a traffic light. "Maybe she thinks he needs to be saved from something he did."

"Or something *they* did," Ivy replied. "So now we have even more suspects."

"Because Corinne was a cyberbully."

"Looks that way. And if she was," Ivy added, "our suspects could range far beyond River Gardens." She reached behind the seat and dug out a folder of maps she had printed. "We should check out the shop where Corinne worked as well as her school, to see if she was upsetting people there, too."

Tristan nodded. "Before we do, let's stop at her house and talk to the grandmother who is supposed to like me. After that, we should probably cut out of the neighborhood, before word gets around about us."

Fifteen minutes later they pulled up in front of a tall frame house surrounded by a chain-link fence. Two mailboxes with locks on them stood just inside the gate.

"So who's going to ring the doorbell?" Tristan asked quietly, pointing to a sign on the gate: BEWARE OF DOG. "Which one of us runs faster?"

"Me," Ivy whispered back, "but I bet you're quicker getting over a fence, so you go and signal me when it's all clear."

Tristan laughed softly. "It's awfully quiet, and the windows are open. Let's see if Fido barks." He opened and closed the gate with a bang.

The only sound was a motorcycle rumbling down the street.

"You'd expect a path to be worn around the edge of the yard," Ivy said. "Dogs don't just run up and down a sidewalk."

"Maybe the dog is her stepfather," Tristan joked.

"Right. It'd be better for you not to run into him. I'll see who's home."

"No," Tristan said quickly, his pride getting the better of him. "It's both or neither of us."

"Stubborn angel!"

Together they walked up the front path and rang the doorbell.

After the second ring, a lace curtain was pulled aside, then let go. A short, squarely built woman with expressive eyes and thick white hair opened the door. Tristan removed his sunglasses. Her eyes widened as she peered up into the shade of his baseball cap. Before he could react, she reached and pulled the hat off his head. "Luke! It *is* you." Tears filled her eyes.

It was hard for Tristan, the way the old woman gazed at him. He felt so . . . unworthy around people like her and Alicia, who looked at him with a love that he had done nothing to deserve, people who were desperately glad to see him, a mere pretender.

"I missed you, Luke. It broke my heart, losing Corinne. And then I lost you, too." One worn hand cupped his cheek. "Come in, come in." She turned to Ivy, then cocked her head at Tristan. "A friend?"

"This is Gemma. She wanted to meet you, Gran." Although Alicia said everyone called the old woman that, it was hard for Tristan to, because he suspected, coming from "Luke," it would mean something to her. The look she gave him, her eyes glistening, told him he was right. He wanted to look away, but he knew that he couldn't. "Gemma went to art school with Corinne."

Gran reached and took Ivy's hands in her own, then turned and led them through a living room of assorted dark wood furniture. Her kitchen was scrubbed clean and made bright by chipped, colorful dishes.

"Still like your coffee strong?" Gran asked, and, without waiting for an answer, poured Tristan a cup. "How about you?"

"Thank you, but no for me," Ivy said

Tristan sipped the coffee. It made Starbuck's espresso taste like flavored water.

"Tea?"

"That would be perfect," Ivy agreed.

Gran turned on the kettle. "How have you been, Luke? Where have you been? There were so many rumors."

"Different places," he replied.

"Why didn't you write me? I wouldn't have told no one. I knew you could never hurt my Corinne."

"And I knew you wouldn't tell anyone, but other people might have seen the letter and the postmark before it got to you."

"Excuses!"

Tristan smiled—she sounded less like a scolding grandmother and more like a flirtatious girl who was letting him know she hadn't gotten the attention she wanted. She smiled back, then placed a mug and two boxes of tea in front of Ivy. "You *look* like art school," she remarked.

"Thank you. . . . I think."

"How have you been, Gran?" Tristan asked.

"You know, you know, nothing different 'cept I don't have my Corinne. *He's* the same."

Tristan figured that *he* was Corinne's stepfather. "How's her mom?"

"Acting like a fool."

Tristan wondered what that meant, but nodded like he knew what she was talking about.

"Corinne had some issues with her mom," Ivy said.

"Don't we all," Gran remarked.

"But she always talked about you and—"

The front door banged back against the wall. Ivy jumped, but Gran appeared used to it; her only response was to turn off the kettle, which was about to whistle.

"Whose car is that?" a deep male voice demanded from the living room.

Gran put her finger to her lips.

"Gran?" he yelled. "Gran? I smell your stinkin' coffee."

Tristan slipped on his sunglasses and hat.

A large man with a shaved head entered the kitchen. He was neatly dressed in a white shirt, black tie, and black pants, his clothes seeming more refined than his manners. His high bald dome made his facial features look low on his face, pushed down toward his chin with a kind of mean-ness. *Hank Tynan,* Tristan thought.

"Who the hell are you?" Tynan asked, looking from Ivy to Tristan.

"Friends of Corinne," Ivy answered.

"Are you now." He turned his back on them and opened the refrigerator door, standing in front of it for a while as if he wanted to cool himself down. "I don't ever remember seeing you before."

"I went to art school with Corinne."

"You're a liar," her stepfather said, then reached in and pulled out a soda. "Corinne wouldn't tell anyone where she came from."

"Yes, you're right about that," Ivy said. "But she talked a lot about Gran. She also left behind a lot of photos. And photos have clues, you know."

Tristan guessed that Ivy was testing for a reaction, and she got it. Tynan stared at her for a full minute in a way that made Tristan want to step between them. Then he yanked the top off his can, threw it at the table where they were sitting, and kicked closed the refrigerator door.

"And you have these photos with your little clues?"

"A lot of people have them. She was always sending them out to friends and posting them online."

"But you had enough to trace her back here," Tynan noted.

"I was a big fan of her work."

Tristan could see that Ivy was making Tynan uncomfortable.

"Corinne and her photos—she was a snoop." Tynan took a swig from his can. Beads of moisture coated his upper lip. "She could never get enough dirt on people. She thought herself high and mighty, but she was a bottom dweller—she loved mud."

"She was a wonderful photographer," Ivy said.

"She was a tattler with a camera. And in the end she was a fool, because she didn't know when to stop."

"Stop what?" Ivy asked.

Tynan smirked. "Tattling, what else?" His smile faded as he studied Tristan. "And you, you some kind of a silly artist?"

Tristan simply looked at him.

"Got a voice?" the man asked.

Tristan removed his sunglasses. "Yes, I do, Hank."

Tynan's small eyes grew larger. "Well, well, well. *He returns.*" Tynan's voice was smooth and sarcastic, but his eyes darted from one to the other as if he suspected some plot against him.

Tristan decided that the less he said the better. Let the man imagine Luke, who might know all kinds of things about him, had returned and was keeping a smug silence.

"I could turn you in," Tynan threatened.

Tristan nodded. "You could."

"But I owe you."

Tristan forced himself to gaze blandly at the man, as if he could care less what Tynan had to say.

"Life's a lot more pleasant in this house now, know what I mean?"

A hiss escaped Gran's lips.

"And it's going to stay that way." It sounded like a threat. "Did you kill the other girl too?"

"Neither," Tristan replied.

"Alicia hasn't been in River Gardens for two years," Gran said, "and it happened on the Cape."

Tynan spun around. "Where do you think *he* was?"

Gran snorted. "I know murderous rage when I see it," she said, never taking her eyes from Tynan.

The man glanced at the kitchen clock, cursed, and grabbed a large bag of chips from the counter. Pulling a set of car keys from his pocket, he paused in the kitchen doorway. "Here's a bit of advice, Luke. Don't let Corinne's mother catch you here." He laughed and made a gesture with his keys, handling them like a knife. "She's liable to cut your throat."

AFTER TYNAN LEFT, IVY SIPPED HER TEA AND watched Gran over the rim of her cup.

"Yeah, *he's* the same," Tristan said.

"Don't get me started," the old woman replied. "Between him and my daughter—" She made a dismissive gesture.

"Where is Corinne's mom?" Ivy asked.

"At work. Waiting tables at the diner. Somehow she's managed to keep the job," Gran said. "Luke, I was sorry to hear about Alicia. She was a good friend to you. She was better to you than Corinne was."

Tristan nodded and stared down at his coffee. Ivy wished she could reach across and rest her hand on top of his. When she glanced up, Gran was watching her closely. The old woman didn't miss much.

Ivy set down her cup. "Who killed Corinne? Do you have any idea?"

"I have a lot of ideas," Gran replied, "but no answers."

Because there were so many people who wanted her granddaughter gone?

"Is her room still—what did her mother do with her bedroom?" Tristan asked.

"Mia moved things back from Corinne's apartment—took the new stuff, the nice stuff for herself, of course—and piled the rest in Corinne's old room. Sometimes I sit on Corinne's bed, the way I used to, but it's not the same. I know she's not coming back." Gran studied him. "Maybe you'd like some time in there."

"If that's okay with you."

She led the way, and Ivy followed Tristan.

The room was crammed with boxes and bags that were piled on the floor, bureau, desk, and a pair of old kitchen chairs. Despite the chaos, Corinne's bed was neatly made, her coverlet lovingly turned down as if prepared for someone to climb in bed. Ivy had the feeling Gran had done that, even though she'd acknowledged Corinne wasn't coming back.

On the table next to Corinne's bed sat a broken piece of pottery that had once been a glazed jar with a lid. Ivy picked up one of the fragments. "She made this, didn't she?"

"Yes. Her apartment was broken into, some of her decorative boxes and jars broken."

"When?" Tristan asked.

"Several days after her death, you remember." Gran frowned. "No, you must have been gone by then."

"Was anything taken?" Ivy asked.

"Her computer and iPad. I didn't care about those. But I hated the way they destroyed things that Corinne made with her own hands. Hoodlums!"

Or someone looking for something in a hurry, Ivy thought, exchanging glances with Tristan. What if Corinne was more than a cyberbully? What if she was a blackmailer? Tony's sister had called her "a world-class snitch," and Hank Tynan, "a tattler with a camera."

"What a shame," Ivy said aloud. "Luke, you probably want some time alone here. I'll wait back in the kitchen," she added, hoping Gran would follow her, allowing him to search the place. After a few minutes, the old woman did.

"I told him we'd be in my room," she said to Ivy. "He

and Corinne both liked to sit there and talk while I did my sewing. Bring your tea."

Gran's room was pleasant, with floral slipcovers and framed photographs of family members, pictures that went back all the way to sepia-toned portraits. The old woman pointed to a chair, then took the one opposite, which had bright light coming in over her shoulder and an array of sewing tools around it—a basket of yarn, a box filled with a rainbow of shining thread, and a large jar of buttons. "Corinne used to thread my needles for me. I need a white one—the heavy cotton—and a black polyester. I'd better match this one myself," she said, holding a peach colored blouse next to the box of spools.

Ivy threaded the needles, adjusting the lengths of thread according to Gran's directions.

Gran poured a small heap of buttons onto the table between them and sorted through with quick fingers, finding the ones she wanted.

"So are you an item?" Gran asked.

"Excuse me?"

"You and Luke."

"Uh, no. I met him when he came to see Corinne at school. We're just friends."

Gran's dark eyes were piercing. "So far."

"So far," Ivy said, acquiescing to Gran's perceptiveness.

"Don't hurt him. That boy's been through hell and back."

Ivy nodded.

"Did Corinne have a rich boyfriend at school?" Gran asked.

The question caught Ivy off guard. Of course, Ivy realized, Gran saw her as a source of information, just as she saw Gran.

"It was hard to tell if Corinne had someone steadier than the rest. She didn't have any trouble finding guys interested in her," Ivy ventured.

"*Never* had trouble," Gran confirmed.

"And she was kind of private about some things."

"Secretive," Gran said. "We may's well tell it like it is. She was secretive and sometimes sneaky."

"She never asked anyone from school over to her apartment," Ivy went on, realizing there was a limit to what she could fake; even if Gran had never been there, she would have seen the objects they brought back.

"She had some very nice things," Gran said, "and I had hoped she had a rich lover. Corinne always liked expensive things, and sometimes she bent the rules."

Bent the rules—as in stealing? Ivy nodded as if she understood.

"If rich people didn't show off their nice things, other people wouldn't steal them now, would they?"

It was a strange way of seeing the world, but perhaps it worked for an older woman defending a grandchild she loved.

"The last time I saw Corinne, she was very nervous," Gran remarked.

"She was? I'm surprised," Ivy said. "Of course, people at college have different personas than they do at home."

"You're right, it wasn't like Corinne," Gran replied, and sewed fiercely for several minutes, fastening a button to a man's shirt so tightly Ivy imagined that the collar would rip off before the button could be lost again.

"Something was wrong. Corinne came home and asked me to mend a sleeve for her, and sat where you are sitting, just like she did when she was a little girl and in some kind of trouble. She didn't always tell me what trouble she was in—told me less and less as she got older, but still she would come in and sit. This was her safe place, and when she came that evening, I knew something was very wrong."

"Did she give any hint of what it was?"

"No. I thought maybe you knew."

"Sorry, no."

"Nothing going on at school?" Gran persisted. "Not that anything to do with school ever rattled her."

Ivy shook her head. "I'm surprised the police didn't follow up on that."

"I told the police nothing," Gran said. "The trouble was for me to know, not them."

So Gran must have suspected that Corinne wasn't involved in a completely innocent thing. . . .

"Finding out is for my peace of mind, no one else's."

Except, Ivy thought, *others' safety could depend on it.*

Gran put aside the shirt she'd mended and picked up the jar of buttons. She shook it, held it up, squinting at it, then poured what was left in the jar on the table between them. Picking out a gold button, she studied it for a moment then held it out to Ivy.

"This is the only clue she left."

Twenty-two

IVY OPENED HER PALM, LETTING THE PIECE OF GOLD drop in. "A cufflink."

"Ever seen one like it?" Gran asked.

"No. My stepfather is the only person I've known to wear them to work. What is this design?" Ivy turned it around. "An arrow?"

"Looks it to me," Gran said. "Nobody you know at school makes jewelry?"

Ivy hesitated. "No one I'm friends with. But Corinne and I didn't share friends. It's not like high school when you have a clique you belong to. I assume Corinne gave this to you."

"Left it here that night. Hid it in the button jar."

Ivy turned the cufflink this way and that, looking for a fine engraving of initials or a jeweler's signature. "I don't see anything but the arrow on it. Are you sure Corinne was the one who dropped this in the button jar? You're sure she put it there the night she was killed?"

Gran nodded. "When she was a little girl, she used to play with the buttons while I sewed, made pictures around them, used them for faces and flowers and things. The night she was murdered, she emptied the jar and was moving the buttons around like she did when she was little, then she put them all back. I didn't think about it till after her funeral. I was sitting here, missing her, and poured out the buttons. There it was."

Ivy wished she could take the cufflink and wondered who else Gran had shown it to. "And no one else who you showed it to had any idea where she got it?"

"I haven't told nobody. Her mother'd sell it for its weight in gold. The police would put it in a plastic baggy and I'd never see it again. It's the last thing I have from Corinne. It stays with me."

Ivy handed it back to her.

"I'll show it to Luke. Maybe he knows something," Gran said.

"Let me get him," Ivy offered, rising quickly, not wanting

Gran to walk in on Tristan searching the room. "Luke," Ivy called out before reaching the bedroom door, "Gran has something curious to show you."

Tristan followed her back to the room and studied the round cufflink. "Sorry," he said, handing it back. "Never seen it."

They stayed an hour longer, looking at old photos of Corinne, several of which had a young Luke in them, and listening to Gran's stories. It occurred to Ivy that Corinne's grandmother had not been able to share her grief with anyone else, including Corinne's mother.

She held Ivy tightly when saying good-bye. "Just your age," she kept repeating. Ivy walked ahead, letting Gran say a private good-bye to "Luke." Then Tristan and Ivy drove off silently, not speaking till they were beyond the boundaries of River Gardens.

"That was hard."

"Yeah," Tristan agreed softly,

"When Gregory died, his dad cried like a baby. Andrew was horrified at what Gregory had done, but he still grieved for him."

Tristan nodded. Ivy was wondering when he would ask about his own parents; whenever he was ready, she told herself.

"Art school next?" Tristan asked. "Think anyone will be there for summer session?"

"It's worth a try. There should be dark rooms and computers where photography students hang out. And it's not far from the mall where Corinne worked. Grab the maps in the back seat."

They set their course, then Ivy recounted her conversation with Gran.

"So what do you think was going on?" Tristan asked.

"Gran wasn't supporting Corinne, not if she was wondering if Corinne had a rich boyfriend to pay for her stuff. And I've worked at a mall shop. Even if school tuition was completely covered by scholarship, there's no way Corinne was paying for her own apartment and buying nice things with a part-time salary from a store."

"Then you're thinking the same thing I am," Tristan said. "The elementary school snitch—"

"And middle school cyberbully—" Ivy interjected.

"Figured out how profitable real blackmail could be."

"Sure looks that way," Ivy agreed. "All her electronics are gone—anything which might have photo files that could be used for blackmailing."

"I wish I'd had more time to search," Tristan said.

"Was anything damaged other than the handmade boxes and jars?"

"No. I think they were broken because someone was looking for a small object, like a flash drive."

"Or a cufflink!" they said at the same time. Ivy added,

"Corinne anticipated that someone would come looking, so she put it where her victim wouldn't think to search, in an old woman's button jar."

"So why is this cufflink so important?"

Ivy didn't respond until she had merged off the exit ramp. "Well, if you lose a piece of jewelry somewhere, it proves you were there. And if you weren't supposed to be there—"

"But you could always deny it," Tristan pointed out. "You could claim you were set up, that someone else put it there. Although I suppose enough damage could be done just by others believing you left it there."

"Not that many people wear cufflinks," Ivy said.

"Yeah, only classy guys like me, working as a waiter at your mom's wedding."

Ivy laughed at the memory. "I guess it was the weight of those cufflinks that made you spill the trays. You also wore them for the prom."

"So it's possible Tony's worn them," Tristan said.

"And Hank, driving the execs around."

"Or a professor type from her school. Or someone she caught doing something at the mall where she worked. The list is getting long," Tristan noted.

"Or maybe she *did* have a rich boyfriend," Ivy suggested, "one that was married, and she blackmailed him." Ivy sighed. "We need to find out as much about her life away from home as her life in River Gardens."

For the next three hours they tried and had little success. The two students they found working on photos in the school lab shrugged off their questions, saying Corinne hung around a little with everyone but not much with anyone; no one was close to her. The people in Corinne's apartment building shut their doors in Ivy and Tristan's faces, all except one neighbor who, after an extended interview, was discovered to have moved in after Corinne left. Ivy guessed the man was lonely for company. At the mall they received strong opinions from her coworkers. The two twenty-somethings clearly didn't like her. She was "always watching us" they said, and she "sucked up" to the owner; Ivy figured that Corinne the snitch had made their lives miserable.

At last, tired from a long day of faking and questioning, Ivy and Tristan collapsed at a local Panera. They didn't say a word till they were both digging into sandwiches, enjoying the comfort of a cushioned booth. They sat side by side, Tristan putting his long legs up on the bench opposite, Ivy leaning happily against him. She wondered if Tristan had any idea how precious these ordinary moments were to her.

During the meal Ivy told Tristan that Beth was continuing to act strange, but she stopped short of mentioning the attempt on her life. There was no need to worry him more, Ivy decided; it wasn't going to happen again.

"Will's keeping a close eye on her," Ivy said, then

checked her phone for messages. "No news, and no news is good news."

"Did you bring in your laptop?"

"In the big bag," she replied, pointing.

He retrieved and opened it so they both could see the screen. "Let's search for cufflinks and see what we can find out about designs and makers."

They discovered that cufflinks came in every imaginable shape and color, and that there were a million specialty cufflinks featuring sports teams, rock stars, college seals, and animals, along with cufflinks with designs that made them "perfect gifts" for bankers, teachers, gardeners, gamblers, computer geeks, fantasy players . . .

"We should take a photo of the cufflink and send it to Suzanne. She'd enjoy this kind of research," Tristan remarked. "It's going to take days."

"Try *cufflink* and *evidence*," Ivy suggested. "I've been assuming that the owner of the cufflinks, our blackmail victim, has the matching link. But that would result in the situation you mentioned: Corinne claiming the link was found in a certain place, and the owner denying it. What if the police had the matching cufflink? What if they found it at a crime scene?"

Tristan typed the terms in the search box, then read aloud. "*CSI: Miami* Season 8—several entries for that. And a case in Colorado where the cufflink is forensic evidence, and then there's 'evidence' of 'cufflinks' in seventeenth-century England, and evidence they existed as far back as King Tut's dynasty—who knew—and . . . Ivy, look!"

She leaned closer. "Click on it!"

The article had appeared in a Springfield, Massachusetts newspaper.

A 43-year-old motorist was killed early Saturday morning by a hit-and-run driver along Route 20, southeast of Brimfield, Massachusetts. Genevieve Gilchrest was found severely injured about fifteen feet from her car, a gray Nissan Altima, which was parked on the side of the road with a flat tire. She was flown to the Trauma Center at UMass Memorial in Worcester, where she died several hours later.

Police recovered a partial imprint of a second vehicle's tire tracks near the victim's car as well as a gold cufflink near the body. The cufflink, which appears to be custom made and bears a design resembling an arrow, may belong to someone who stopped to look at the victim, possibly the driver who struck her. The vehicle which struck Ms. Gilchrest is likely to have sustained obvious damage to its grill or hood as well as a cracked or broken windshield.

Crimestoppers is asking anyone with information

*to come forward. All calls will be kept strictly
confidential.*

"It happened in May a year ago," Tristan observed. He and
Ivy checked through other entries listed by the search engine,
then returned to the article. Mapquest showed Brimfield to
be about an hour and fifteen minutes from Providence.

"That was the end of senior year for Corinne. What do
you think she was doing there?"

"Maybe nothing," Tristan replied. "The police found
the cufflink mentioned here. She simply had to hear about
it, recognize the cufflink, and know how to get her hands
on the remaining one. Let's see if the Providence papers
carried the story . . . no."

Tristan tapped his fingers on the edge of the keyboard,
thinking. "The car would have damage. And the police
would survey body shops in the area—in Massachusetts,
but maybe not Rhode Island. What about—"

Ivy met his eyes. "Tony's? Could be! Tristan, we need to
convince Gran to turn the cufflink over to the police."

"Or give it to us," he said. "We can go back to Tony and
press him for information."

Ivy shook her head. "I think it's too risky, and not just
for us. What if Tony is innocently involved?"

"I guess you trust the police more than I do," Tristan
replied.

Everlasting

"I trust them more than I trust Corinne's killer, and Luke's, and Alicia's. Tristan, at least one person—maybe several—is desperate to cover up something and willing to murder whoever gets in the way. Tonight we should keep our distance from both Providence and the Cape, and tomorrow, tell Gran what we've discovered. Then, after I drop you back at the church, I'll call the police and let them take it from there. Okay?"

She looked into his eyes, not the hazel they once were, but a brilliant blue, and yet she knew from the way he looked at her, they were the windows to Tristan's soul.

"So where are we spending tonight?" he asked, brushing her cheek with his fingers. "Another state park?"

She thought for a moment, then smiled. "I know a great tree house high on a ridge in Connecticut."

Twenty-three

FROM THE TIME TRISTAN HAD REALIZED WHO HE was, he had thought about his parents and wondered about their life now. The dangers of the moment had often pushed back these thoughts, but during quiet stretches when he was alone in the church, he had recalled memories of his life with them with both joy and sadness. His meeting with Gran had made these memories weigh heavier on his heart.

Ivy had been driving for an hour and a half, and they were approaching the outskirts of his hometown, Stonehill, when he said, "Gran will mourn Corinne for the rest of her life. She'll never get over losing her."

Ivy slowed the car down and looked over at him. "That's how it is when someone you love dies."

"My parents," was all he could get out.

She nodded as if she understood what he was asking. "It's been very hard for them. I think they've poured all the love they showered on you on the people they work with, your mom's patients, and your dad's. He's still a chaplain at the hospital."

"I can't believe how self-centered I've been," Tristan said. "I thought watching you from afar, being dead and not being able to reach you, was the worst thing that could ever happen. I felt sorry for myself. But it's the people left behind who are most badly hurt."

"Everywhere we looked," Ivy said, "we saw places we had been with you. Everything we did, we thought of how we had done it with you, and longed to be able to do it again. It was incredibly painful. And yet, to try not to think about those things—to forget—was to lose you forever.

"After you died, Gregory encouraged me to forget. One day he became furious with your mother and told her to leave me alone, that it was over. Your mom said, 'When you love someone, it's never over. You move on because you have to, but you bring him with you in your heart.' Your mom and dad, they still carry you with them in their hearts."

Tristan swallowed hard, then watched the town of Stonehill unfold around him, the pretty houses and shops, Celentano's Pizza, where he and his buddies used to eat, the home of his swim coach, the high school where he had met Ivy. He had seen the town at six p.m. a million times, the bustle around the commuter train station, the rush at the grocery story, parents and little kids and teens, and yet he watched it now with wonder, these scenes he once took for granted.

Someone waved at Ivy—who had washed off her makeup and changed back into her own clothes before leaving Panera. Ivy gave a little beep of the horn.

"Love the car!" the woman called—it was Pat Celentano, but she didn't recognize Tristan. Nobody here would recognize him.

"Could we drive by my house, my parents' house?" he corrected himself.

"*Your* house," Ivy said. "Sure."

It was real, yet dreamlike to him, riding along the tree-lined streets over where he had biked and skateboarded. He saw landmarks he knew but had never paid much attention to: a striped awning off a side porch halfway down the block, a blossoming vine that came back each year to twine around a lamppost at the end, the white picket fence on the corner of the next block with tall spikes of flowers that always seemed to lean against it.

Ivy pulled up in front of a clapboard home with gray shutters, old shutters that had taken him and his friend Gary an entire summer to scrape and paint.

"The cherry tree. It's gone." Tristan had spent a lot of time under the shade of that tree.

"We had a really bad storm this spring."

"Right. Of course. Things change," he replied quickly, and saw Ivy biting her lip. "It's okay," he told her, resting his hand on hers. "I can handle this."

Then the front door opened, and he gripped her hand hard as he watched his mother emerge. There were streaks of silver in her hair—maybe she'd had them before and he'd never noticed. She was carrying her medical bag, and he could guess where she was going: on a house call, which few pediatricians made these days.

His mother saw their car and stopped. "Ivy!" She rushed over.

Ivy glanced toward him, then got out. Tristan watched her and his mother hug.

"Look at that suntan! You look well. I heard some scary stuff from your mom."

"Yes, but I'm fine now, just home for a few days, then back to the Cape to work."

"Steve and I have missed you, but I'm glad you, Will, and Beth are enjoying a summer at the beach. How are they?"

Tristan saw Ivy hesitate. "Fine. Good."

His mother leaned down and peeked in the car. It made him ache, seeing her smile at him as if he were a stranger. "Hello."

He couldn't move.

"This is my friend . . . Gabriel."

"Hello, Gabriel."

"Hi."

"He's a little shy until he gets to know people," Tristan heard Ivy say. "Then you can't shut him up," she added, leaning down to look in the window as if she were teasing him. She straightened up again and he couldn't see either of their faces. "Gabe works at the inn with us, lives on the Cape year round."

"I'm glad you're making new friends."

Knowing his mother, Tristan could hear the quiet message in her words: *It's okay, Ivy.*

He heard his mother's phone buzz.

"On call?" Ivy asked.

His mother's hand reached into her pocket to retrieve the phone. He was glad he was in the car, hidden enough to stare at a hand he had held onto so tightly as a child. "Same patient," she said. "First child—new parents always get a little nervous. I had better go. But listen, Steve will be home any minute. Stay and see him—he'd love it. I'll let you in the house."

Ivy leaned down, her face appearing in the driver's side

window. Tristan shook his head quickly. He couldn't bear to go in the house. It was too much.

"Thanks, but we'll wait in the garden for a few minutes. I've always loved it there. "

Tristan's mother gave Ivy a second hug, then she leaned down to peer in the window again. "Sorry I can't stay. Come back, okay?"

His heart felt pressed against his ribs.

He watched her hurry off to her car and back down the driveway too fast—as always—cutting the wheel too soon as usual.

"Mailbox!" he yelled when she was still ten feet from slamming on the brakes. She gazed at him with surprise, her hazel eyes holding his for a moment, then she laughed and continued out of the driveway on a safer path.

Ivy got back in the car and sat silently, waiting for him to speak.

"I don't think I can take anymore. Can we go on to your house?" Tristan asked.

She took his hand in hers, cradled it in both hands, then kissed it. It took her a long time to answer him. "Are you glad you saw your mom? If you could push the delete button, would you erase the last few minutes?"

"No!" he said, the passion in his voice surprising him. It was painful, but no matter what, he couldn't part with those moments.

"Then I think we should wait for your dad. You can stay in the car and we can make it as quick as with your mom."

"What if I—" he hesitated, feeling as vulnerable as a child. "What if I . . . break down?"

"Your dad's work is to be with people when they break down. It'll be all right."

Tristan kept his hand in hers, and when a dark blue car drove up and he saw the clergy sticker, he wove his fingers through hers.

He watched as his father got out and walked toward the house, his dad's mind elsewhere, as it always had been, not noticing Ivy's car.

Tristan's throat tightened. "He looks old. Not his face, but the way he walks." Tristan didn't want to think of his parents growing old, their bodies becoming worn.

His father turned suddenly, saw their car, then his face lit up, making him look years younger, the father Tristan remembered.

"Ivy! What a wonderful surprise!"

Ivy got out of the car and Tristan watched them meet halfway across the lawn, his father's arms opening wide, then closing around her. She and his father talked for a few minutes, moving slowly toward the car, then his dad leaned down to look in. For a moment, Tristan was eight and saw the face of his father staring at him, under his Spider-Man bedcovers, where Tristan had buried himself due to some kind of second-grade catastrophe. Tristan couldn't remember the catastrophe, just his father kneeling on the floor next to his bed, his face suddenly appearing under the covers. "How are you doing, buddy?"

"Hello, Gabriel," his father said, his voice gentle but formal. "I'm Steve Carruthers."

"Hello."

Ivy went through the same explanation as before about shy Gabriel from the Cape, and Tristan somehow found the strength to move his arms and legs and climb out of the car. His father reached out to shake his hand. Tristan tried to remember if he had ever shaken his father's hand, except when he was being taught as a little boy.

"Would you like to come in?"

Tristan felt Ivy watching him. "Well, how about the garden?" she asked. "Are you growing tomatoes again?"

Tristan remembered how amused Ivy had been by his father's garden, in which vegetables and flowers were mixed together, cucumbers hanging on a trellis next to climbing roses, squash running over petunias, tomatoes surrounded by zinnias. The garden had looked like their house, especially the living room, the first place where Ivy and Tristan had been alone together, the day she gave him her cat, Ella. He remembered how politely she had peeked around at the piles of medical journals, sports magazines, and books of prayers that left no place to sit but the floor, not mentioning until much later that she had seen the tub of carryout chicken he had stashed behind the sofa.

Now Ivy offered to show "Gabriel" the gardens that extended around the side yard, perhaps to save Tristan from walking through the house, but he spoke up and accepted his father's invitation to come in and get a cool drink. Ivy took his hand, twining her fingers in his as they entered the house.

It looked the same, except no sports magazines were left open on the floor. His books were still in one of the many bookcases that lined the walls, and there were pictures of him at every age, more than he remembered.

"We have a new member of the family."

Before his father could explain, a black and white cat flew out from a pile of laundry that had been dumped on the sofa, pounced on Tristan's sneaker, and began pulling on his shoestring.

Tristan bent down. "She looks like Ella!"

His father looked at him surprised. Tristan couldn't believe he had blurted that out. He picked up the kitten and tried to recover from his mistake. "Doesn't she look like your cat Ella, the one you showed me pictures of?" he asked Ivy.

"Yes, very much." Ivy petted the young cat under her chin.

"Her name's Lacey," Tristan's father said.

Tristan saw Ivy's jaw drop. "Lacey! What a cute name! What made you think of it?"

"It's an odd kind of story," he said as he led them into the kitchen. "Lynne and I were having dinner on the back patio, enjoying one of the first warm spring evenings. A girl came around the corner of the house—a teenager, not a little girl—saying she had found our kitten. We explained to her that we didn't have one. She said it was on our front porch, its paws up on the screen, crying to get in. 'Really, it's not ours,' we said. Then I noticed it had a collar and tag."

"This one?" Ivy asked. Both the collar and little metal heart were purple.

Tristan's father nodded.

Ivy flipped it over. "Lacey," she read aloud.

"While Lynne and I were looking at the tag, the girl ran away. She was gone in a flash, nowhere to be found, and there we were, holding a cat. We advertised, put signs up in town, and an ad in the paper. By the time it became apparent that no one was going to respond, Lacey had made herself at home here."

Tristan held the cat away from him to study her: she was mostly black, but had one white foot, with a splash of white on her face and the tip of her tail. Did Lacey think his parents needed a companion and, finding a kitten that was a double for Ella, decide to drop by with it? Did cats have souls—could they come back?

He handed her to Ivy, who cradled little Lacey in her arms. The cat blinked her large green eyes at Ivy and purred.

"She has a big motor for such a little thing," Tristan said.

"Oh, she's a purr-ball, all right. We think she's about six months old."

Ivy rubbed her cheek against the kitten's, and Tristan saw a tear sparkling at the end of Ivy's lashes.

"Bring her leash with us. She enjoys the garden, but Lynne and I don't want her wandering off."

Ivy picked up the long leash from a hook by the door, and Tristan and his father carried their glasses of lemonade outside.

They talked for a half hour, Ivy catching up on all the news of Stonehill, Tristan drinking up the familiar smells and colors of the garden, and, most of all, the sound of his father's voice.

When Tristan was a child, he had thought his dad had Superman's X-ray eyes, the way he could read him and guess when Tristan had been into something he shouldn't have. Tristan had that feeling again, every time his father's eyes came to rest on him.

"Would you two like to stay for dinner?" his father asked. "Something simple. Pizza or Chinese. Lynne ought to be back soon."

Ivy glanced at Tristan. *Enough,* he thought, aware suddenly of how emotionally exhausted he was. He stood up, hoping she could read his body language.

"Thanks so much. Another time," Ivy said.

Tristan's father put the cat inside, then walked Tristan and Ivy around the house. When Tristan reached the car, he saw his father had caught Ivy by the arm and was talking to her quietly.

Tristan waited. The tilt of his father's head told him that he was asking Ivy questions.

"He knows, yes. Gabriel knows all of what happened," she said, looking back at Tristan, before turning to his father again. She was nodding at whatever his father was saying, then suddenly leaned against him and started to cry. For a moment, he was an angel without a body again, unseen by Ivy and his father, an outsider, powerless to comfort either of them. He watched his father put his arms around Ivy and saw the age and sadness in his father's face.

Then Ivy turned to Tristan, smiling through her tears, and said, "Reverend Carruthers says that there's something about you, Gabriel. Despite how different you are from Tristan, when he looks at you, he keeps thinking of his son."

Tristan stared at his father. What reasonable response could he make to that? *None.* He walked toward his father, put his arms around his him, and hugged him. It was almost unbearable letting go again. "Thank you," Tristan said quietly. "Thank you."

Twenty-four

"SO WHAT DO YOU MAKE OF LACEY JR.?" TRISTAN asked Ivy as she drove past the edge of town, following the two-lane road that led to her home.

Ivy laughed out loud. "Well, we know *who* is watching out for your parents, but where exactly did Lacey get the kitty? Philip has always said that Ella became an angel, and we all went along with the idea, since it seemed to help him get over her death." Ivy told Tristan about the graphic novel Will and Beth had been collaborating on, and he smiled.

"But who knows?" Ivy added. *Who knows anything for*

sure? she thought. She'd never dreamed she'd be driving this road again with Tristan.

She turned into the driveway that led to her house, climbing the long hill through stretches of trees that opened here and there to small clearings made bright by wild-flowers. When they parked, she turned to look at Tristan, trying to read his feelings about seeing his parents again. The first thing she had learned from loving him was that, when you love deeply, pleasure and pain can be intertwined. "How are you doing?" she asked softly.

He smiled into her eyes as if knowing she needed to look into them to be convinced. "I'm good. I'm glad we went."

She kissed him lightly on the cheek, then got out of the car.

"You're sure no one's here?" Tristan asked, standing next to her, gazing up at Ivy's home.

It was an imposing house, three full stories with a two-story wing on each side, massive double chimneys, and heavy black shutters. For Ivy, moving from their Norwalk apartment to this house had been difficult, the residence seeming too large and too cold, and later becoming a place of fear, thanks to Gregory. After her stepbrother's death, Andrew had asked her mother, herself, and Philip whether they wanted to stay there or move to another house. Knowing Andrew's attachment to a house and land that had been in the Baines family for several generations, they decided to replace the bad memories with good ones. Ivy believed it was proof of their and Andrew's love for one another that they'd been slowly able to do that. The only place she avoided in the house was Gregory's old room, which was now used for storage.

"While they're in California, Henry's taking off," Ivy told Tristan. Henry was Andrew's longtime cook, who'd been out of a job for just three weeks before Andrew realized the kitchen wing was in danger of being burned down by his bride. "The groundskeepers come every Wednesday. We've got the place to ourselves."

"The music room," Tristan said. "That's where I want to go. And the tree house."

Ivy unlocked the door and punched in the security code. Tristan stood in the middle of the kitchen, gazing about, then peeked in the dining room, almost as shyly as the first time he'd been invited to a family dinner.

There had been too many serious thoughts and feelings for one day, Ivy decided. "Tag! You're *It*!" she cried, and took off.

Tristan spun around, surprised. They raced down the hall, in one door to the living room and out the other, through the dining room, kitchen, family room, Andrew's office, and library. Tristan had more speed, but she was more agile and knew better the curvy obstacle course. She danced around a floor lamp that threatened to tip; he flew across a polished floor on an Oriental scatter rug; a pillow fight stripped the sofas and chairs in the family room. With a main staircase and two smaller ones, it was easy to keep from getting cornered, so the chase rolled like a wave upstairs and down. Ivy suspected that Tristan let her get away twice when he could have grabbed her. She finally sprinted from her bedroom up the steps to her third-floor music room where he caught her—or she caught him.

They held on to each other out of breath and laughing, which made them even more breathless. He covered her face with kisses. "Let's dance," he said.

When they were first together, he had danced with her here in the silent moonlight. Now he provided the music, humming off-key, which made Ivy giggle.

"Excuse me, Miss Lyons, do you find something funny?"

"Yes, *you*," she said.

He kissed her smile with a smile.

She played their favorite songs on the piano, then they returned to the second floor.

"I'd like to see Philip's room again," Tristan told her.

He stopped at the entrance in front of a picture of himself and Philip, snapped on Philip's ninth birthday. Tristan picked up the frame, holding it gently for a moment, then returned it to the bookshelf.

A baseball game was laid out on the floor next to Philip's bed, a diamond and four bases painted on a green rug, with players' cards assigned to positions in the field. Philip liked to move the cards around and call the game like a sports announcer.

"I see Mark Teixeira is up at bat, and the bases are loaded," Tristan said, then knelt down. He moved a Red Sox outfielder to the edge of the green rug, lined up the three Yankee base runners as if they were ready to greet Teixeira at home plate, and put Teixeira between third and home, as if he were running out a grand slam.

"You know, Philip never forgets where he left his cards."

Tristan grinned. "Good!"

They retraced their steps, though in a more orderly fashion, straightening everything they had knocked crooked, then went outside.

Just a puzzle piece of sun was left, shining dark orange through the trees above the horizon. They walked hand in hand toward the stone wall marking the edge of the property. The ground fell away sharply there, eroding into a steep hillside of rocks, spindly trees, and brush. Several hundred feet below was the town's station for a commuter train, its track following the river. In the approaching twilight, the dark green river valley and distant hills were lapped in violet shadows. Standing near the wall, Ivy leaned back against Tristan, the evening's peace settling softly around them.

After a few minutes they turned to the tree house. It had been Gregory's as a child, and Andrew had it rebuilt and expanded for Philip, putting a new two-floor structure in an adjacent maple and a boardwalk that connected the two sections. A rope ladder dangled from one side and a rope swing from the other. Ivy sat on the swing as Tristan eagerly climbed the ladder. She heard him cross the boardwalk and tread on the heavy planks directly above her. She looked up just as he peeked over the edge. No longer worried about being seen, he had taken off his hat. His gold hair looked like a halo as he smiled down at her.

"Coming up?"

You fly down here, she was tempted to say. "In a minute. I want to see how high I can swing."

"Then I'm going to the other side, in case you pull over the tree."

Ivy loved the feeling of her hair flying back when she sailed forward, then rushing forward over her face as she was sucked back up to the sky. When she had finally had enough and climbed the ladder, she could feel the pink in her cheeks. Tristan's hands gathered up her wild hair and pulled her to him for a long, sweet kiss.

They sat together on the top level of the tree house, listening to the leaves rustle around them and the last birds of the day singing.

"They always seem to sing loudest just before it gets dark," Tristan said.

They lay down, Ivy in Tristan's arms. Was it possible?

she wondered. Had they been given a second chance for a lifetime together? Were they one cufflink away from many more nights like this?

"I love you," Tristan whispered. "I've loved you from the first moment I saw you. My love for you will never die. It's everlasting. I swear it to you here, halfway between heaven and Earth."

TRISTAN HAD TRIED TO STAY AWAKE AS LONG AS POSSIBLE, not willing to give up one moment of holding Ivy asleep in his arms. Both of them had wanted to stay in the tree house, and they had retrieved blankets and pillows from her bedroom. The night felt gentle, as if all of nature high on the ridge wanted to wrap them in peaceful sounds and tender breezes.

At last the need for sleep overtook him. A long, heavy sleep gave way to a lighter one. Waking at dawn, finding Ivy still in his arms, he happily fell back into dreams of his time with her.

Then the voices began—murmuring, menacing, inhuman voices. They crept in like a tide, washing over him. Dread pooled in his soul.

He could hear distinct syllables—he heard words! *Now. Ever. Ours.*

What did they mean? What did they want from him? From their tone, he knew they were not simply telling him something, but demanding it—*Now. Ever. Ours.*

"Mine," he replied, knowing that whatever the hellish voices were claiming, he couldn't let them have it.

Now. Ever. Ours, they insisted.

"Leave me alone!" he shouted.

Ours!

He heard the squeal of tires against a road and jolted awake.

Their laughter exploded in his head. *Which way? Which way?* they taunted. The voices faded. *Which way?* one voice asked softly.

"Tristan?" Ivy's hand reached up to touch his face. It was morning, the sun already high in the sky and dappling the tree house floor. Ivy lay next to him, gazing up at him, her finger tracing his cheek. "Are you okay?"

He nodded.

"You don't look okay." She sat up. "What's wrong?"

"Nothing. I was dreaming."

"A nightmare," she guessed. "What was it about?"

He hesitated, then lied. "I don't know. I only remember the feelings."

"You shouted. You sounded angry."

"I was."

She began to gather up the blankets, watching him as if waiting for him to say more, then told him, "It's okay, Tristan. After all that's happened, you have many reasons to be angry."

They climbed down the rope ladder and walked together across the grass. Tristan felt like he was emerging from a movie theater on a hot summer day, the sun so bright that details of his surroundings were washed out, and the frightening movie seeming more real.

"Hungry?" Ivy asked.

"Yes," he lied a second time, not wanting to worry her.

In the kitchen she picked up her recharged phone and checked her messages.

"Beth and Will okay?" he asked.

"Looks like it."

She seemed so happy, flipping pancakes and drizzling syrup over a stack. While cleaning up, she sang. He hummed—the only way he could, off-key—trying to hide his anxiety and make her laugh, which she did. Her laughter helped ease the fear within him, and by the time they were halfway to Providence, the voices seemed farther away.

They arrived in River Gardens at noon and drove directly to Corinne's house, hoping to find Gran alone. No one answered the door. Circling the house, they saw that the windows, which had been opened yesterday, were now closed. They didn't want to draw the attention of neighbors, with many of them home on Saturday, so rather than waiting in front of the house, they drove in loops, leaving the neighborhood and returning, looking for a sign that someone had come home.

They were exiting River Gardens for the third time when Ivy's cell phone went off. Tristan recognized the ringtone—Will.

"I'd better get this," she said, pulling over to the side of the road. "Hi, Will."

Tristan watched Ivy's face as she listened, her slight frown deepening to genuine concern.

"So when was the last time anyone saw her? . . . She took your car without asking? . . . I see . . . No, Will, listen to me, there is nothing you could have done. Maybe—maybe she just needs some space."

The lines in Ivy's forehead told Tristan she didn't believe that.

"Right. Right." She nodded silently as Will talked. "Good idea. No, no, I'm coming back. . . . I am! Don't argue with me!"

Ivy shook her head, rejecting whatever Will was saying. "If she shows up, then just call me, and I'll turn around again."

"Beth's missing," Tristan guessed, after Ivy clicked off her phone.

Ivy nodded. "She had off from work today, so Will was texting her, but she didn't respond. When he got a break at the inn, he checked the cottage and his room. She was gone and so were his car keys. Until now, she's always asked before using it."

"Any idea where she'd go?"

"She has been so strange with Gregory inside her mind, I can't even guess. Will's checking her laptop for clues. He's called Chase, but Chase has been hanging around Dhanya lately. Beth doesn't talk to Dhanya and Kelsey now, any more than she does to me. She could be anywhere, Tristan, anywhere!" Ivy's voice broke. "I have to go back."

"I know."

"I'm going to take you to my house for a few more days. You'll be safe there till Wednesday, and—"

"No, I'm staying with you."

"As soon as she's found," Ivy continued, "you and I will go back to Gran's."

"I'm staying with you," he said again.

"That makes no sense!" she snapped. "You'll be safer in Connecticut, and it will be easier for me if I'm not trying to hide you."

He blinked and pulled back.

"I'm sorry," she apologized. "That didn't come out right."

Tristan didn't reply immediately. *Deal with it,* he told himself; the need to keep him hidden had made it hard for Ivy—that was no surprise. But he suspected that something else was going on here. "Ivy, what's scaring you? I know Gregory has slipped into Beth's mind, but there's more, isn't there? Something you haven't told me."

Ivy looked away from him.

"What is it?"

"Several nights ago, she tried to kill me."

Tristan slammed his hand against the dashboard. "What?!"

"She didn't know what she was doing, Tristan. It was Gregory, not Beth. Gregory!"

"Oh my God," he said, leaning forward, both hands holding on to the dashboard.

"It was my mistake," Ivy continued. "I should have learned from experience and done more to protect myself. If you could save me last year by slipping inside Will and getting him to act, then of course Gregory could kill me, slipping inside Beth, urging her on."

Tristan couldn't stop shaking.

"I thought that we were reaching her, Will and I. We had gotten through to her with the amethyst we gave her. I hope she has it with her now, and that we can reach her before she—" Ivy broke off.

"Before she . . . does what?"

"I don't know, Tristan. *He* is capable of anything."

They sat side by side in the car, staring straight ahead. There were too many enemies for him to fight: whoever wanted Luke dead, the police convinced of his guilt, and most powerful of all, Gregory. Tristan couldn't do it all. But he didn't have to tell Ivy that, he decided; he simply had to convince her to take him with her. He'd fight the one battle that Ivy had to win, and when the others caught up with him . . .

"Ivy, listen to me. I am a part of what's happened to Beth as much as you are. Don't leave me out of this. Don't make the mistakes I made when Gregory was alive. I was proud—I wanted to save you myself, but I needed the help of others—I needed the help of Will to fight him.

"Gregory's powers have grown really fast. When I slipped inside other people's minds, I couldn't make them do something they didn't want to. You and I know that Beth would die before she'd hurt you, and yet she tried to kill you. That tells us just how powerful Gregory has become. Bryan, Kelsey, and Dhanya don't know what they're dealing with. You, Will, and I—we know—we need to work together."

She gazed into his eyes. "I'm so afraid—for Beth and for you."

"I'm afraid too, but fear's okay. Letting it divide us is not," he said. "That's exactly what Gregory wants."

Ivy took a deep breath. "That's what I told Beth, not to separate herself from Will and me."

Tristan held Ivy's face in his hands. It was as pale as the night he had given her his kiss of life. "We can't let Gregory separate us."

"It's your choice, Tristan, but please be careful. I don't think I can survive losing you again."

Twenty-five

"WE NEED TO CONTACT LACEY," IVY SAID AS SHE AND Tristan drove toward Bourne Bridge, one of the two car bridges that connected the mainland to Cape Cod. "She's more likely to come if you ask her."

"I called to her when you were talking to Will the second time."

Will, knowing Beth's computer password, had accessed her accounts and was surprised to find that she had deleted all of her mail and texts from the last six months. This was Gregory's doing, Ivy thought, another attempt to isolate Beth from those who loved her.

The only leads Will came up with were the Internet pages Beth had visited most recently and most often: Provincetown, especially its mile-long jetty, Chatham beaches, the ferry ports of Hyannis and Woods Hole, and Nickerson State Park. Chase and Dhanya were now headed to Provincetown. Max, knowing Chatham better than anyone, was searching it with Kelsey. Bryan was driving Will to Hyannis Port. Ivy—and, unknown to the others, Tristan—was checking out Woods Hole. Whoever finished first would check the lots at Nickerson in search of Will's car and Beth.

Inching along in the Saturday afternoon traffic, it was taking forever just to get back on the Cape.

"Does it seem odd to you," Tristan asked, "that the kinds of places Beth was interested in would be mobbed this time of year? I mean, do they seem like places she'd like?"

Ivy had been thinking about that. "If she was still writing, yes. Beth loved to sit and watch people—it gave her ideas. But the presence of Gregory has blocked her writing and has made her withdraw from almost everything around her. So it scares me a little. I keep wondering what Gregory is planning."

Ivy beat her hands lightly on the steering wheel, frustrated by the traffic ahead. "Do me a favor, grab my phone and text Suzanne," she said, then glanced at the dashboard clock. "It's two thirty here—eight thirty in Italy. Maybe she'll be checking messages between forks of pasta. See if she's heard from Beth."

At last they crossed the bridge high above the Cape Cod Canal. Out of the corner of her eye, Ivy saw Tristan looking to the right, toward the train bridge.

"It's an awesome bridge," she said, "but even before Alicia died there, I found it kind of spooky."

A tower rose up at each end of the railroad bridge, its metal fretwork topped by a square house-like structure with a cone-shaped "roof," these two tall steel points dominating the outline of the bridge. The bridge itself, its horizontal span, was suspended far above the canal, just beneath the gothic-looking towers, and was lowered only when a train crossed.

"I can't imagine what she felt, being up on that bridge," Tristan said.

"I prayed that she didn't feel anything, that she was drugged by then and didn't know where she was."

They touched down on the other side of the canal and soon after entered a traffic circle.

"I hate this rotary," Ivy said. "Which spoke takes us to Woods Hole?"

"I don't know—I can't read all the signs fast enough. Just keep circling till we're sure."

They circled twice.

"There! Route 28 South," said a voice from the backseat.

Surprised, Ivy glanced at Lacey through the rearview mirror, then made a quick exit, drawing a loud blast of a horn from the guy she had just cut off.

Lacey quickly lowered her window and hung out of it. Ivy couldn't see what gesture she made to the unhappy motorist, but she was pretty sure he didn't appreciate it.

"Thanks for the tip, Lacey," Tristan said, "but it's better not to encourage road rage."

"Me?" Lacey replied. "Talk to the one who's driving."

Ivy smiled.

"Why are we going to Woods Hole?" Lacey asked. "You two taking off for the islands?"

"We're looking for Beth," Tristan replied.

"The radio has disappeared? Does she have the amethyst with her?" Lacey asked.

"Will said it's gone but—" Ivy's voice trailed off.

"But you don't know if she took it with her," Lacey said, "or if Gregory convinced her to throw it away again."

Ivy nodded, and Tristan related where the others were searching. "It's all that we have to go on, Lacey. Can you find her?"

"What do you mean, *find* her?"

"Use your powers and tell us where she is."

"What d'you think I am, all-seeing? I can locate people only when they ask for me—I trace it kind of like a phone call. But without a signal from Beth, the best I can do is guess, just like you."

"All right," Ivy said, "what are some guesses?"

"As it happens," Lacey continued, "Beth called me yesterday."

Ivy braked in response and quickly pulled onto the shoulder of the road. A car blew by, horn blaring. "Sorry."

"Don't worry about me; I'm already dead."

Ivy and Tristan turned toward the back seat. "What happened yesterday?" Tristan asked.

"Beth was, like, really upset, her eyes kind of wild, though they had a lot of blue in them."

"So she was still stronger than Gregory," Ivy said hopefully.

"She was clutching the amethyst."

"That's good," Tristan said.

"She had a lot of questions, more than I've ever thought of. I knew the answer to only one," Lacey added, then suddenly lowered her head.

"What was the question?" Tristan asked.

Lacey chewed on a purple fingernail. "Same question you had," she said to Ivy, "how a demon is expelled from the world."

"The person occupied by the demon has to die," Ivy replied slowly, then recalled Beth's words—*Ivy, if ever I hurt*

261

you, I couldn't live with myself! "Oh, God! She's going to kill herself."

"It never occurred to me!" Lacey said quickly, defensively. "When she asked me—I mean, if I had suspected for one moment—if I'd had any idea—"

"It's all right, Lacey," Ivy replied. "It didn't occur to me either."

"But won't Gregory stop Beth to save his own neck?" Tristan asked.

Lacey chipped nervously at her fingernail. "Depends. I don't think demons know any more than angels do, when they first come back. So Gregory might not realize how things work. But if he does, and if he figures out what she's up to, he'll cut out and leave her to die."

Oh angels, protect her! Ivy prayed. *Angels, help us find her.*

"I'll make some inquiries," Lacey said. "Maybe someone will know where *Gregory* is. He'll stand out more."

After Lacey departed, Ivy drove to Woods Hole as fast as the traffic would allow. There were five different lots for ferry parking. She and Tristan toured row after row of cars looking for the one Beth borrowed. At first, Ivy's heart quickened each time she spotted a silver Toyota. But by the time they reached the third parking lot, a dull feeling had set in. She'd see a silver car and tell herself "that won't be it," guarding against disappointment. Repeated disappointment gave way to desperation. When they reached the final lot, every car that looked like Will's made her angry. "What difference does this make?" she cried to Tristan. "So we find it and it's empty, where do we go then?"

Tristan put his arm around her. "Do you think this could be a decoy? Beth knows that you and Will would start searching for her as soon as she was missing. Could she have gone to these websites deliberately, to keep you from guessing where she is and what she's planning? Maybe she is trying to fool us as well as Gregory."

Tears ran down Ivy's face. "I don't know. I just don't know."

Her phone rang, and she fumbled for it. Tristan picked it up from the ground and handed it to her.

Ivy struggled to compose herself. "Hi, Will. Any luck?"

"No. How about you?"

"Nothing."

"And nothing from the others yet," he said.

"We're looking for a needle in a haystack!" Ivy told him.

"I know."

"Will, I'm afraid Beth's going to kill herself. She's going to make sure that she—Gregory—doesn't hurt anyone else."

There was a long silence.

"Are you there?" Ivy asked.

"I'm here." His voice sounded as if it was coming from

the deepest part of him, as if he could barely bring his words to the surface.

"What next?" she asked. "Where are you now?"

"We're almost finished with the lots in Hyannis Port."

"We're done here," Ivy said. "So I guess we should head to Nickerson."

"Bryan and I will meet you there, at the main entrance. There must be some kind of information or nature center. If the place is crowded, stand in front of that."

"Okay. We'll be there."

"Drive safely," Will said. "Ivy? Who's *we*?"

"Luke and I," she replied, and clicked off before he could ask any more.

TRISTAN FELT EXPOSED, WALKING SO OPENLY IN A part of Nickerson that he had visited only under the cover of darkness. Even more, he felt as if his inner self was going to be laid out in the open for Will and Bryan to examine. The strangest part of this "reunion" was that the person he had worked closely with to save Ivy was sure to be antagonistic toward him, and the person he'd never met before would welcome him as an old friend, almost a brother.

As he and Ivy walked toward a building marked Nature Center, Will spotted him—that is, he saw "Luke"— and turned away. At the same time, Bryan broke into a smile. He moved quickly toward Tristan, meeting him halfway. He clasped Tristan's hand, then gave him a team-mate's hug.

Tristan knew that he was walking a tightrope with Bryan, especially after acting as if he remembered things when he was around Gran and Hank Tynan. Gran had wanted to talk, and for the most part, Tristan simply had to echo her. But if Bryan was Luke's close friend growing up, there were too many things Tristan could get completely wrong. So here was another bit of irony, Tristan thought. Bryan might be the easiest person in the world to convince that "Luke" had amnesia, given all the opportunities Tristan would have to say the wrong thing.

"What's this furry stuff on your chin!" Bryan exclaimed, stepping back. "You trying to look like a professor rather than the best damned hockey player born in Providence?"

"So I was better than you?" Tristan replied, guessing—and hoping he had guessed right—that Luke and Bryan had been competitive friends.

Bryan grinned. "I missed ya, Luke." He eyed him up and down carefully, and for a moment, Tristan feared that Bryan had noticed something not quite right.

"Looking good," Bryan said. "Thin, but I guess that's to be expected. You need some of my mom's cooking."

"At this point, I wouldn't mind *your* cooking. How is she . . . your mom?"

"Great. Completely outfitted in BU sportswear. There

for every game—she'd come to practices if I let her. You should have seen it Parents' Weekend, when Joan got out there and demonstrated her hockey moves to my team-mates."

Tristan smiled.

Bryan's face suddenly grew serious. "You really don't remember, do you? You would have found that really funny. You used to tease her about her moves."

"Oh . . . sorry. If I saw her again, it might help. Ivy and I went to River Gardens, and it helped a little," Tristan added, with a glance toward her. "I couldn't remember the names of the streets, but I could find my way around."

Ivy nodded to confirm.

"So some things are coming back," Bryan said.

"But not what needs to," Tristan replied. "I have no idea how I ended up on the beach at Chatham. I can't remember anything about the night Corinne died or how you got me out of Providence—Ivy told me about that. I know I owe you big time."

"Give me an honest answer," Bryan said, peering at him so hard that Tristan felt as if he were looking into his soul. "I promise not to get my feelings hurt: Do you remember me?"

Tristan hesitated.

"Thanks for the honest answer," Bryan said. "Oh well." Then he glanced over his shoulder and rested his hand on Tristan's. "Just a head's up: Will's not real happy to see you."

"No kidding," Tristan replied as the three of them walked toward Will. Tristan held out his hand. "Hi."

Will kept his hands in his pockets, nodded, and turned immediately to Ivy.

Tristan could read Will's feelings toward Ivy and the surprise she had just delivered in the lift of Will's eyebrows—not anger as much as disbelief—a sense of betrayal. And Tristan couldn't blame him.

"Okay, let's look at the park map and figure out who covers which lots."

The four of them walked to an outdoor display. Tristan studied Will closely as he and Ivy conferred and divvied up the eight parking areas. Something had changed about Will. His brown eyes were years older than those of a guy starting college. Was it pain or knowledge? Tristan wondered. Both. The pain that came with knowledge, the knowledge of evil and what it could do to people.

"I don't know where we go after this," Will was saying to Ivy.

"Did Beth keep a journal?" Tristan asked.

Will spun toward him. "Do you think I'm stupid? Of course, and I looked for it right away. It's gone."

"So then we need to remember conversations with her and—"

"We?" Will interrupted Tristan. "Have *you* been talking to her?"

"Will," Ivy chided softly.

"No, I haven't," Tristan replied calmly. "So it's just a suggestion that everyone who's had a conversation with her, even the most ordinary, think back on it. Sometimes, in the heat of the moment we miss something really important."

"*We* miss something?" Will repeated sarcastically.

"Luke knows you don't like him, Will. You don't have to keep making that clear," Ivy said.

"And do you know why I don't like him, Ivy? Because of the way he treats you. If Luke really cared about you, he wouldn't drag you into his messed-up life."

"What if he's not the one who messed up his life?" she countered. "What if he's a victim?"

"Keep your voice down, Ivy," Bryan reminded her, with a glance toward park visitors crossing the lot.

"Unbelievable!" Will exclaimed softly.

Tristan said nothing; after all, it did seem unbelievable, and Will only wanted was best for her.

But Ivy grew angry. "Luke is innocent!" she said, her voice low but intense. "And we're going to prove it."

"Let it go, Ivy," Tristan said. "It's not important."

"It *is* important," she replied, and turned back to Will. "Someone else killed Corinne and let Luke take the rap."

Will glanced toward Bryan as if asking whether that was possible.

Bryan nodded. "It's old news."

268

"To you, Bryan, but not to Will," Ivy replied, turning back to Will.

"Let's everybody stay cool," Bryan said. "No need to make a public announcement."

"We think that Corinne was blackmailing someone," Ivy continued in a calmer voice, "and her victim had finally had enough."

Bryan raised his eyebrows. "Are you sure? Did you find out something when you went back to the Gardens?"

"Don't you get it?" Ivy continued to Will. "Luke is innocent. You're angry with the wrong person. And your distrust is making everything harder. We're all on the same side, Will."

"In the end," Will said, his voice dark with misery, "it doesn't really matter. If I lose Beth, nothing else matters."

Tristan saw Ivy's anger evaporate. She rested her hand on Will's arm. "Then let's find her."

Bryan and Will took the lots on the east side of the large park, and Ivy and Tristan headed for those on the west side. Despite the shade of acres of trees, the air had grown hot and sticky, with the kind of stillness that precedes late afternoon storms. Ivy peered up at the yellow-gray sky, closed the car windows, and put the AC on full blast. They were halfway through their trolling of the lots when her phone beeped.

"Suzanne," Tristan said hopefully.

Ivy stopped her car and read the text aloud: "Can't get through to Beth, not since scary dream."

"Anything else?"

"Just that she'll keep trying."

Tristan remembered that some of Beth's dreams were prophetic. "What is she talking about?"

"About a week ago, Beth dreamed that a snake was coiled around my neck, strangling me."

Tristan stared at Ivy. "Why didn't you tell me?"

"Because I interpreted it as her fear that you—I mean Luke—would kill me the same way she thought he killed Corinne. I knew I was safe with you. There was no point in upsetting you with the dream."

Tristan struggled to remain patient. "Except you weren't safe. Beth has the snake in *her*, and he has already tried to kill you once."

"Not by strangling," Ivy argued, "by suffocating."

"Either way, you cut off oxygen."

"Even so, she was just thinking about Corinne and—"

"Think back, Ivy," he interrupted. "Were there other dreams or odd things Beth said—an image, *anything* that might give us a clue."

Ivy shut her eyes, then opened them again wide and nodded. "Last Sunday night, when the others were out, I found Beth lying in bed so still it looked like she was dead, with a red candle flickering on the table next to her. When I got closer, I saw the amethyst. Its chain was fastened to the headboard of my bed. The other end had been shaped into a noose. My china angel was hanging by her neck."

Tristan grasped Ivy's hand.

"I figured it was a warning to me, the same kind Gregory used to send through Ella, when he cut her foot, then mine, and when he hung her: *What happens to Ella, will happen to you.* You remember, that's how he worked."

Icy fear ran through Tristan's veins. "I remember, but I don't think this warning was for you. Ivy, we have to get to the bell tower! Last weekend, I saw Beth standing outside the church, gazing up at the bell as if in a trance. I thought that she had sensed me there—that she knew I'd climbed up there. I was afraid that Gregory had picked up some sign of me. But I think it's much worse. I think the angel to be hung is Beth."

Twenty-six

THEY WERE JUST MINUTES FROM THE CHURCH, BUT IT seemed to take an eternity to get there. Will and Bryan, whom they had called immediately, had pulled out of the park right behind them.

"Angels! Angels, protect her," Ivy prayed aloud.

Tristan called to Lacey, but she didn't respond.

Turning into the lot behind the church, they spotted Will's silver Toyota.

"She's here!" Ivy was both relieved and terrified— relieved to have found Beth, terrified that they had guessed her plan correctly.

Bryan and Will swung into the lot next to them. Tristan raced ahead to the window with the broken latch and shoved it upward. The three of them rushed through the opening and followed him to the steps. On the main floor they ran down the aisle of the church toward its front entrance, calling Beth's name.

Ivy knew that the boys' deep voices would carry up to the tower, but would they keep Beth from hurting herself or would they push her to action?

She can't be dead, Ivy thought. *Somehow, I'd feel it, I'd know it. Angels, please.*

The ladder in the vestibule was gone. Beth must have pulled it up through the trapdoor. *How did she have the strength?* Ivy wondered, then remembered how strong Beth was when she tried to suffocate her. Gregory had made it possible. Perhaps, then, he hadn't figured out his fate if Beth died.

"Get on my shoulders, Will. Help him up, Luke," Bryan directed.

Tristan cupped his hands, giving Will a step up to Bryan, then Will pulled himself through the open square in the ceiling. Ivy followed, propelled by Bryan and Tristan through the trapdoor.

It took a moment to regain her balance and see the scene before her. A shaft of light slanted downward from the open door beneath the bell, shining like a spotlight on

Beth. Beth stood high on the ladder, one hand grasping it, the other fingering the coil of rope around her neck.

"Beth, please," Ivy begged, her voice shaking. "Please hold on."

Beth stared straight ahead, stroking the snake of rope.

"Beth, look at me!"

She didn't react. Ivy's fear mushroomed into panic. Beth was already dead to them—they'd never get her back—she was already part of Gregory's world.

Gregory. He was the one Ivy had to convince. "If she dies, Gregory, you die," Ivy said, her voice low, quivering with fear and anger. "You'll be gone from here forever. Leave Beth alone. Leave her now before she can do that to you."

The ladder creaked; Beth was shifting her weight. Ivy eyed the rope, which was connected to the bell wheel above. If Beth stepped off the ladder, she would drop several feet, but not far enough to touch the floor.

"Don't move, Beth!" Will shouted. "Keep both feet on the ladder."

He stepped on the first rung. "Listen to me," he pleaded. "We'll get through this together. We're stronger than he is."

Will pulled himself up slowly as if fearing to upset Beth. Ivy watched and held her breath.

"Our love is stronger than his hate, Beth," Will said. "Don't let go." He was on the third rung . . . fourth rung. "I need you, Beth, more than you know. Please don't let go."

Beth slowly moved her head, looking down on him and Ivy. "Take care of each other," she said, then removed her hand from the ladder rung and stepped into the air.

"No!" Ivy cried, her heart jerking with the rope.

Will rushed upward.

As Beth's body dropped, pulling the rope, the bell in the tower clanged. Will grabbed Beth and yanked her body toward him. The return swing of the massive bell threatened to tighten the rope around Beth's throat. Will struggled to hold Beth with one arm and anchor the rising rope with the other.

Ivy hurried up the ladder behind him. She grabbed hold of the taut rope, pulling down on it hard. Will loosened the noose and pulled it off. The bell, swinging free, clanged loudly.

Beth lay limp in Will's arms. Tears streamed down his face. Ivy bent over her friend, cradling Beth's head, crying.

"Please live," said Will.

Feeling as if her hands were not her own but being guided by an angel, Ivy tilted back Beth's head and lifted her chin. "She's breathing!" Ivy reached for Beth's wrist. "There's a pulse. Weak, but it's there."

Ivy remembered what she had learned in CPR. "We need to get her on the floor so we can—"

Suddenly Beth's chest heaved upward. Her mouth opened wide. A stroke of lightning flew up the rope and struck the

275

bronze bell with a deafening blow, shaking the tower until it felt as if it would tumble down. For a moment they were bathed in jagged light. Then the knife of lightning blew out of the tower, leaving the bell to rock and clang madly.

"What the hell?" Bryan exclaimed from below.

"Ivy!" Tristan shouted.

A clap of thunder sounded a short distance away.

"We're okay. Okay!"

A siren wailed.

"The tower was struck," Bryan said.

Ivy shakily climbed down the ladder then held it as Will descended with Beth in his arms. He laid her on the floor.

A second siren sounded, its wail surging over the rise and fall of the first.

"Someone must have seen the strike and called it in," Bryan hollered to them. "Cops'll come. I've got to get Luke out of here."

"Yes, go!"

"No, Ivy—" Tristan began to protest.

"Now," Ivy insisted, looking down from the tower at Tristan's upturned face.

"But—"

"Luke, the police'll recognize you," Bryan argued. "If they find you here, it's over."

"Go!" Ivy shouted. "Bryan, get him out of here. Call you later."

Then she knelt down by Will and Beth.

"She's going to die, Ivy."

Ivy felt Beth's wrist. "She's hanging in there. Her pulse is steadier now."

"I don't know how to help her."

"Help's on its way."

"What's taking them so long?" Will's voice was panicky.

"They sound close," Ivy said, trying to reassure him.

"They're taking forever."

Ivy watched Beth's chest rhythmically rise and fall. "She's holding her own. Help me move her into recovery position."

"Ivy, if I lose her, I can't go on!"

Ivy met his eyes, then rested her hand on his. "I know, Will. I know just how that feels."

BRYAN SWORE AND STEPPED BACK QUICKLY INTO the shadow of the church's exterior wall. "Luke, wait! More cops."

"They're not stopping," Tristan observed as the second police car raced past the entrance to the church lot, heading down the narrow road that led to the bay.

"Better for us," Bryan replied.

A third car—State Police—sped toward the beach.

"But if Ivy and Will need help—"

"They have phones," Bryan reminded him. "We have to

get you out of here." He started across the lot, then stopped. "Where'd she come from?"

"Who?"

"The skinny girl with the purple hair."

Lacey stood in the tall grass of the church lawn. "Looks harmless," Tristan said.

"Yeah, until she takes down license plates numbers."

"Just keep going." The last thing Tristan needed was a conversation with Lacey; if she acted like she knew him, things would get very complicated. "Walk to your car like we belong here."

Bryan glanced sideways at him. "I guess your survival skills are sharper than mine now."

They crossed the lot, Tristan following Bryan. As soon as Bryan was focused on his car, Tristan glanced back at Lacey, who was looking up at the sky, frowning. Was Gregory gone from Beth? Tristan wondered. He pointed toward the tower, trying to signal to Lacey that she was needed there.

By the time Bryan opened his car door, Lacey had disappeared. Bryan turned quickly around, looking for her, then shrugged. "No one's watching at the moment, but I hear more sirens. Get in the back, down between the seats, till we clear this place."

Tristan nodded and pulled open the back door. "Oh great."

"Sorry about the mess."

Tristan climbed into the pile of worn workout clothes, then Bryan covered him up.

"Are you trying to asphyxiate me?"

Bryan laughed. "Keep quiet, and I'll open the windows."

"I don't think that'll help."

Bryan drove slowly to the edge of the lot. "Volunteer fire and an ambulance," he said softly. "Hang on."

His tires spat stones as he spun out of the driveway onto the road.

"Some smooth driving!" Tristan remarked from the back seat. More than ever he felt split in half, his heart and soul back with Ivy, Will, and Beth, the superficial part of himself preoccupied with playing Luke. "Hungry, Bryan? There's something back here that looks like part of a hotdog."

"I was wondering where that went."

"It's got some fuzzy stuff on it," Tristan continued.

"Car lint or mold?"

"Can't tell."

"Shut up a minute—we're stopping at an intersection."

The car slowed and idled, then made a sudden turn. A horn blared.

"So how close did he come to hitting us?" Tristan called from the back seat.

"A few inches," Bryan replied, laughing. "You can come up for air now. But stay in the back seat, just in case."

"Yeah, that'll look real normal, you chauffeuring me."

"Best we can do, buddy. We're headed toward Harwich, my uncle's rink. I got keys to the storerooms. You'll be out of sight till things settle and we hear from Ivy."

"Thanks."

"You in love?"

Tristan hesitated for a moment, wondering if Luke would admit it, then grinned. "Yeah. Yeah, I guess I am."

"She's awfully smart, you know." It sounded like a warning rather than a compliment.

"I can handle her," Tristan replied, glad Ivy wasn't there to hear him playing macho.

"You're going to have to finish high school. She's the kind to want a college guy."

"I guess." Tristan shrugged. "I'm not thinking that far ahead. Hey, there's a warm can of Coke back here. Can I have it?"

"If you open it outside the window. I don't want you to mess up my clean car."

Tristan laughed, opened the can, and watched the foam blow off the top.

"How's the drinking?" Bryan asked.

Tristan was about to answer "warm and stale," then realized Bryan was referring to Luke's alcoholism. "I've stayed away from it."

"Completely?" Bryan sounded as if he wanted to believe it but couldn't.

"Yeah, well, when you wake up finding yourself beaten to a pulp and have no memory of how you got that way, you don't have that much desire to keep drowning yourself in alcohol."

"Then maybe it was worth it," Bryan replied. "Was Ivy telling the truth or just trying to make you look good to Will? Did you really find out something about Corinne's murderer?"

Tristan quickly weighed the pros and cons of revealing what they knew. "She exaggerated a little, but it seems kind of obvious that someone was being blackmailed by Corinne and decided to put an end to it. Considering what I heard about her yesterday, I should have figured it out back before my memory was wiped clean."

"The police should have figured it out!" Bryan answered quickly. "But you made yourself such an easy target, Luke."

"Looks that way. Things are going to be different from now on."

"Not a moment too soon," said Bryan.

IT SMELLED AS IF IT HAD RAINED JUST ENOUGH TO dampen the church's stone lot and make the leaves of nearby trees glisten. The freshness of the evening air seemed to help Beth: She opened her eyes for several seconds, gazed at Will, who was carrying her, then rested her head against his shoulder. Ivy opened his car door, and he laid Beth gently in the back seat.

As he did, the amethyst necklace slipped out of her pocket.

"Ivy," Will said, surprised. "Beth knew what she was doing! She had the amethyst with her so she could fight him. *Beth* was in control, not Gregory. She wanted to die."

"No," Ivy replied, and recounted what she and Beth had learned from Lacey about expelling demons from the world. "Beth was doing it to save me and anyone else Gregory might hurt through her."

"Is he gone?"

Beth's mouth moved as if she were trying to speak. Ivy leaned close. "Beth, open your eyes."

She did, and Ivy gazed into irises that were a full, clear, luminous blue, eyes that made a perfect sky seem pale. "He's gone."

Beth nodded and smiled a little, still weak. "Gone."

The police and ambulances had bypassed them for whatever was going on at the end of Wharf Lane. Ivy moved her car to another lot, then was picked up by Will. Beth had shut her eyes again, but the color had returned to her face and she seemed to be sleeping peacefully in the backseat.

"I think she's going to be okay," Ivy said.

"Even so," Will replied, heading west on 6A, "I don't think we should go back to the inn right away. There's going to be a lot of questions."

After discussing the simplest and most believable story,

Ivy called Bryan, who agreed it was best to keep the truth quiet and not call attention to Luke's hiding place at the church; he offered to keep Luke hidden at the rink until Ivy could pick him up. Then she called the others, informing them that they had found Beth in "Hyannis Port" and that she needed some time away from the inn. "Sorry, what's that, Chase? I can't understand you—you're breaking up, Chase. Talk soon," Ivy said, and clicked off her phone.

Will smiled. "I know a nice place this time of day."

By the time they reached the beach in Yarmouth Port, Beth was sitting up. With Will on one side of her and Ivy on the other, they linked arms and walked toward the bay. Like the beach near Alicia's, the sand, now gold with the slanting sun, gave way to the salt marsh: tiny islands of brilliant green sea grass, set like puzzle pieces in the deepening blue of the bay. A long boardwalk stretched over the marshes. They strolled along the pathway, stopping from time to time to lean over the wood rails and point out the fiddler crabs and schools of tiny fish.

They spoke only of what was around them—imagining the bubble secrets of tiny bay creatures, enjoying the earthy smell of the marsh, gazing at the far shore, where a red hull glided past a shimmer of sand. They lived only in the present moment—not halfway between heaven and earth, Ivy thought, but halfway between land and sea—which was joy enough, because they were together again.

Twenty-seven

BEING WITH IVY BACK IN STONEHILL HAD MADE IT even harder to be away from her now, which meant Tristan cared much less about his safety than Bryan did.

Bryan had unlocked for him a storeroom as far away from the rink as possible, then returned with a steak sub and fries twenty minutes later. "Look what I found in the back of my car. And it's not even fuzzy."

As they shared the food on a carton top, Bryan talked about life in River Gardens. "Does any of this sound familiar?"

"It sounds like somebody else's life," Tristan replied. Sometimes it was ridiculously easy to be honest.

"Luke, why don't you let me help Ivy with the detective work? Gran will protect you, but Hank Tynan will blab—by now it's probably all over the Gardens that you came back. And if you can't remember people, you won't know who you're dealing with. Whoever wants to get you will be one step ahead. I think you should lay low."

"It's too late for that."

Bryan shook his head. "You're so freakin' pigheaded! You should have lost your thick skull rather than the memories inside."

Tristan laughed. "I wonder if I can still skate."

"Don't try it here. My uncle is lousy at faces, but he never forgets the skating style of a great player."

Ivy called Bryan an hour later. When she picked up Tristan, Bryan handed him a care package, tossing it in the car after him, telling Ivy to "Gun it, babe," at which she laughed and pulled carefully out of the rink's driveway.

"So what's the plan?" Tristan asked.

"We're meeting Will and Beth in Yarmouth Port, then you and I will drive Beth back to Stonehill tonight and home tomorrow."

"How is she doing?" Tristan asked.

"When I left, she looked much better—tired, but like the real Beth."

Tristan could hear the relief in Ivy's voice. "Did Lacey know what happened—whether Gregory has slipped into someone else's mind?"

"Lacey? I haven't seen her."

"She was in the parking lot when Bryan and I left. I couldn't talk to her, but I pointed to the tower. I thought she'd help you."

"Maybe she saw we were doing okay, and moved on."

Tristan nodded, but still looked puzzled.

"What's in the bag?" Ivy asked.

Tristan reached in the back seat, rummaged through Bryan's care package, and laughed. "Enough caffeine for an army, sports bars, fudge, chips—oh, geez—a bankroll."

"Don't worry, we'll pay him back."

It was twilight by the time they reached the small café where Beth and Will had eaten. They were sitting on a bench outside, talking, their faces lit softly by a ship's lantern hanging from the café's sign. For the moment they looked normal and happy, Tristan thought. Why couldn't Beth, Will, Ivy, and he have normal lives? Did people living everyday lives have any idea how lucky they were and how fragile it all was? Two years ago, he didn't.

But Will knew, at least now he did. Tristan could see it in Will's face and in his hands—the way he held onto Ivy and Beth before they got into the car, the way his eyes lingered on Beth as if he feared he might never see her again.

She'll come back safe, I promise you, Tristan wanted to tell him, but now more than ever he knew he couldn't make such rash promises.

They arrived at Ivy's home a little after midnight. Beth had fallen asleep early in the trip, and Ivy and Tristan helped her upstairs to Ivy's bed. Ivy wanted to stay close by, in case Beth had nightmares. Carrying blankets and pillows, Tristan and Ivy tiptoed up the stairs from her bedroom to camp out in the music room.

The crescent moon, rising early, had dropped low enough in the sky to look like a Christmas ornament hanging in the dormer window. Tristan watched Ivy's hair catch the light as she laid down the bedding. She was humming a song from *Carousel*. He hummed with her.

Ivy glanced up at him, her eyes bright, looking as if she were trying to hold back laughter.

"It's harmony," he explained.

"Oh."

He pulled her to her feet, laughing, then found himself close to crying. "Come on," he said. "One last dance."

BETH SLEPT LATE SATURDAY, AND IVY TOOK HER TIME that afternoon, strolling and talking with her, making sure she was all right before driving her home to her parents. Later, after changing into "Gemma the art student," Ivy headed to Providence with Tristan. Finding a dark limo parked outside Corinne's home and figuring it was Tynan's company car, they circled the block every fifteen minutes, hoping he would leave. At eight o'clock, they got lucky. When they knocked on the door, Gran answered and said she was alone.

She was surprised to see them again so soon—and too smart to think that this was just a pleasant visit. They had sat down in the kitchen for five minutes, making small talk as she poured coffee and tea into her colorful mugs and opened a tin of lemon bars, when she said suddenly, "Oh, stop the bull. You've learned something. Out with it."

Ivy and Tristan exchanged glances.

"We found an article online which mentioned a gold cufflink with an arrow on it," Tristan said.

Ivy pulled from her purse a printed copy of the article.

Gran read it, and after a long delay looked up. "I told Corinne when she was just a little whip of a thing she'd better learn to play fair or she wouldn't have no friends. And I told her when she was older if she wasn't going to play fair, then she'd better play smart." The old woman shook her head. "Didn't listen."

"Gran, we'd like to take the cufflink to the police," Tristan said.

The old woman closed her eyes.

"Please."

She got up and walked around the kitchen. "So where'd

she get the cufflink?" Gran asked. "How'd she hear about the hit-and-run? It happened in Massachusetts."

"I don't know," Ivy answered. "Maybe just luck. Maybe the person took his or her car to Tony's when she was photographing the place."

"You think this is going to get you off the hook, Luke?" Gran asked. "People believe what they want to believe."

"It's my only chance."

Gran sat down again, thinking. Tristan nibbled a lemon bar and Ivy sipped her tea, waiting.

"So," Gran said at last, "we'd better search her room and see if we can find something more to give the police, a photograph of the car or a note."

They searched for the next two and a half hours, going through every drawer, every shirt and pants pocket, every single piece of paper as well as boxes of photographic prints that Gran brought from her own room, finding nothing that seemed related to a hit-and-run accident. At Gran's suggestion, they pulled the drawers all the way out of the bureaus and desk to look behind them, lifted the rug and stripped the bed, checking the mattress and box spring. They discovered nothing. Ivy remade the bed, turning down the spread as it had been before. Gran gazed down at it, then leaned over and pulled the spread back over the pillow, smoothing it gently with her hand. Corinne's death had become real and final to the old woman.

Without speaking, Gran turned out the lights in the room and waited for them to follow her out. She closed the door behind them. Handing Tristan the cufflink, she said, "I'll vouch that Corinne left this the night she died, and that I gave it to you tonight, but I fear for you, Luke. Gemma should take it to the police. You should stay hidden until they have a killer in custody. Are you listening to me?"

"I'm listening," Tristan said, and handed Ivy the cufflink.

Gran walked them to the front door. Tristan hugged her good-bye.

"Thank you," Ivy called back softly through the screen door. She wasn't sure Gran heard her.

"It's as senseless as her dying," Gran said, gazing beyond Ivy, "an old woman like me living this long."

Ivy and Tristan didn't speak until they were beyond River Gardens. "I—I didn't know what to say back to her."

Tristan nodded. "Anything comforting would have seemed like a lie."

Beyond Providence, on the long stretch of road that dropped down to New Bedford, then hugged the coast, traffic grew light. Ivy checked her rearview mirror and saw only two sets of headlights a distance behind her. Few people were driving to the Cape at eleven o'clock on a Saturday night.

She drove in silence, reviewing everything they had discovered in the last several days. At last she said, "I wish we could have found a photograph of a car with front damage.

With all those that Corinne took for her photo essay, there wasn't a single one there, which tells me someone had a reason to scoop them up."

"I've been thinking about that. One incriminating photo could be sent to a million places on the Internet, which means the person who is being blackmailed could never be sure he or she had gotten rid of all the electronic copies. And maybe, with software like Photoshop, a picture alone isn't considered evidence. But a matching cufflink would be, especially a custom-made one, especially if the person who found it was still alive to testify where and when she found it."

"Which is why Corinne is not."

"Looks that way," Tristan agreed. "Let me see it again."

Ivy reached in her pocket. Tristan turned on the cabin light and studied the cufflink. Ivy blinked as a car passed them, its headlights catching in her side mirror, momentarily blinding her.

"This is a rounded kind of arrow," Tristan observed, "not straight like a graphic symbol. It sure looks custom made."

Ivy glanced in the rearview mirror. Just one set of headlights followed her now, the same set that tailed her when getting on the highway, she thought, then laughed at herself. How could she possibly tell in the dark?

"I think our only choice is to turn the cufflink over to the police as soon as possible," Tristan went on. "I'm a little worried about Gran's safety. The police should give her some protection."

"I'll go to Rosemary Donovan, rather than the police in Providence. She'll help us out."

Tristan nodded.

"In the meantime, we need to figure out where to hide you. People must have heard the church bell ringing this afternoon, and they may have investigated that or the lightning strike. If we left anything behind—food wrappers, footprints—it's not going to be safe for you anymore. What do you think—back to Bryan?"

"No. I know he wants to help, but the less people we involve the better. "

"Nickerson?"

"Home sweet home!" Tristan replied with a smile.

Ivy glanced in her mirror two more times, then flipped the switch to the night view as the car behind them drew closer.

"Something wrong?" Tristan asked.

"Uh, no, not anymore. He—or she—is finally passing us. What kind of car is that?" she asked as it went around them.

"A little black one," Tristan replied, then laughed. "I'm not up on expensive sports cars."

"I saw one just like it when we were leaving Providence."

"There are probably a lot of them roaming the East Coast," Tristan pointed out calmly.

"Of course," Ivy said, but she shifted in her seat, unable to shake an uncomfortable feeling.

"Tired?"

"Yeah." She turned off the AC, opened the window, and let the fresh air blow through the car. The road was mostly straight and flat, edged with sandy stretches of grass and scrub pine. They drove for miles in silence, then Tristan suddenly turned in his seat.

"Where'd that car come from?" he asked sharply.

"The shoulder of the road, I think. There's no exit along here."

"If so, he was sitting with his lights off."

Something most people don't do, Ivy thought. She picked up speed. A half second later, the car behind them picked up speed. Ivy slowed. The car behind them slowed. "I don't like this."

"The headlights are low to the road," he observed.

"Like a sports car's."

"Drive steady," he said. "The other guy could be zoning out, or drunk, or simply entertaining us with a little game."

"Or it could be Corinne's killer." She said it like a joke, but she was getting scared.

The car behind them began to close the gap between, creeping closer and closer. Ivy's heart beat fast.

Suddenly the sports car accelerated, bumped the rear of Ivy's car, then pulled back. Ivy swore. "What's he doing?"

"Keep going!"

"Here he comes again!" Ivy exclaimed and stepped on the gas, barely escaping a second bump from behind.

"He might be trying to create an accident, just enough to make you pull over. Keep your eyes on the road and keep moving."

Ivy tried, but it was impossible not to glance in the mirror and watch the car behind her shifting back and forth, moving dangerously close to her left side, then dangerously close to the right.

In the final stretch of road to the canal, there were no highway lights. Only the high beams of the two cars marked their path through the night. For a moment, Ivy flashed back to the night of her collision on Morris Island, when she was floating high above her wrecked car, looking down on the lights of another car racing away.

The car pursuing them jolted her out of the memory, locking on her left side, chafing the metal, then disengaging again.

"You're a pro!" Tristan praised her, his hand lightly covering her whitened knuckles as she gripped the wheel. "One mile to Bourne Bridge," he read. "It's lit—and probably has security cameras. Maybe he'll back off."

"And if he doesn't?" Ivy asked.

As Tristan predicted, the car hung back while crossing the bridge, but as soon as they cleared it, he was on their tail.

"Rotary coming," Tristan warned.

"Hold on!" Ivy made a quick right off the traffic circle. The car behind them kept going.

"Well done!"

"Except I have no idea where I'm going."

"Safety in numbers. Go wherever you see a bunch of lights."

On a straight road now, Ivy accelerated, her eyes darting between the pavement ahead and her rearview mirror. Moments later, when she saw a car behind them picking up speed, her stomach tightened. "Someone's back there." She took another quick right, then hooked left. The road grew bumpy.

Tristan leaned forward. "I see a tower with a light on top. We may be headed back to the canal."

She made another turn.

Tristan turned around in his seat. "I think we've lost him."

Ivy continued along the narrow road, then began to slow. Black pines crowded the margins of the route. "This looks like a service road."

"There are some lights ahead."

She drove a little further. "Dead end!"

A one-story building, well lit by security lights, faced an empty parking lot. The road continued on only as an unpaved path, barely wide enough for a car. In the distance, from beyond the trees that lined the path, she heard a soft *clang-clang*. "A train."

"We must be near the railroad bridge," Tristan replied. "I bet that was the tower I saw."

"Listen—"

They strained to hear the whining of another motor above the idle of theirs.

Suddenly a car gunned its engine. With lights off, it shot out from an entrance they hadn't seen and came barreling down the road toward them.

Twenty-eight

"FLOOR IT!" TRISTAN SHOUTED.

They sped toward the unpaved path, then flew down it, bumping over potholes, taking a sharp curve, scraping against pine branches. Tristan saw a clearing ahead. Then he saw the train. "Stop! Stop!"

Ivy slammed on the brakes. The car that was chasing them braked as well and spun next to them, kicking up sand and dirt, coming within an inch of slamming into their car and flinging them into the train. The driver punched on his headlights, momentarily freezing the scene in halogen brightness. Tristan wrenched around and saw that they were trapped between their pursuer and the slow-moving train.

He had wedged them in. To return to the unpaved path, they would have to back up and make a three-point turn. The other option was to drive over the tracks after the train had passed. But it wasn't a paved crossing and the tracks were high. Ivy would have to ease over them slowly in her little VW—if the car could make it at all.

"Windows up. Doors locked," Tristan said, hoping the sports car was the pursuer's only weapon.

The black car's lights went out. The bridge lights, about fifty feet away, designed to warn airplanes and boats, did little to illuminate the area. Were they dealing with one or two people? Tristan wondered. The Beetle's taillights picked up a single dark figure moving toward them.

Tristan glanced sideways at Ivy. If they had been followed from Providence, their pursuer was here for "Luke." Tristan figured there was a way to be sure the pursuer left Ivy alone. After stealing one last look at her, lingering just a second longer, Tristan unlocked his door and got out.

"Tristan!"

"Get ready to go," he said, closing the door, moving quickly away from the car.

"Tristan, get back in!"

He could hear her screaming at him through the glass.

He moved toward the bridge, but not too fast, wanting to make sure the hooded figure followed him, allowing Ivy to escape.

"Where you going, Luke?"

At the sound of his voice, Tristan's stomach clenched. Without stopping or glancing over his shoulder he said, "You're acting like a jerk, Bryan."

"Playing a little bumper cars, that's all," Bryan replied.

Tristan turned to face him.

"Just having some fun. You used to be more fun, Luke."

"You're drunk."

"A little, but I'm careful nowadays," Bryan replied. "I don't let myself get out of control. Can't—not anymore—don't think I got nine lives, like you."

Tristan stepped backward onto the bridge. There was a maintenance walkway and handrail on one side.

"I'll never know how you climbed out of that ocean alive," Bryan continued, walking toward Tristan. "I dumped you several miles out. Did some fisherman help you?"

The train had disappeared around the bend, but Ivy's car was still there. Tristan's heart sank when he saw a shadow separate from the car. She had climbed quietly out of it and was following Bryan. Tristan wanted to shout at her to go back, but he couldn't give away that she was there.

Continually walking backward, he kept Bryan waiting for a response, drawing him onto the bridge. "Something like that. How'd you get me out in the boat? You shot me up with something, didn't you?"

Ivy had stopped at the edge of the bridge. Tristan saw her look quickly toward the base of the tower, which he suspected housed the gears that raised the bridge. She looked back at him and pointed upward with her hand.

Tristan stopped and rocked slightly on his feet, trying to signal to her that he knew the entire span would rise, hoping to keep her from shouting to him.

"What do you want from me?" he asked Bryan, moving more quickly than before.

Bryan, who had kept pace with him, was now twenty feet from Tristan and a hundred feet from Ivy on the canal's bank. "*You* know. The cufflink. Hand it over."

Tristan felt a jolt and tremor in the steel bridge. "You're talking crazy," he said as the bridge began to rise. "I've never owned a cufflink in my life, and far as I know, neither have you."

"Oh, but I have," Bryan replied. "They were a gift from my uncle, who knows that money and opportunities come to big college stars. 'For your sports banquets,' he told me, 'and when those rich businessmen take you out on the town.'"

"Tristan!" Ivy shouted.

"Stay there, Ivy!" he yelled back.

Bryan glanced over his shoulder and laughed. "Isn't

this fun? I took this ride with Alicia, but she was kind of slumped over."

"Tristan!" she cried out again.

"Who the hell is Tristan?" Bryan asked, suddenly uncertain, turning back toward Ivy as if looking for a third person. "She calling the dead guy?"

"She thinks he's an angel," Tristan replied.

Bryan laughed but kept his eyes on Ivy, then took a step toward her.

If Bryan had enough brains, Tristan thought, he'd figure out that he could get "Luke" to do whatever he wanted by threatening Ivy. Needing bait, Tristan dug in his pocket. "Does your cufflink have an arrow on it?"

Bryan spun around, his eyes immediately going to the glint of gold in Tristan's hand. "A *top*, stupid. You gave me the nickname."

A simple finger top, Tristan thought, studying the shape.

"You've called me that since we were eight," Bryan said. "You *have* lost your memory. Too bad that Ivy talked you into proving your innocence."

One thing was clear: Bryan wouldn't end his killing spree with "Luke." Ivy knew too much.

"When you hit that woman, you should have manned up and gone to the police."

"I was drunk, coming home from an awards banquet. And anyway, when I left her, she was still breathing."

"So you call an ambulance."

"Like I've said a million times, you're naïve. Yeah, they might've looked the other way if I was playing in the Stanley Cup, but not for me, a kid from River Gardens who hadn't yet shown what I can do in real competition. My career would've been over before it started."

"So you took your car to Tony, knowing Tony's the loyal kind. And Corinne was there."

"Doing her damn photoshoot. She got there early, while I was sleeping off the banquet in Tony's house.

"I come out and see that lens pointing like a big nose into my personal business. She was always messing with other people's things. She found the cufflink in the car."

Tristan kept moving and kept Bryan talking, all the while drawing him away from the shore and Ivy, and trying to work out a plan in his head. "So she started blackmailing you. You must have paid her a lot—she had her own apart-ment."

"It got old. So I offered her a large lump sum for the cufflink."

"And told her to bring it to Four Winds. But you didn't really expect her to give back the cufflink. You knew Corinne well enough to know you were safe only if she was dead. And me being your naïve best friend, you couldn't ask for an easier person to frame for her murder. I've got to tell you, that wasn't a real friendly thing to do."

"C'mon, Luke, you were wasted," Bryan replied. "I had worked hard. I had everything to lose—you had nothing. Why should I be the one on the run?"

"So then, why did you help me get away?"

"It seemed a good plan at first," Bryan said with a shrug. "As long as the police were focused on trying to catch you, they weren't going to think about searching for anyone else. But I couldn't trust you to stay out of trouble. You forced my hand, Luke.

"A few drinks and you were out of control. Sooner or later you would get yourself caught. I started thinking: What if the State gave you a decent lawyer, one who realized the police case had holes? That would be just my luck." Bryan grimaced. "You had to die—and without the police knowing you had, so they would keep looking for you."

They were more than halfway across the bridge and about twenty feet above the water. Tristan started walking faster. "What about Alicia—did you have to kill her?"

"Once you and Ivy got to her, I did."

Tristan felt sick to his stomach.

"I followed you to the beach that night and caught up with her after you left. She happily told me that you were innocent, and she was your alibi. I knew it was just a matter of time before they'd be looking for the guy who texted you from Corinne's phone, asking you to come to Four Winds."

"The cell phone they found. You took it from me the

night you tried to drown me. Why'd you leave it on the Mass Pike?"

"I know you, Luke—I'd already seen you in love with Corinne. And Ivy is so much nicer. I knew you wouldn't leave her. I needed to get the police off your back and mine, till I could win Ivy's trust and finish things off."

By slowly increasing his pace, Tristan had widened the gap between them. The dark water and confusing reflections made it impossible to tell how far they were above it, but each foot that the bridge rose would make it more dangerous to jump. Tristan figured the center of the canal was deep enough for container ships and would have a strong current between the ocean and bay. He wanted to be close enough to shore to have a chance of swimming. But too close, and he'd crash onto the shoreline.

Tristan took off. Bryan charged after him. Their footsteps banged against the metal walkway. With a quarter of the span left, Tristan looked over his shoulder. Bryan, in excellent shape, was gaining fast. Tristan had just a few seconds left.

He's a competitor, Tristan thought. Above all, Bryan was an athletic competitor. Tristan pulled the cufflink from his pocket, held it high for a second, making sure Bryan saw it, then flipped it back over Bryan's head.

Bryan couldn't help himself. Gifted with excellent reflexes, he couldn't keep himself from going after the thing he had obsessed about. He spun like a top and chased the cufflink.

Tristan quickly climbed down under the bridge. As he hung from the steel fretwork, the wind buffeted his body and sang in the bridge's cables. For a moment, he heard the voices. Then he said a prayer and jumped.

IVY RAN FROM THE TRAIN TRACK TO THE PATH ALONG the canal, trying to see what was happening on the bridge. She had watched Tristan and Bryan as they moved along it, Bryan keeping pace with Tristan.

Suddenly, Tristan had taken off. Ivy had screamed to him, but he was too far away to hear her. As the bridge rose, she lost sight of both of them.

Now she stood on the path next to the water, gazing up at the bridge. "Help him, angels!"

She saw a figure coming back, moving toward her side of the canal. He stopped at the center of the bridge, and she recognized the silhouette: Bryan stood tall against the star-lit sky. As the bridge rose higher, he stretched his arms out in triumph. She thought she heard laughter, then she saw him leap. He fell to the water like a dark angel.

A siren on the other end of the bridge went off. Had someone seen him? Where was Tristan? If he had fallen or jumped, he'd be closer to the opposite bank. Ivy ran back to her car and drove to the rotary, then sped across Bourne

Bridge, joining the emergency vehicles heading toward the train bridge.

When she got close to it, a police car quickly pulled in front of her, blocking off the street. The officer got out of his vehicle and signaled her to turn around. When Ivy didn't move, the officer strode toward her car.

She lowered her window. "Something wrong?"

The man looked at her as if she were crazy for asking that. "Do you need to get somewhere?"

Ivy's heart was pounding, and she wanted to scream: *I need to get to Tristan.* "I was just curious."

"We're busy here, miss. A night fisherman thought he saw someone jump."

Just one person? Ivy wondered.

"U-turn," the officer said, then waited for her to follow directions, his hands on his hips.

Ivy turned around. "Lacey, where are you?" she cried out as she drove off. "Help him, Lacey, please."

A quarter mile up the mainland side of the canal, just past the Bourne Bridge, she pulled over and got out of her car. She could see a helicopter hovering above the train bridge, shining its light down on the water.

She watched the helicopter, joined by police boats, trolling the area. She prayed that Tristan would suddenly emerge from the canal's bike path, shaking off water, smiling at her, but he didn't. A little after three a.m., the helicopter wheeled across the sky and left. Boats continued to search and several police cars remained with their lights flashing. At last Ivy returned to her car and drove toward Sagamore Bridge.

Had Bryan survived his leap into the canal? She guessed the bridge had risen fifty feet before he had jumped.

And Tristan? He had to be alive. He couldn't die now. *Angels, if I lose him again—Lacey, where are you?*

She crossed the Sagamore and drove the Mid-Cape Highway, her mind racing. Where should she go? Who could she trust? How would she find him?

She exited the highway, and when she stopped the car, saw she was at the church on the corner of Wharf Lane. A wreath woven with flowers and black ribbon had been hung on the sign pointing to the beach. In the predawn light she read the message scripted on a wide strip of satin: IN LOVING MEMORY.

Ivy started to cry—for Tristan? Alicia? Herself? She wasn't sure. She remembered the rush of emergency vehicles to the beach after Gregory left Beth in a streak of lightning. Had he struck and killed someone?

Ivy turned into the church lot. New NO TRESPASSING signs were posted outside the church, but she ignored them. This was her and Tristan's refuge—she needed to get inside and think. She tried the window with the broken latch, then all the others, and the door, but the church was locked up tight.

Ivy sat on the lowest step to the church porch, leaning forward, her head on her knees. Even more than her body and mind, her heart and soul were worn thin. If Tristan were dead, she couldn't go on.

Then she felt a presence next to her, someone leaning against her, and she looked up. "Lacey."

"I don't know where he is," Lacey said. "When he jumped, I couldn't help him. He didn't see me, didn't hear me."

"He's alive," Ivy insisted. "He has to be!"

"If he's dead," Lacey replied, "he's lost more than his life."

Ivy drew back. "What are you saying?"

"The voices that Tristan has been hearing—"

"What voices?" Ivy interrupted.

"Like those the night Gregory fell from the train bridge. They've been haunting him. Tonight, even I heard them. If Tristan is alive, he's almost out of time."

Glancing over her shoulder, raising her eyes to the belfry, Lacey shuddered. High in the tower, the dark bell tolled.

Acknowledgments

MANY OF THE SETTINGS IN THIS TRILOGY ARE REAL, such as the towns, parks, and beaches. Some—the inn, homes, churches, and secondary streets—are based on real places, but have been moved to new locations, built upon, and renamed, so that I could weave a good story. Still other places exist only in my mind: The real city of Providence is a wonderful place to live and to visit; the neighborhood of River Gardens sprang up completely from my imagination.

I'd like to thank Joseph W. Dick, who took the time to guide me through the lovely Yarmouth New Church.

Thanks for letting me climb the ladders—and double thanks for ringing the bell! Thank you to Walter Chapin, who made the contact for me, and to the Yarmouth New Church Preservation Foundation, Inc., which is dedicated to restoring and preserving this American Gothic building; they have made it an excellent place to enjoy cultural and artistic community events. Thanks again to Karen of The Village Inn, who made me so comfortable while I was doing research.

A writer needs good editors—the longer I write the more I know it. Many thanks to Joelle Hobeika and to Emilia Rhodes.

And thanks to my sister, Liz, who lives on Cape Cod and fields last-minute calls and requests as I'm writing—"You know that beach in . . ." As always, thank you, Bob. You're the best. Love you! And finally, thanks to Puck, who sat on my desk and slept on my bookshelf for sixteen years, and who is now playing in a sunny garden with Ella.